Dinnusos Rises

Dinnusos Rises

Tej Turner

Elsewhen Press

Dinnusos Rises

First published in Great Britain by Elsewhen Press, 2017
An imprint of Alnpete Limited

Elsewhen Press, PO Box 757, Dartford, Kent DA2 7TQ
www.elsewhen.co.uk

British Library Cataloguing in Publication Data.
A catalogue record for this book is available from the British Library.

ISBN 978-1-911409-03-8 Print edition
ISBN 978-1-911409-13-7 eBook edition

Printed and bound by CPI Group (UK) Ltd, Croydon, CR0 4YY

Contents

For my father, Julian Turner.

And his father, Jack.

My other grandfather, Fred Jackson.

And also David Beck.

1
Dreamwalker

He was that typical doctor that, by some cruel and yet comical twist of fate, a girl will always end up being placed before when they have come to discuss womanly matters. Balding, and what is left of the wispy vestige of his hair, grey. His face seems to be in a constant state of frown. You are not sure if he is frowning presently or the lines have seasoned after spending much of his life bearing such an expression.

There are a few things you can be almost certain of though, such as that he plays golf at the weekends and his newspaper of choice is *The Daily Telegraph.*

That doctor.

I am beginning to believe it is a mass-scale prank orchestrated by a secret network of surgery receptionists.

And do you know what else is funny? Usually when a sixteen-year-old schoolgirl is skipping out on one of her classes it'll be for reasons which are exciting, or possibly a little juvenile. She'll go on a shoplifting spree, or hide behind a shed and smoke some cigarettes – or even a joint, if she is a bit edgier. Maybe she'll just be in the park somewhere with one of her girl friends. The two of them giggling the day away, high on their act of teenage rebellion.

Not me. I chose to miss biology class so I could visit the doctor. And I even went to the trouble of obtaining a note of permission from my school.

I'm a bit boring like that.

"Faye Steepleton?" he said.

"That's me."

He turned his eyes back to the screen – to that database of me that they have assembled over the years – and scrolled through a rather intimate history of my anatomy.

It was nothing terribly exciting. Vaccinations were a little late but, knowing my mother, it probably took them a while to convince her they weren't an evil conspiracy. Chickenpox when I was two. Who *didn't* have chickenpox when they were two? Some minor surgery on my teeth, when I first became acquainted with laughing gas at the age of twelve.

"I went to the chemist for my prescription," I interjected, in an effort to save him some time. "But they said I needed to see you."

He ignored me and carried on staring at the screen. Then he found it. *Click.*

"Microgynon..." he murmured, narrowing his eyes.

He swivelled his chair around to face me. "It's just general procedure that after the first three months we have a quick chat before I renew your prescription... now... let's see... you're..." he turned back to the screen to check my date of birth.

"*Sixteen*?" he said.

A new element to this scenario passed between us. It was without words, but I felt it in the disapproving expression he pulled at me.

I had only just turned sixteen. The prescription for birth control started a little before that.

Now *that* was an awkward appointment. This one, in comparison, should be a walk in the park.

"Are you still sexually active?" he asked.

"Yes."

"Have you, since beginning the medication, experienced nausea?"

"No."

"Headaches?"

"No more than usual."

"Tenderness in your..." he hesitated, and then pointed to his chest. "Bosom."

"Definitely not."

"Have you bled at any times you would deem as being 'irregular'?"

I shook my head.

"Well... good," he then harrumphed and turned back to his keyboard. Started tapping away, and then, shortly after, the printer began its laser-dance with a sheet of paper.

My new prescription.

He handed it to me.

"You should use condoms as well, you know," he advised, just as I was getting up from my seat. "Teenage boys can be–"

"Oh, don't worry. David is different. He would *never* cheat on me," I replied, knowing how delusional I sounded even as the words came from my own mouth.

If this doctor was a more emphatic person he would have probably rolled his eyes. But he didn't. He just nodded and turned his attention back to the screen.

I could almost telepathically hear his altering frame of mind – *Next!* – as I left, and he prepared himself for the next quandary to step through the door.

Okay, so now I should probably tell you something.

I was lying. I don't really have a boyfriend called David. I am not 'sexually active'. In fact, I am a virgin (well, sort of, I will get back to that later) and I, most definitely, do not need birth control.

'*So why?*' You're probably thinking. Why would a sixteen-year-old girl invent a fictional relationship just to get her hands on the pill?

Maybe you suspect that I'm an attention seeker – that I have a cunning plan to carry the pills around until someone notices them, because I am craving an oh-so-dramatic intervention – and you're beginning to worry that this story is going to turn into a painful saga about me celebrating my adolescence by engaging in phantom pregnancies and theatrical self-harm.

Or maybe I just *really* didn't want to go to Biology class that day.

In both cases, you would be wrong.

Have I mentioned yet that I'm a lesbian? Well I am. And I'm not one of those girls who's going through a phase because she thinks it's a bit edgy and boys will find it salacious, either. I have experimented and, trust me, I am one hundred percent gay.

Another reason why I don't need this prescription that I'm currently queuing for.

They are really for a friend of mine, and her name is Tilly.

"Did you get them?" she asked, when I met her at our usual lunchtime retreat on the green.

I nodded and, after carefully looking around to make sure no one was watching, handed her the white paper bag.

"Are you sure you know what you're doing?" I asked her. "They sound like some pretty hardcore shit. They fuck up your peri–"

I stopped myself mid-sentence, realising that I had just trodden upon thorny ground.

I should probably tell you something about Tilly.

She is not a real girl. No, wait. Scratch that. That's horrible. That is not the right way to explain it.

Sorry, let me begin again:

Tilly's chromosomes are XY. At birth she was assumed male.

But it turns out that her mother, the doctors, and even biology itself – to some degree – were mistaken. Tilly's mind, her essence, her instincts and impetus, are all of female gender.

The cause for why some people are born this way is still under investigation. These days, they think it's most likely caused by a hormonal abnormality in the mother's womb during pregnancy, but they aren't completely sure. Most of the experts seem to agree the evidence is pointing towards nature rather than nurture though. That it *is* biological rather than psychological.

What we *do* know is that, somewhere along the line, nature sometimes does something a little bit differently and we have people like Tilly.

I forget most of the time. She is just my friend. She is a girl. She looks like one, acts like one, thinks like one, and she is even – thanks to the hormones – undergoing a puberty right now which is similar to what I am going through. Although she hasn't started her period yet. And she never will (which is something that, in my opinion, she *really* isn't missing out on, but I don't think she would appreciate me saying that).

She is fifteen. Doctors won't prescribe her the hormone treatment she desperately wants because they say she is too young. They only give her these things called 'puberty blockers' to try to keep her quiet and contained, but I guess Tilly is impatient.

She used to order the treatment online, but she can no longer afford it.

I know that we are breaking the rules and self-medicating is generally inadvisable and all of that stuff but, what you've got to understand is, Tilly was close to suicide when I first met her. Some friends of mine saved her life, and at her old school she was bullied horrifically.

But that's a different story.

We became friends after that all happened, and she transferred to my school. I had just 'come out' myself at the time and it seemed to make sense. I think there is much truth to the concept of safety in numbers because, all things considered, we haven't been picked on too much since then. We are part of a diverse and dynamic group of friends and surrounded by many weird and wonderful people.

Although her life is much better than it was, I still think that the hormone therapy is pivotal to Tilly's happiness. That is why I do this for her. She has come a long way since I first met her. I don't want to see her regress to the timid, scared girl she used to be.

And that is how a sixteen-year-old virgin ends up with a prescription for birth control.

Tilly opened the bag and inspected the contents.

"Thank you," she eventually said.

"Are they working?" I asked.

"I think so..." she said. "Things take time... it's hard to tell..."

"Just promise me you know what you are doing," I said.

"I do," she nodded. "Honest. I did loads of research."

"Please tell me it wasn't on Reddit or something," I said, dryly.

Tilly rolled her eyes. "Of course not, and I looked it up in more than one place. Please, Faye... I need this."

"Fine," I said. "But just... be careful."

"You've got your flute with you," Tilly's eyes went to the

case dangling from my shoulder. “Are you gigging tonight?”
“We’re just practicing. It’s no biggie.”
“At Dinnusos?” Tilly asked.
“Yes,” I said. “At Dinnusos.”

Dinnusos is on the other side of town. A forgotten side of town. A place which is known as ‘Yesterville’ by the locals. Its original name has been lost to time. Some say that it is used to the epicentre of the city, and that it was once bustling and it thrived. It is also said to be the oldest district.

I can believe that. It certainly looks old now. At the turn of the century – when the borough expanded, a new high street was erected and modern neighbourhoods were entrenched – the megastores and international chains swooped in like magpies and the residents wriggled over like worms. Yesterville was abandoned. It fell into neglect. It is now a ghetto. A place of urban decay and broken streetlamps. Vagrants and outcasts. Faded signposts and overgrown gardens. Thrifty means and humble dreams.

And tucked within this wasteland is Dinnusos.

I pushed the door open and the hinges groaned. The main bar was empty with the exception of Neal, the owner, who was standing behind the counter.

“Slow day?” I asked.

He nodded sombrely.

It wasn’t unusual. It was Tuesday, after all, and most of the residential houses around here are empty. This is not the sort of place people stumble upon by accident.

It is the kind which enchants people. There is something beguiling about it. It is a little dusty around the corners, sure. And the jumble of tables and chairs are a little creaky and mismatched, but to me that’s just part of its charm. There is much to love about Dinnusos.

The building is Victorian, with high ceilings and sash windows. It’s big, too. Rumour has it the place was once a fancy hotel. If the main bar ever gets too rowdy and you fancy some quiet, there’s a whole labyrinth of rooms on the upper floors you can get lost in. One of the city’s old canal ways runs along the back of the building. Each floor has a balcony and, at night, when all is still, it can be very eerie watching the abandoned neighbourhoods of Yesterville from them.

But the thing I love the most about Dinnusos is the people. Neal's boyfriend Tristan, for instance. He's an artist and has covered the walls with beautiful murals. Kev always has some new wild theory he wants to tell you about. Pag can make anyone feel at ease with his crooked smile. Namda is always eager to engage in a bit of gossip, as long as it's harmless, and Frelia's dry cynicism isn't always what you want to hear, but it's usually true. Dinnusos is frequented by remarkable people and, for many of them, it is a second home. Which is a valuable thing to have if you are from a broken family.

But this isn't enough. Not to keep the place going. Most of us are young and on the fringes of society. We don't have much money to spend, and it takes more than a sense of community to keep a place like this afloat.

Neal hasn't said it outright yet, but I suspect he is struggling to break even.

"I am sure things will pick up," I said, trying to sound as optimistic as I could.

He nodded. "They will… I hope so, anyway."

I patted him on the back. Neal is one of the older members of my social circle. He carries his middle-age well and possesses a smile which is so bewitchingly handsome it can make even my head turn after a few pints of cider. He is somewhat of a patriarch – a father figure. It wasn't pleasant to see him despondent.

I made my way up the stairs. I am in a band called Sunset Haze, and Neal lets us practise in one of his rooms.

When I opened the door, Jack was in the middle of playing a riff on his acoustic guitar and he smiled at me and carried on playing as I stepped inside.

"Do you like it?" he asked when he had finished.

I nodded. "Is it a new song?"

"I would like it to be. It just kind of popped into my head last night... it needs work though," he said, humbly. "And you guys would need to figure out your parts, too. I think I remember some lyrics Ellen wrote a while back which might be right for it..."

"It's got potential," Patrick said, making me jump at the sound of his voice – I didn't even realise he was there. I turned around and saw that he was sitting on a chair in the corner. "But it's a bit repetitive. You should break it up."

"You scared me!" I exclaimed.

He shrugged and turned his focus back to his violin. He was tuning it.

Patrick has a tendency to act like he's got a stick up his ass but I think beneath that persona his heart is in the right place. He can actually be quite thoughtful sometimes. We used to hate each other but have reached a truce over time.

"Isn't Steve coming?" Patrick asked as he tested one of the strings by drawing his bow across it. He then twisted one of the pegs a little and tried again.

"He'll be here later," I replied. "He wanted to get changed."

"I see..." Patrick said, briefly looking me up and down, smirking – I was still in my school uniform.

Steve and I are the babies of the band; the others are all in their late teens and early twenties.

I cleared my throat and claimed a chair next to Jack, freeing my flute from its case. Jack began to play the main riff from his new song again, and I started experimenting with different melodies to accompany it. He smiled at me.

I have always liked Jack. With his long hair and billowy, faded clothes, he reminds me of some of the friends my mother and I made during my childhood summers we spent touring festivals selling strawberries.

After a few minutes of testing different sounds, I eventually found a tune which pleasantly accompanied Jack's rhythm and, shortly after, a warm note entered the ensemble. I looked over to see that Patrick had joined in. Grudgingly.

The three of us gently tested different sounds for a while. Our experiments frequently went wrong, but that was just the way of it. We were patient with each other. Starting from the beginning again, each time.

Eventually Ellen arrived and she paused in the doorway and watched for a while, her little mouth parting into a smile.

"I think you have something there," she said when we finished. She walked over to the rail to hang her coat.

When I first joined the band, Ellen used to make me nervous. Which sounds ridiculous when you take into account that she is barely five feet tall and softly spoken, but it's true. It wasn't fear I was feeling; it was awe. With her grey eyes, pale complexion, and jet black hair, Ellen possesses an unearthly quality. She's one of those people who just has an ambience – an aura, if you will – which doesn't demand regard, but draws it from people all the same.

"Jack came up with it," Patrick said. "We're just trying to figure the rest of it out."

Ellen nodded. "Play it again. From the beginning."

Steve arrived shortly after. He had just returned from a holiday in France so Jack and Ellen rose from their chairs to greet him, and they spent a while catching up. Patrick, however, brought the pleasantries to a swift end, pulling Steve aside to discuss a harmony he had in mind for him to play on his cello. It was back to business again.

I waved at Steve from behind Patrick's shoulder. There was no need for the two of us to have a hearty reunion – he's my classmate and I sit with him during many of my lessons in school.

Last to enter the room was Amelia, as usual, and she made a beeline straight to her drum kit. With only her loud footsteps and the clatter of the door slamming shut behind her to announce her presence.

"What are we playing?" she said flatly, after she had parked herself on a stool and picked up her drumsticks.

We warmed up with some of our usual material, and then Jack introduced Amelia and Steve to his new song and the two of them began considering their own contributions. Ellen sat on the floor and leafed through her collection of poetry and lyrics.

A few minutes later, Neal stuck his head through the door and we all stopped.

"Sorry," Jack said. "We'll turn it down. I–"

"No," Neal shook his head. He was smiling. "Don't worry about that! A load of punters just walked in! The bar is packed!"

"That's awesome!" Steve grinned.

"I know!" Neal beamed as us. "And it's a *Tuesday*! Can you believe it? They're all new faces, too!"

Neal then looked down, suddenly becoming coy, and poked the toe of his boot into a crack in the floorboards. "Anyway..." he said. "I was just wondering if you could do me a favour… You see, I want to create a buzz. Something to make them want to come back. Now, I know you are–"

"Do you want us to play downstairs?" Ellen finished for him.

He turned his head back up and he grinned so widely I knew that none of us – not even Patrick – would be able to refuse.

"I mean, not for too long," he added. "I know some of you have school in the morning."

"Sure," Ellen smiled. "Just give us a few minutes to get ready."

"Brilliant!" he exclaimed. "I best go! There's a queue to the door! Thanks!"

We hurried downstairs, instruments in hand, and began to set up. Neal had not been exaggerating when he said the place was busy. In the six months since he had opened I had never seen the bar so full. Tristan had been called in to help and he was dashing around behind the counter serving drinks.

I carried a section of Amelia's drum kit down the stairs while Jack, Patrick and Steve set up all of their equipment. It took a few trips and a bit of fiddling for us to get ready but, in that time, we drew a lot of attention. Some of the guests started eyeing up the stage.

By the time we had finished preparing, many of the tables and chairs had been rearranged and we found ourselves looking upon an expectant crowd. Ellen switched her microphone on.

"Testing. One. Two. Three," she said, causing a few more heads to stir. "Good evening everyone. We are called Sunset Haze, and Neal," she gestured to the landlord standing behind the bar. "The lovely owner of this place, has asked us to play some songs for you. Welcome to Dinnusos."

Jack started strumming a riff on his acoustic guitar. I

recognised the tune he was playing, and smiled. It was the intro to one of the jauntier tracks from our catalogue of songs.

It was a good way to begin. It was March. Spring had come early this year and the air was getting warmer. Even though we were just about to enter the evening hours, the window was still glowing with sunlight.

I know a lot of bands say this, but our music is hard to categorise. Our style is a fusion of folk, ethereal wave, dark rock, and sometimes we have even been referred to as 'classical'. The mood of our sound ranges from festive and uplifting, to sombre and melancholy. Even the instrumental line-up varies. I mostly play flute, but we do have a few tracks where I tap keyboard and sing backing vocals. Jack will often switch several times, during gigs, between his electric and acoustic guitar, and Steve sometimes plays bass instead of cello.

I could tell, before we even began this set, that this was the sort of crowd our music would go down well with. I took in just a fleeting glance across the bar and saw a whole kaleidoscope of different styles. Purple pigtails. Blonde braids. Frilly black dresses. Patchwork tunics, denim jackets, and tweed waistcoats. There was a girl resting her legs on the table who had beads in her hair and a ring in her eyebrow. She was smiling. Some of them were just dressed plainly, but that was fine, too. They all had the air of artists and students. Poets and thinkers.

A few of them got up and started dancing, so we upped the tempo. Choosing our songs as we went along to match the shifts in mood.

It was almost an hour later – after Ellen had just finished singing the last verse to one of our songs and the rest of us were preparing for the instrumental bridge – when something remarkable happened.

To the audience it probably just seemed that Ellen had become enthralled by the music. She began to dance. Wildly. Her arms making shapes in the air and her hair flinging back and forth as she careened, her head swerving from side to side, up and down.

To Jack, Patrick, Jack, Steve, Amelia, and I – the ones who

knew Ellen's secret – it was something much more significant. Ellen was catatonic. Ellen had gone to another place. Ellen was not even aware of herself anymore.

Ellen was being possessed by Jessica.

So here's the thing – and you are going to think the whole lot of us are crazy, but just hear me out.

Jessica is the ghost of Ellen's deceased twin.

She died shortly after the two of them were born and now Jessica is a ghost. She lingers. She follows her twin through the journey of her mortal life. She haunts Ellen. She haunts all of us, in a way. Her spirit is rooted into the essence of our music.

You are probably sceptical, but trust me, if you had seen or experienced half of the things I have since I joined the band, you would believe it too.

Ellen is known by many people as a psychic, a mystic, a wisewoman – whatever you want to call it. She just has a way of knowing things which, in a wholly rational world, she shouldn't. People come to her for advice because Ellen often knows the answers to mysterious things which are going on in their lives.

It is through Jessica that Ellen gains much of this wisdom. Her deceased twin's voice whispers to her from across the ether. To Ellen, Jessica is very real. An apparition floating around her, guiding the course of her life.

Ellen can even, when the timing is right, be possessed by her.

The five of us turned to each other as Ellen's body swayed back and forth, knowing all too well what was happening and what was expected of us.

We finished the song and then Jack swiftly placed his acoustic guitar down and turned on his amplifier. Steve did the same, swapping his cello for a bass.

Ellen – or Jessica, more accurately – grabbed the microphone and playfully winked at me before turning her attention back to the audience and bringing it to her mouth. She let out a wail, one which sent shivers down my spine. Patrick brought his violin back to his chin and began to play one of our songs.

The audience – even though they were not privy to our band's secret – must have noticed something had changed. Jessica has a different style to Ellen, so we play variant songs for her. Both of the twins will often, during gigs, abandon conventional lyrics and cascade into catenations of glossolalia but Jessica's vocal range is much more rampant and tumultuous than Ellen's. The rest of us play a different style of music to match her. Jack and Steve switch their amplifiers to distorted settings, and the notes I play with my flute are more drawn out. I often feel, when we are playing with Jessica, that we are channelling something arcane and intangible.

The audience began to sway, rather than dance, and some of them closed their eyes. Almost as if we had taken them to a different place. There was no sound of chatter in the background anymore. Everyone's attention was rapt upon us. They were mesmerised.

Even I lost myself. I became only vaguely aware of the transitions we made between different songs. It all became one symphony.

When Jessica drew the performance to an end, it felt a bit like I was being dropped and, when I landed, I became very aware of the sensation of my feet pressed against floor.

I grounded myself, reluctantly.

After the audience had finished applauding I left the stage and made my way towards the stairs.

"You were fantastic!" Neal exclaimed, appearing in front of me. "One of the best sets I've seen you do. Here," he pushed a glass into my hand. "Have this. It's on the house."

"What is it?" I asked.

"Lemonade," he said. And then he winked in a way which made it immediately clear that it was somewhat more than lemonade.

It was a kind gesture: the authorities don't come to Yesterville very often, but Neal still worries about his licence sometimes.

"Thanks, Neal," I said. "Can I leave it down here for a minute though? I just need to put my flute away."

"Sure," he said, and I handed it back to him. "I'll keep it behind the bar."

I made my way up the stairs and back to our rehearsal room to place my flute back in its case.

It was while I was walking back down again that a pair of hands appeared behind me and grabbed my collar. My heart lurched against my chest and I screamed.

"Get off me!" I yelled, as they pulled me through a doorway and into a dark room. I fought, driving my elbow back to try to catch them in the ribs, but missed. I called out again, making as much noise as I possibly could in the hope that someone would hear me.

They finally let go and I turned around and saw their face.

"Ellen!" I exclaimed. "What the fuck?"

But then, when I looked at her properly – noticed her posture and expression – I realised that it wasn't Ellen at all.

"*Jessica*?" I exclaimed. "What are you doing? Why are you still here?"

"Is that any way to greet me?" she asked, grinning devilishly as she drew close. She put her face up close to mine.

And then she kissed me.

So now I should probably tell you something else about Jessica.

She is my girlfriend. Well, sort of. It's hard to put a label to it really, considering that our relationship – until this moment – has never been physical.

I don't have Ellen's gift to see nor speak to the dead, so the only time I ever get to spend with Jessica is when she visits me at night during my dreams. They are rather intimate dreams. The kind which bathe you in bliss and you wake up from feeling suspended and craving something more.

"No," I said, pushing her away. "We can't."

"What's the matter?" she asked, frowning.

"That's Ellen's body," I said. "Not yours."

"Me and Ellen were identical," Jessica said. She tried to close in on me again, pressing Ellen's body against me, but I stepped away. "What difference does it make?"

"It's weird," I said. "What are you doing here, anyway? You usually leave when we finish playing."

"I decided to stick around for a while," she shrugged.

"It's not fair on Ellen," I folded my arms over my chest. "Let her come back, Jessica."

"This," Jessica said, pointing a finger to the body she was using. "Is between me and Ellen. You let *us* worry about that. Just come here," she implored. She put those hands upon my waist and tried to draw me into her, but all I could think was that they were *Ellen's*. "Enjoy it."

"No!" I said, flinging her away. "Sorry Jessica, but I can't. It's just not right!"

I reached for the door.

"Faye! Wait!" she said as I opened it.

I slammed the door shut and raced down the corridor, towards the stairs.

I knew that if I went straight to the bar Jessica might find me there so I made a detour to the balcony on the second floor. It's usually a quiet place where one can be alone for a while, but when I stepped outside and into the moonlight another girl was already there.

"Hello," she said, looking me up and down before drawing a cigarette to her lips. She inhaled and blew a cloud of smoke into the air between us. "You're from the band," she said.

I nodded, feigning a smile as I hugged myself. It was dark now and beginning to get a little chilly. I didn't have my coat.

"Do you smoke?" she asked. "Or did you just come here for the fresh air?"

For some quiet, I almost said, but then I realised that might have sounded a bit rude. "Just air," I replied. "I don't smoke. Well... only sometimes."

"Is this one of those times?" she asked, holding out her packet to me and popping open the lid.

"Go on then," I said, taking one. She passed me a lighter too, and I lit up.

"Long night?" she asked, as I exhaled.

I nodded. "You wouldn't believe it if I told you. What's your name? I haven't seen you here before."

"Naomi," she said. She looked at me. Her eyes were very striking. Hazel, with leafy green in the centre. They were earthy and dazzling at the same time.

I looked down and saw that she was wearing a black dress and there were several necklaces dangling from her neck. She was very pretty.

"What's your name?" she asked me.

"Faye."

We shook hands.

"Lots of new faces tonight," I commented. "Where have you all come from?"

"We're students at St Bridgets. An art college down the road," she said. "Kelly heard about this place and talked us into checking it out."

"Do you like it?" I asked.

"It's been an interesting evening..." she said, turning her eyes to the sky ponderously. "I was particularly intrigued by your band's... *encore*."

I looked at her, wondering if she knew about Jessica. I couldn't tell. She was staring out at the rooftops of Yesterville with a peculiar expression on her face.

"Now that was quite extraordinary…" she finished, turning back to me.

"Ellen gets quite into it once she's warmed up," I said guardedly.

"Oh, so it's nothing to do with that ghost then?" Naomi said, looking at me with a frank expression.

I gasped, but Naomi simply raised her eyebrow.

I knew then that there was no point in denying it.

"How do you know about that?" I asked.

"I can sense things," she shrugged. "It follows you, you know. But I think you're already aware of that," she hesitated. "She's rather... attached to you..."

I blushed and turned away, not knowing what to say. I had never told anyone about Jessica. Not even my closest friends. I think Ellen and some of the other members of the band had guessed though.

I then felt a hand on my shoulder. It was Naomi. She was close to me now and I could feel her breath on my ear. "If you ever want to free yourself from her, let me know," she whispered. "Spirits can be restless and unpredictable. There are ways to banish them."

I opened my mouth to reply, but before I could she leaned into me and brushed her lips on my cheek. It was only brief, but sensuous. It surprised me. I didn't know how to respond.

"You're an interesting girl," she said, while I was still trying to figure out what I should say. "If you ever want to talk to me, you can find me at St Bridgets. I'm usually in my workshop till about seven most weekdays."

She then turned and walked away.

"It was nice to meet you, Faye."

That night, while I was sleeping, I was visited by Jessica.

"Why didn't you want me?" she asked.

We were lying together on the grass. Naked. It was night, but the trees around us were beset by a hazy glow which didn't seem to come from any particular source.

When Jessica visits my dreams, they are always a little like this. I *know* that I am dreaming. The colours, sounds, shapes and sensations, however, are always much more vivid than they are in a normal dream. It almost feels real.

"Why didn't you want me?" she repeated, with a little more urgency in her voice this time.

She pressed her forehead against mine so that our noses were touching.

"I want *you*. Not Ellen," I said. "That's why. You can't use her like that, Jessica. It's not fair."

Jessica's features rippled like water disturbed by a stone. Her face changed. Her hair grew, her cheeks became rounder.

She turned into Naomi.

"Or is it really me that you want?"

"No!" I exclaimed, flinging her away. She tumbled onto the grass, rolled, and, when she righted herself, she was Jessica again.

"You like her," Jessica said. "I know you do! You can't hide it from me."

"Maybe I do..." I admitted. "But that doesn't mean things between us have to change."

"I am not enough for you anymore!" Jessica said. "You want to feel real flesh against you! Don't deny it. I *know* you,

Faye. More than anyone else. I am losing you. That's why I did it. I wanted to pleasure you like a mortal."

"You're not losing me," I croaked.

"Don't lie to me!" she howled, and her voice echoed around me. The trees around us were stirred by a sudden gust of wind which made the branches quiver. Brown leaves fell from the sky like rain.

"Jessica!" I yelled. But, as I opened my mouth, I felt myself spinning. Spiralling. I reached out for her, but she was gone and I was falling. Falling. Falling.

I bolted upright with my hand held to my chest, gasping for breath.

I was back in my room.

I turned to the window, and the curtain was rippling. There was a storm blowing by outside.

Coincidence? I wasn't so sure.

"You look like crap," Tilly said flatly, when I saw her the following morning.

I groaned as I sat myself next to her. I had just come out from my first lesson of the day and it was hell.

"Didn't sleep much last night," I admitted, pressing a fist to my mouth to stifle a yawn. "We ended up playing in the bar."

"I thought you said it wasn't a gig?" Tilly said, and her face fell a little. She seemed almost hurt.

"Oh, sorry," I said, remembering our conversation the previous day. "It wasn't at first but loads of people turned up and Neal asked us to."

That wasn't the only reason I didn't get much rest; after I woke up from that dream with Jessica I dared not go back to sleep again. But I didn't tell Tilly about that.

"Sorry, Tilly," I said. "It just kind of happened. And it was late as well. I didn't think you would want to come all the way to Dinnusos at that time."

"It's okay…" Tilly said. "Did it go well?"

"Yeah," I replied. "It was a really good one. Everyone said they enjoyed it. There was this girl called Naomi – I met her on the balcony – and she goes to this college called–"

"You fancy her!" Tilly exclaimed.

"What?" I blurted, not quite managing to disguise my reaction. "What do you mean?"

"When you said her name you were smiling," Tilly giggled triumphantly. "I could tell."

"Was it a bit like when you talk about Jack?" I asked, tartly.

Tilly blushed.

Gotcha, I thought, feeling smug.

I knew there was a reason she was always so keen to come to our gigs.

"So, anyway," I carried on. "She goes to this art college called St Bridgets, and she invited me to go there and see her work sometime."

"Are you going to?" Tilly asked.

"I don't know..." I murmured. The thought of it put me on edge. I was going to have to go back to sleep eventually and, when I did, I would have to face Jessica.

"I think you are…" Tilly said.

I convinced myself all day that Tilly was wrong. That I wasn't going to see Naomi. When I finished school, I even walked all the way home.

But, once home, I undressed, showered, towelled myself dry, and I even spent a few minutes deciding what to wear.

And then, after spending an extraordinary amount of time fussing over my hair, I found myself leaving the house and walking towards St Bridgets.

It took me a while to find it. It was near the park; a large neo-Gothic building with a domed roof.

I stepped inside, expecting to find a reception there or at least someone to talk to, but the foyer was empty. I wandered around and nobody asked any questions as to my purpose – I guess they all just assumed I was another student. Eventually I approached someone.

"Do you know where I can find Naomi?" I said.

"Naomi?" he repeated, scratching his head. He was one of those people who seemed incapable of looking someone in the eyes. In the few moments we conversed, he looked at almost everything else. The wall behind me. The door. The window. Another door.

"Yes... she's a student here," I said.

"I'll ask... hold on."

He shuffled away and returned a few minutes later with a girl in paint-stained dungarees. "I recognise you," she said as she adjusted her glasses, lifting them back up to the bridge of her nose. "You're in that band – the one which played in Dinnusos last night – aren't you?"

"Yes," I said, feeling a little embarrassed and not knowing why.

"You were awesome!" she exclaimed, and then she took my hand. "Hi. I'm Hannah by the way. Are you looking for Naomi Thorne?"

"I'm not sure what her surname is," I admitted. "I met her last night and she said I could find her here."

"That'll be Naomi then," she nodded. "She was there with us. Follow me. I'll take you to her studio."

Hannah engaged in a bit of chitchat as she led me through a series of corridors and then outside and through a courtyard, towards a smaller building. As we approached it Naomi emerged from the door.

"Faye?" she said as she came out to meet me. "I saw you from the window."

"She was looking for you," my bespectacled escort informed her.

"Thanks, Hannah," Naomi said, and then turned back to me. "I wasn't expecting you so soon. Come in."

Hannah winked at us as Naomi ushered me inside. I followed her through a large hall which was filled with unfinished sculptures, scattered tools, and installations, and smelt acutely of paint and glue.

Naomi led me through another door and then into a small room. "This is my studio," she said, casting her arms out widely. I could tell this place was a source of great joy for her.

"You have your own room?" I asked.

She nodded. "I pay a little extra to use this space. This building isn't *technically* part of St Bridgets. It just happens to be next door and everyone who has a studio here is from St Bridgets. It's partly funded by grants and community projects, so the fee is reasonable."

It made sense. I had done a little bit of research into St Bridgets before I came – as I had never heard of the place until now – and it was actually a very highly regarded college. Most of its students were between sixteen and nineteen years old, and they all had to either earn a scholarship or pay a large tuition fee to enrol.

I looked at the walls. They were covered in paintings. At first sight they appeared to be typical depictions of landscapes and natural settings. Beautifully illustrated, but mundane.

I began to notice hidden details. In one, I saw a man's face in the furrows in the bark of a tree. In another, there were spritely creatures camouflaged in the undergrowth of a forest. I found something unusual in all of them if I looked for long enough. One of the most striking ones was of a canyon during sunset, and, between all of the enchanting colours glowing in the horizon, was the silhouette of some kind of mythical creature with wings.

There was an easel by the window where Naomi was working on a new piece. It was of a woman walking down a dark pathway, unaware of the shadowy hands behind her, reaching for her.

"Are they *all* yours?" I asked.

She nodded.

"They're really good," I said. There seemed to be a recurring theme. Unseen forces lurking in day-to-day places. A sense that all was not quite what it seemed. A challenge to the materialistic milieu.

I could relate to that.

"So what's your story?" I asked, looking her up and down. "Are you a Wiccan or something?"

"No," she laughed and shook her head. "I am not a Wiccan... but I guess you could call me a 'witch'. What made you think I was Wiccan?"

"My mother has lots of friends who are into that stuff," I confessed. I was getting the impression from the slightly deprecating tone when she uttered the word 'Wiccan' that they were not a group she particularly desired to be associated with, so I mentioned some others she might find more agreeable. "Pagans, Druids, Shamans... and, well, you remind me of them. A little. And this art," I added, gesturing to the walls. "It's all quite... magical. Isn't it? And you knew about–"

I cut myself short. I almost named her then – Jessica – but I stopped myself. I didn't even know this girl.

Naomi nodded. "Yes, I sensed your... friend. It was hard not to really. She was buzzing all around the bloody place."

"Ellen – our singer – is psychic too," I said. I could tell her that much. It was fairly common knowledge. "She hears voices."

"I don't have the same gift as her," Naomi said. "Not everyone is the same. Some hear voices, others *see* things, some people even smell, or taste. I *feel* things... like impressions. It's hard to explain... How do *you* communicate with her?"

I didn't ask who '*her*' was; Jessica was an elephant in the room. A rift between us.

I felt very drawn to Naomi – so much that I had come here even though I knew it risked Jessica's wrath – but I wasn't quite sure if I trusted her yet.

When Jessica came into my life, I had never really thought about what would happen if I got involved with a girl in the mundane world. It was never something the two of us had reason to discuss, until now.

But last night, Jessica had made it clear that she was tempestuously jealous. I had seen a whole new side to her.

A side which scared me.

I had always assumed that our amour would remain contained. Special, in its own way, but exclusive to my dreams. I never thought that other people would find out about it and it would affect my waking life.

Did Jessica really expect me to never experience intimacy in the flesh? To never have a 'normal' relationship?

"She visits me during my dreams," I admitted.

"And I bet they're interesting dreams too," Naomi said, in a knowing manner which made me blush. "Not everyone is able to communicate with the dead during their sleep... so you must have a gift."

I paused. I had never thought of myself as special or

psychic, so I didn't know what to make of that. I didn't *feel* like I was the gifted one when Jessica visited my dreams. Jessica was the one who was very much in control during those unions.

"She didn't like you meeting me, did she?" Naomi said.

"How did you know that?" I asked.

"I sensed her when we were on the balcony last night. She was watching us," Naomi paused, thoughtfully. "She does only visit your dreams when you *want* her to, doesn't she?"

I hesitated.

I didn't want to lie, but I didn't want to paint Jessica as a villain, either.

But, when I thought about it, I realised that, in all the time Jessica had frequented my dreams, when had she ever asked my permission? Even when it first began – before I realised that Jessica was an actual entity and not just some automaton my subconscious had conjured – she had initiated things with me which, in the mortal world, would have been bordering on assault.

"There are ways you can protect yourself from her, you know. I can teach you," Naomi offered. "I could even banish her, if you ever wanted me to."

I gasped. She said something similar to me the night before.

Could she really banish Jessica? The thought of it scared me. Jessica had been such a poignant force in my life since she burst her way into it. She liberated me. She was the soul of the band, and Ellen would be lost without her.

She had become a bit unstable lately, but I was hoping that mood would pass. I didn't want her out of my life completely... I just wanted her to give me some room to breathe.

"Don't worry. I would never do anything like that without your permission," Naomi said, placing a hand on my arm. She must have noticed something in my expression. "You look terrified... I'm sorry... I just wanted to let you know I can help you. But only if you want me to. Sit down," she said, offering me a chair.

"Could you teach me how to not let her in? When I don't want her to be?" I asked. I felt guilty as soon as the words came from my mouth – I wondered if Jessica was watching us this very moment. It wasn't always easy having a ghost as a lover. It often felt like your every move was being observed.

"Of course I can," Naomi said. "But it might not work instantly. And it will take a bit of time. How old are you, anyway?" she narrowed her eyes and looked me up and down. "I thought that school uniform you were wearing last night was just part of your band's thing, but now I..." she paused. "Are you still in school?"

"Yes," I admitted. "But I am sixteen!" I hurriedly added. "I'm in my final year."

"You are quite young..." she said, looking at me thoughtfully.

"Why?" I asked. "How old are you?"

"Eighteen," she said.

"That's not much difference," I said. "I'm not too young to be your–"

I stopped myself, feeling heat rising in my cheeks. I almost said the word 'girlfriend' then. How embarrassing. "I mean..."

"You've never dated a mortal, have you?" Naomi said dryly.

"How do you know?" I asked, feeling defensive.

"It's obvious," Naomi said. She chuckled. "But kind of cute, too..."

"So you would date me then?"

She laughed again, this time louder. "No. Not yet, anyway. You shouldn't say things like that to a girl you have only just met, you know, but I'll let you off. You're cute, Faye. Even if you don't know how to talk to girls and have a weird psycho-ghost haunting you."

I looked at the floor.

"Anyway," Naomi was the one to break the silence. "Do you want me to teach you how to shield yourself from her?"

I nodded.

She spent a while teaching me methods to protect myself from spiritual entities. It was interesting. And then we chatted for a while. She gave me a charm to hang over my bed while sleeping, but she also said that there was no guarantee any of these precautions would be completely effective. She described them as tantamount to applying insect repellent; they were deterrent, but not failsafe.

I woke the next day not able to recall any particular dreams of import, although I vaguely remembered hearing my name being called a few times. It sounded weak and distant.

I went to see Naomi again the following day. Though only for a short while – with the busy week I had had so far I was beginning to fall behind with my homework, so I spent the rest of that evening catching up. We did arrange to meet at the park the following day, and that was fun.

It was that afternoon I found out more about her. She told me about her childhood, growing up in the countryside and spending much of her youth building dens in the woods and reading books in her garden. It was when Naomi turned twelve that her mother revealed to her that she was a hedgewitch and introduced her to her craft.

It sounded like a fairy tale to a city girl like me. Idyllic. But Naomi said that by the time she was a teenager she began to find rural life a little boring. One of the reasons she applied to study at St Bridgets was because she wanted to meet more people.

I told her about my own mother – a yoga-obsessed, vegan hippy – and she laughed and laughed. She said that our mothers would probably get on very well.

It was then, when we were both heartily laughing, that I got caught in the moment and did something bold.

I leant towards her. I wanted to kiss her.

And, briefly, it seemed she wanted to kiss me too.

But then she turned her head away.

"No," she said.

I was so embarrassed I couldn't even look at her. I faced the lake and drew my knees to my chest, hugging them.

That was the first time I had ever made a move on a girl. It just felt like the natural thing to do. I had assumed that everything would fall into place.

"Why?" I said. My voice – against my will – croaked, only adding to the humiliation. "I thought you liked me..."

"Because you belong to someone else," she said.

"I haven't heard from Jessica for days," I said. "She's in my dreams and you're real… it's different."

"Oh, Jessica is her name, is it?" Naomi said, and I flinched. I had managed to keep that a secret until that moment, but in my dejection I had let it slip. "You've been avoiding her, true, but you are far from free. And I'm not even sure you want to be."

I opened my mouth to reply, but then I realised that there was some truth to her words.

"If you make yourself *permanently* free from her, then we could have something, Faye," she said. "But I am not sharing you."

I looked at her. Into her wondrous eyes which made me think of pine needles glowing in the sun.

I wanted, more than anything, to tell her that I desired her and her only, but the thought of saying goodbye to Jessica forever – and never having her visit my dreams again – bloomed an empty feeling in my chest.

A part of me had been hoping I would find a way to bring Jessica and Naomi around – convince them that they could both be a part of my life – but I knew now that it wasn't going to be possible. They were going to make me choose.

And I had no idea how to make a decision like that.

"Come," Naomi said. She stood up. "I will walk you home."

My mother ended up inviting Naomi in to have dinner with us and, rather predictably, the two of them got on like a house on fire. When Naomi left, my mother asked me some rather prying questions about her, which I dodged masterfully. Ever since I came out to her a few months ago my mother has made a point of being all liberal about it and pestered me almost weekly over whether I had a girlfriend.

I have never told her about Jessica. As open-minded as my mother is, I doubt she would have quite been able to get her head around that one.

That night I dreamt of moons and pentacles and black cats with glowing eyes – all sorts of cliché witchy things – so I guess some of the conversations I had had with Naomi recently must have rubbed off on me.

The cats slinked their way between the trees, and I followed them. I had a torch in my hand. There was something glowing in the distance, and they were guiding me there, occasionally turning their necks back to stare at me with their yellow eyes.

We reached the light. It was a fire, softly smouldering in the middle of the glade. The cats dispersed – I had reached my destination now, their purpose had been served – and I started dancing around the open flames. In that sibylline, dreamlike, bedevilled way, I didn't even know *why* I was dancing. It just felt right.

And then I found myself face to face with Jessica.

"I knew you liked her!" she hissed.

"Jessica!" I whispered. "How did you–"

"That witch! She turned you against me!" Jessica screamed. "You've been shutting me out!"

"I just wanted some space..." I said.

"You're *mine*!" she wailed, tears pouring from her eyes.

"I am not *anyone's*!" I said. "And why are you forcing me to choose? Why can't–"

"No!" Jessica shook her head violently. "She's dangerous! Don't trust her!"

I backed away but she carried on advancing. I looked her in the eyes, suddenly feeling defiant and angry.

"Get away from me!" I yelled.

I swung the torch to at her and she leapt back.

"You can't hurt me," she said. She narrowed her eyes at the yellow flames burning from the torch I was holding between us, and they died. "See!" she said, smiling as she advanced on me again. "You can't escape from me, Faye..." Her expression softened a little. "Just talk to me… Please. Tell me what you want."

"This is *my* dream, Jessica!" I screamed. "You have no right to be here!"

I cast my arm out – I wished she would just *go away* – and, to my utter surprise, her feet left the ground. She flew back several feet, colliding into the trunk of a tree.

She looked up at me, shocked. "Faye," she said. "I–"

There was a network of roots beneath her and, possessed by a new understanding and feeling empowered, I saw them for what they really were – a genius of *my* subconscious mind, a part of *me* – and I imagined them coming to life. They grew, coiling around Jessica's arms and limbs like a family of snakes. She kicked and fought, so I tightened them.

"I get it now, Jessica," I said, walking towards her calmly. "None of this is real. You have no power here, because it is *my* dream."

She vanished before my eyes.

"You don't know quite as much as you think," she whispered into my ear. She had suddenly reappeared behind me. Her body was pressed against my back and her arms were draped around my neck.

"Give up, Jessica," I said. "It's over.

I clicked my fingers and the whole setting around me – the moonlit glade, the trees, the grass, and Jessica with it – vanished. I visualised a new setting. A meadow, dazzled in sunlight and dotted with flowers. And it came to life.

I span around in a full circle, revelling in the control I was wielding over my revelry. And then I walked through the field. Ran my hand through the long blades of grass and caressed the kernels with my fingers.

Jessica appeared again, shortly after, but I envisaged a black hole opening up beneath her feet. She wailed as it swallowed her, but the sound was cut off when the gap closed.

I didn't hear from Jessica again that night, but I remained in a cognisant state – aware that I was in a dream, and still able to effect my will upon it.

I conjured a beautiful forest and, as I strolled through it, plants rose up from the ground. Each one became wilder and more exotic in its shape and colour, as I experimented with creating different forms in this world where I was omnipotent.

I soon discovered I could fly – I pictured my feet leaving the ground, and they *did* – so I took to the sky. I flew, leaving the forest behind and soaring towards something blue in the distance. An ocean. I thought of tropical beaches, and an archipelago of islands with sandy coves appeared below. I envisioned a castle floating upon an island in the sky, and it materialised, too. I glided towards it and landed upon one of the towers. Sat down for a while and watched the aerosols of clouds soar past me as the castle floated through the welkin.

Eventually I thought of Naomi, and she appeared beside me. Her wavy tresses of red hair rippled gently in the wind and, when her big hazel eyes settled upon me, they widened. I laughed gleefully at how lifelike I had managed to make her seem. Even the expression of surprise on her face when she looked at me, was perfect.

"Faye..." she said.

I realised then, as I looked upon her lovely face that, if I wanted to, I could enact all sorts of desires. No matter how base. No matter how sleazy.

But I didn't want to. Even though I knew this girl standing in front of me was just a projection of my own cognition, to turn this wonderful dream into some kind of seedy fantasy would have felt wrong.

If I ever made love to Naomi, I wanted it to be with the real her.

"I know that you are not really Naomi," I said. "But I am just going to say it to you anyway. I am finished with Jessica. She no longer has any power over me. I know how to shut her out now. It's you that I want."

I then kissed her – I would let myself do that, at least – and she kissed me back. Her lips felt warm and soft, like feathers.

I awoke, torn away from Naomi's lips to the sound of my alarm. I let out a groan as I reached for my phone to end the noise.

When I had successfully pressed the snooze button, I lay back into my sheets and smiled to myself as I stared up at the ceiling.

That was the most invigorating night of sleep I had ever had.

I was bounding with energy that day, almost too much. I found it difficult to sit still during my lessons. I just wanted the day to be over so I could see Naomi – which of course, only made the hours drag.

At four o'clock I raced back home and got changed. It was Friday and I had the whole weekend ahead of me. I originally had plans to spend the evening with Tilly, but I gently let her down during lunch hour. She was a little disappointed but gave me her blessing.

I made my way to St Bridgets and, when I reached Naomi's studio, the door was hanging open and she was leant over her easel brushing some finishing touches into that painting she was working on. The one of the girl walking towards the moonlight. It was almost finished.

"Naomi," I said, and she span around.

"Faye," she said, smiling at me. She dropped her paintbrush into a jar of murky water and came to greet me.

"I finished with Jessica last night," I said. "She no longer has any power over my dreams. I know how to shut her out now. I–"

Naomi's jaw dropped, leaving her mouth hanging wide open.

"What's the matter?" I asked.

"That's so weird..." she breathed. "I had a dream about you last night, and you said almost the exact same thing." She ran a hand through her hair. "We were in a castle, and there were clouds around us. You told me–"

"You're kidding..." I gasped.

She shook her head. "You said that you wanted me. Me only. Is it true?"

I nodded.

She drew me into her arms and kissed me. It was a little different to how it felt the night before – a little less sublime, not as velvety, and I was sure I could taste a subtle hint of coffee in her mouth, too – but it was still wonderful in its own way because it was *real*.

"Oh, sorry!" she pulled away and touched my blouse. "I got paint on you!"

"I don't care," I whispered.

"I told you you had a gift," Naomi said, a while later.

She had just returned from the vending machine, carrying two polystyrene cups steaming with tea.

"It could have been you," I said as I took one. She sat herself down next to me. "You're the witch."

"No. It is you who made the connection. I'm sure of it," she said. "I know what I am capable of and entering other people's dreams is not one of them. I have never even had a *normal* lucid dream in my entire life, let alone one like you had. And like I said before, not everyone can communicate with spirits while they're asleep. The fact that you took *control* last night proves it. I think you're a dreamwalker."

"A dreamwalker?" I repeated.

She nodded.

"What does that mean?"

"I am not sure, really," she admitted. "It's a term I heard once, and it sounds an awful lot like what you have been doing. I have never known one before."

"So you don't actually know anything?" I asked.

She shrugged. "I can ask around if you like. My mother or one of my friends might know something."

I sighed. "But if I am really a 'dreamwalker' why haven't I ever done it until now? I only started having dreams like that when I met Jessica."

"Are you sure of that? Have you recorded every dream you have ever had? Have you asked *every* friend you have ever dreamt about if they experienced it too?" Naomi asked, and she looked at me so shrewdly I had to concede she had a point. "And people who have abilities are not always aware of it. All of those films people watch and books they read tell stories about 'special' people who are 'gifted'," she raised her hands and made ersatz quote gestures with her fingers for both of those words. "But the reality is very different. I think a lot of people have dormant skills. Sometimes using them comes naturally, and sometimes it doesn't. Sometimes something needs to happen to help them awaken it. Most people are capable of a lot of things, if they're patient and willing to put the effort in."

She put her hand on mine. "But dreamwalking is something I think you have a knack for."

Whatever it is, I thought.

"Does this mean I am always going to dream like that from now?" I asked.

"I'm not sure," she said. "Like I said, I have never known a dreamwalker before. And even if I did, it would be very likely that their experiences would be different to yours. Everything will become clearer with time."

By the time we had finished talking about dreams and other paranormal phenomena, I looked at the clock and realised that it wasn't even 7pm yet and there was still plenty of the evening left.

It was Naomi who suggested we go to Dinnusos – she admitted that she had taken a shine to the place when we met there earlier that week – and, well... it didn't take much to convince me to visit my usual haunt.

We walked there together hand in hand. I felt giddy and elated. It was still too early to know where it was going, but Naomi and I were much more comfortable and at ease with each other now. We had still not talked about 'us'. And I don't think we wanted to yet because whatever *was* happening between us was still exciting and new. To talk about it so soon could spoil it.

"I remember you," Neal said to Naomi as we approached the bar. "Weren't you here the other night?"

"Yes," Naomi replied. "Tuesday, I think. When Faye was playing," she added, and then smiled at me.

"Well, welcome back to Dinnusos," Neal said, extending his hand over the bar counter. "I'm Neal."

Naomi shook his hand and introduced herself.

"Business seems to be picking up..." I commented as I looked over my shoulder. The door had just creaked open again and a new crowd of people were wandering in. I didn't recognise any of their faces.

"Yes, I know!" Neal grinned.

"I didn't even know this place existed until my friends dragged me here the other night," Naomi confessed. "But as soon as I stepped in I fell in love with it! People at St Bridgets have been talking about it."

"Oh, so that's where you lot all came from?" Neal said. "I thought you looked like studenty types... oh, and that reminds me. Faye," he said, then turning back to me. "I was just talking to Ellen. Are you free to play again on Wednesday?"

"I don't think I have any plans..." I murmured, recalling my rather uneventful calendar. "Is Ellen here?"

Neal nodded. "And Patrick. They're upstairs."

I bought a pair of drinks and then ventured to the upper floor to see if I could find Ellen. I was in two minds about seeing her. On one hand, I had been meaning to discuss our rehearsal schedule anyway, so it was convenient she was there. On the other, I felt a little apprehensive. I was very aware that she was Jessica's twin, and I wondered if she knew what had happened between us recently.

I knew I would have to face her eventually though. And I didn't feel like I had done anything wrong or to be ashamed about so I was determined to not let my spat with Jessica affect my relationship with Ellen and the rest of the band.

I opened the door to our room and Patrick and Ellen were sitting at the table leafing through some sheets of music. They both looked up as I entered.

"Hey," I said, as I walked in with Naomi behind me. "Neal said he wants us to play on Wednesday?"

Patrick nodded, but Ellen simply stared at Naomi.

She often does this when she lays her eyes upon someone for the first time. I remember when she did it to me, all those months ago, and it felt very much like her ghostly eyes were looking through me rather than at me, and it made me feel exposed in a way which I can't put into words.

Naomi, however, simply stared back at her, and, in that moment, I could have sworn the greens in the centre of her hazel irises glowed a little.

I probably should have guessed something like this would happen when I introduced Naomi to Ellen. And not just because of Jessica. They were both psychic, in their own ways, so it wasn't too surprising that they would exchange more than just mere words during their first encounter. There was another level of interaction going on which I couldn't understand, but could feel in the air.

"Errrm," I said, clearing my throat in an attempt to end the awkwardness. "Ellen, this is Naomi."

"Hello Naomi," Ellen said, breaking the eye-contact. She rose from her chair and walked towards her gracefully. "I am Ellen," she said, offering her hand.

Naomi stiffly accepted the greeting. "Hi Ellen," she said.

I opened my mouth to speak again, but then something happened.

Ellen retracted her hand from Naomi's, and she let out a gasp.

"Jessica?" she whispered, and her attention was drawn to the air above Naomi's head. Naomi looked up too, in the same direction, and frowned.

Ellen's body did a sudden lurch – almost as if she was a marionette and her strings had just been yanked – her shoulders, arms and legs were momentarily pulled towards the ceiling.

And then she was released. When her feet touched the ground again she stumbled, struggling to regain her balance, her head swaying dizzily.

"Ellen!" Patrick exclaimed, coming to her aid, but, as he approached, one of her arms struck out and flung him aside like he was a toy. With a ferocity which seemed impossible from a girl as small and weak as Ellen. He skidded across the floor.

I realised that Ellen was not in control of that slight body anymore.

Jessica leapt upon Naomi, pinning her down. The space around the two girls swiftly turned into a blur of movement as they kicked and thrashed, arms and legs flailing wildly. Naomi screamed.

I waded in, but Jessica already had a handful of Naomi's red hair clenched in her fist and Naomi was wrestling with Jessica's leg – the only part of her that she could still reach in the position the two of them had managed to get themselves in. I grabbed Jessica's arm – the one which was pulling at Naomi's hair – and tried to prise her away.

"Jessica! Let go!" I yelled. "Patrick!" I called out to him. He was just sitting on the floor, staring in disbelief. "*Help* me!"

He got up and ran over. Together we managed to drag her away, but she took a handful of Naomi's hair with her, and she carried on thrashing and screaming, her feet rattling noisily upon the wooden floor.

"Hold her down!" I said to Patrick, seizing both of her wrists and pinning them to the floor.

Patrick tried to grab her legs, but one of her feet swung at him, almost catching him in the face, and he ducked. Eventually he managed to catch her ankle mid-thrust, and he held onto it.

By this point Naomi was back on her feet. She marched towards us.

"Stay back!" Patrick yelled, seemingly fearful that Naomi was going to reinitiate the brawl.

"Shut up," Naomi replied, irritably. Her face was a grim expression. "I know what I'm doing. I'm going to help."

Jessica spat at Naomi as she neared but missed, and the cloudy glob of spittle struck the wall behind her. Naomi calmly ignored the gesture, crouching down beside me and reaching for Jessica's face.

The moment Naomi's palm made contact with Jessica's forehead, Jessica's eyes rolled into the back of her skull and her body trembled. She let out a moan – a sound which set my teeth on edge.

And then she went silent.

"Ellen?" I said when she opened her eyes again. I could tell it was Ellen who was in control of that body again from her expression.

Naomi withdrew her hand.

"Faye?" Ellen whispered. She looked at me and then at Patrick. I could tell she was deeply confused. "What happened..." she hesitated. "Was that Jessica?"

I nodded. "What's going on, Ellen? I thought she only came when we played."

"She usually does," Patrick said. "She hasn't come like this since..."

He never finished that sentence, but he and Ellen shared a look. I remembered then that the two of them had been friends for a very long time – since they were children – and I came to a realisation.

I was a fool to assume I knew more about Ellen, Jessica, and the mysterious channel which existed between them, than Patrick did. I could sense now, in the way he was looking at Ellen – his expression bearing concern but not all that much surprise – that they shared a lot of history I wasn't privy to.

I turned back to Ellen. It was time to get some answers out of her. "Why is she–" I began, but my words were interrupted. Ellen gasped. I looked into her eyes. Caught the moment that they changed. Clouding over, as Ellen's essence left and something else assumed control.

I seized Ellen's wrists as she began to wriggle fitfully. She lurched with such a sudden force that Naomi, Patrick and I – all three of us together – could not hold her down. Her whole body left the floor and, for a few seconds, she was suspended, floating mid-air. Her neck tilted towards the ceiling and a terrible groan – one that I didn't recognise as either Ellen or Jessica, but something in between – escaped from her throat.

"That is it!" Naomi said. She rose to her feet. Her expression was grim. It was the first time I had seen her angry and, from the wrathful expression on her face, I hoped I would never have cause to again. "That is bloody it. I have had *enough*!"

She turned away and, for a terrible, heart-wrenching moment, I thought she was going to leave. That she meant that she had had enough of *me*. Not just the dreadful situation she had found herself in by associating herself with me.

I thought I would never see her again.

She strode to the other side of the room and reached for her bag – the one she had discarded when Jessica attacked her – and picked it up.

And then she came running back with one of her hands buried inside the opening.

She drew out a small phial and opened the stopper.

"What is that?" I asked.

"Salt," she said, matter-of-factly. She leant down and tilted the phial so that the contents poured from the neck and began walking in a circle around us, leaving a white trail in her wake.

"What are you doing?" Patrick asked.

"I am helping Ellen," Naomi said. "Now come here!"

She seemed so composed and confident that I complied without question.

"*No*!" a coarse voice shrieked behind us, as Patrick and I crossed over the white line.

I turned around and saw that Jessica had, once again, assumed control over Ellen's body.

And I had never seen her so enraged.

But there was more than just rage in those red, swollen eyes that were staring into me. There was desperation, too.

She rose to her feet and reached for me, but her hand was repelled by an invisible force and I heard the air crackle like charged static. Jessica looked down and then she saw the circle which had been made around her. A threshold, it seemed, she could not cross.

"What have you done?" she whispered.

"I am sending you to where you belong," Naomi said. She was sitting on the floor now and she was burrowing into her bag, unveiling more items. A large ball of black thread. A little bag filled with leaves. A candle.

I realised, feeling a stab of betrayal, that she had prepared for this, but, just as swiftly, I forgave her.

Because I knew now that this was the right thing to do.

"You have lingered in this realm for far too long," Naomi said, as she drew out a second candle and placed it upright on the floor. And then a third. Making a triangle.

"What are you doing?" Patrick stared at Naomi, wide-eyed.

"I am banishing Jessica," Naomi replied.

"*Banishing* her?" Patrick gasped. "What, as in *permanently*? Gone?"

Naomi nodded.

"But..." Patrick mumbled. He turned to me.

"Let her," I said, and the heartbroken way Jessica looked at me when I said those words made me feel wretched.

"But Faye," Patrick said. "Jessica's a part of... I mean..."

I shook my head. "She's out of control, Patrick. You saw it. It's not fair on Ellen. She can't treat her like this."

It was over in a surprisingly short amount of time, but that didn't make it any less painful.

Naomi placed a small piece of white cloth on the floor and wrote Jessica's name upon it with a black pen, followed by a series of peculiar symbols I didn't recognise.

Sprinkling a handful of leaves over it, she began to chant. It was in Latin, I believe. I didn't understand the words, but even I – uninitiated and inexperienced in this arcane world I had been dragged into – felt something in the air when Naomi gathered the cloth into her hands and crumpled it into a ball.

All the while, Jessica was screaming.

"No!" she cried in desperation. "Don't do this! Please! Faye!" she implored, turning to me. "Stop her!"

Naomi threaded the black yarn through a large, thick needle and then pierced the ball of cloth with it.

As she did it, she looked at Jessica.

"Jessica," she said. "I bind you."

"You bitch!" Jessica screamed, raising her voice, abandoning her act of repentance and shifting back into a state of rage. She spat at Naomi, and this time she didn't miss. The saliva oozed down Naomi's curly red hair, but Naomi didn't even flinch. She carried on winding the black yarn around the ball of cotton, chanting the next line to her spell.

"I bind you from before. I bind you from after."

"You can't do this to me!" Jessica hollered. "You *can't*! I will get you for this!"

"I bind your lips from sound," Naomi said, and, immediately after, Jessica's voice was cut off. It was like someone had pressed the 'mute' button. She opened her mouth to scream but nothing came out. "I bind your feet from mortal ground."

Jessica fell. Somehow, the silence when she opened her mouth was much more harrowing than the ear-piercing wails she was making before.

I'm sorry, Jessica, I thought as I watched her. She didn't seem so scary now. She was scared. Terrified. For the first time, she seemed unsure.

I hated seeing her face like that, but I knew, deep within my gut, that Jessica had gone too far. Way past the point where she could be given a second chance. She attacked Naomi and she had abused her connection with Ellen. She was out of control. I knew that this was the right thing to do.

But that didn't stop me from crying.

Naomi placed the ball of cloth – which was now completely enveloped in the black thread she had been winding around it – within the centre of the three burning candles. I do not know if it was just the sleeve of her coat disturbing the air around the flames, but they seemed to flicker, angrily.

Naomi then dipped her hand into her bag again and unveiled a dagger. I could tell from its design the implement was for ritual purposes; its blade was darkly grey, rather than shiny, and the hilt was gilded and encrusted with crystals.

She held the blade directly above the threaded ball, and struck. I heard a loud thud and turned back to Jessica. She was writhing.

And then, finally, Naomi drew a lighter from her pocket and set the ball aflame.

I wish I could forget those last moments. But the image of what happened next would haunt me forever.

Jessica clawed at herself – her fingernails digging into Ellen's flesh and drawing blood – and her entire body contorted like a burning worm. Like a slug dropped into a jar of salt.

She stared at me. Her entire body was in a state of seizure. Riddled by convulsions. One of her arms was clawing blindly at the air behind her, with her elbow bent at an impossible angle. Her legs were entangled, like they were trying to strangle each other. Her back was gnarled, morbidly.

But, throughout it all, she stared at me.

And, while our eyes were connected, I witnessed – *felt* – the moment that she left. The moment she was torn away from his world. Pulled to another place, her soul kicking and screaming. Betrayed. Lost. Scared.

I think she took a part of me with her, too.

"What have you done?" Ellen whispered.

She pressed her palms against the floor to help lift herself up and then she looked at the air around her. She turned to me, her lower lip trembling.

"Where is Jessica?" she asked. "I can't feel her..."

She looked at Naomi, and then at the three candles on the floor which were still burning. And the ceremonial dagger surrounded by ashes. Her eyes widened.

"Ellen," I said, gently. To end the chilling silence. "We had no choice. She–"

"No," Ellen whispered, putting a hand to her chest. Her arm was still bleeding from the scratches Jessica had made and her dress was covered in streaks of crimson, but she didn't even seem to notice. "You wouldn't..."

"She was–" I tried to explain, but I was cut short by a pained wail.

Ellen buried her face in her tiny hands and sobbed, uncontrollably.

Patrick walked over – I had almost forgotten he was even in the room until that moment – and he put his arms around Ellen. She wept into his collar.

"Ellen," I said. "I'm sorry. Jessica was–"

"Go away!" she howled, between tears.

"But Ellen," I croaked. "You don't understand. She–"

"Go away, Faye!" Patrick spat. There was something in his expression when he looked at me then which made me realise that, even though he had reluctantly agreed to it, he would never forgive me for what had just happened. "Get out of here, *now*! Leave!"

I walked home silently. Emptily. I didn't even say goodbye to Naomi. I am not even quite sure when it was that we parted ways, but it was without a word or gesture of farewell.

I guess even she was a bit disturbed by what had just happened.

I tried to call Ellen the following morning but she didn't answer. I did, however, receive a text message from her.

I will never forgive you.

I didn't even bother turning up to band practice the following week. I knew that it had most likely been cancelled. I knew that my days in Sunset Haze were over. I went straight home that night and cried into my pillow.

I experienced a few more lucid dreams over the next couple of weeks, but they felt empty. I conjured up settings from my wildest fantasies. I even created characters from my favourite childhood books and lived out their adventures with them.

I felt nothing.

I tried to summon an image of Jessica once, to tell her that I was sorry, but nothing came.

I guess there were limits to my powers in dreamland.

A couple of weeks later, Naomi called at my house.

"What's got into you?" she said once we had reached the safety of my room, away from the ears of my mother. "You haven't come to see me..."

I had thought of going to see her. Almost every day after I finished school I had battled with myself over which direction to walk but, for some reason, I had always found myself heading home.

I thought of calling her, but Naomi doesn't own a mobile phone. She says they are too distracting. It is one of her personality quirks which I both adore and find irritating.

I just couldn't face her. Whenever I thought of her, I thought of Jessica, and her face, too, appeared in my mind. The two of them were now entwined in my psyche. Intrinsically linked in a way which made it impossible to think of one without reminiscing on the other.

"You need to get over it," Naomi said, after she had given me a few moments to speak and I had still said nothing. She sat down on the other side of my bed, making herself at home with that self-assured confidence she always seemed to possess, and looked at me with a frank expression. "Stop blaming me. It was a shit situation. There was no pleasant way out. Would you have done anything different if you could go back? Because I know I wouldn't."

"You planned it," I said. "You had those things with you…"

Naomi eyes went to her lap. "No… I didn't plan it…" she then said. "Not as such. But if you think I was going spend time with you – a girl with a powerful ghost haunting her – without being prepared…then…" she shook her head and sighed. "I was putting myself in danger getting close to you, Faye, and I was quite within my rights to make sure I was able to protect myself."

It was quite reasonable logic, I guess.

"They kicked me out of the band," I said, weakly.

"I had figured as much," Naomi said. "I'm sorry about that, Faye. I really am. But you need to move on."

She put her hand upon mine and stroked my fingers.

I then realised that I had not been touched, physically or in my dreams, by anyone since that incident.

And I missed it.

I pulled Naomi to me and wrapped my arms around her. My bed bounced a little as we lay together, but once the rocking was over she nestled into my shoulder.

"Let's stay in tonight," she said, stroking my hair. "Just me and you."

"Okay," I said, realising that there was nothing I wanted more in the world.

I had agreed to meet up with Tilly that evening, but I guess I was going to have to let her down again.

2
Roots

Occasionally, in life, you will cross paths with a person who is in need of help.

It is not always as visceral and obvious as hearing cries of pain, or noticing in someone's emaciated face that they are ill or malnourished. Woes are not always physical or loud. Sometimes people need help for reasons which are subtle and, just because they don't need an ambulance, food, or shelter, doesn't mean that they don't need another human being to enter their sphere. To intervene.

You feel something in the air. It is almost as if they are emitting a distress call.

They probably are, in a way. All of the incredible discoveries humankind have made about the universe, and yet we still can't fully explain how schools of fish are able to swim in perfect unison, or how the monarch butterfly knows when it is time to begin the long journey back to the very same tree that their ancestor hibernated in last winter. Maybe it is that same mysterious force which tugs upon us sometimes. Triggers something within you and puts your life to a halt.

You drop what it was you were doing, or on your way to, and instinct takes over.

Such was the case when I encountered Tilly that evening.

When I found her she was sitting on a bench. The lamplight was dim. It was definitely the wrong sort of place for a girl her age to be alone. I couldn't see her face. It was obscured by strands of her black hair, and the rest by her hands – as if she was trying to shut out the world – but I recognised that coat she was wearing. On almost every occasion I had met her in the past, she had donned that tattered old thing. And those boots, too.

She was the very image of lost youth.

"Tilly?"

She jolted in surprise at the sound of her name, like a small creature caught somewhere they are not supposed to be. There was a measure of relief in her eyes when she saw that it was only me, but it swiftly transitioned to embarrassment. Her face turned red.

"It's me. Jack," I said. "You remember me, don't you?"

She nodded and then pretended to smile, tucking a lock of hair behind her ear.

"Are you okay?" I asked. "I mean... you look..." I hesitated.

I didn't even know this girl all that well.

"Do you have somewhere to go?" I finished.

"Faye was supposed to meet me..." she said. "But she didn't turn up, and I..."

Her voice trailed off, and the name she uttered lingered awkwardly in the space between us. The fact that we both knew Faye had recently become a rather barren connection.

I never found out why Faye and Ellen fell out. It was all very strange.

"Do you want me to walk you home?" I offered.

"No..." Tilly shook her head. "I can't... my grandmother... she would kill me if she found out I was out this late. I..."

I never knew Tilly lived with her grandmother. It raised a few questions, but I didn't pry. Rarely is there a pleasant story behind it when a teenager lives with their grandmother.

"You can stay at mine, if you like," I said. "I have a couch, and a sleeping bag... somewhere. Well, I think I do, anyway." I scratched my head. "It's no trouble."

She smiled.

"So this is your... home..." she said as I lit a candle.

I could tell she was trying very hard to be polite. The expression on her face, however, betrayed her, as she cast her eyes across my ramshackle abode.

It's not much to talk about. It's technically not even mine. I'm one of those dirty squatters you hear about. This house is one of the many abandoned hovels which make up the neighbourhood affectionately referred to by the locals as 'Yesterville'. The water still runs, but there is no electricity.

Hence, the candlelight.

“I know it’s a dump,” I said, as I flung my hat across the room. It landed on a pile of clothes. “But it’s free.”

“It suits you,” Tilly said.

It was true, I guess. The image conjured in your mind when you found out I am a squatter is probably not a far cry from the mark. I’m a gangly young man, with tangled mousy-brown hair. That day, I was wearing a stripy green tunic made from hemp and baggy corduroy trousers. Pretty standard affair for me.

“You can go back to that lovely bench if this isn’t good enough, you know,” I reminded her.

She giggled and put a hand to her mouth. “I’m teasing you, Jack,” she said. “I actually like it...”

Just then we both heard a scuffing and turned our eyes to the window.

“What’s that?” Tilly asked, her jaw dropping as something small and fluffy leapt from the window pane and landed on my elbow.

“This is Nuttles,” I said. He scurried up to my shoulder and greeted me by nuzzling my cheek. “He’s a... pet of mine.”

“If he’s your pet, then why do you look so surprised?”

“He usually avoids me when people are around,” I explained. “Doesn’t like strangers, you see, but I guess he must like you.”

She carried on staring at me, wide-eyed, as I sat myself down on the nearest chair.

“But...” she struggled for words. “He...”

“Is a squirrel?” I finished for her. “I have a knack for animals... let’s just leave it at that for now.” I reached for a half-finished joint I left in the ashtray and lit up. “Sit down, Tilly.” I said, after taking a few drags. “You’re making me nervous.”

She claimed a seat opposite me.

Nuttles, I thought, turning my eyes to him. *Seeds. Crunchy crunch. House-tree, climb.*

He jumped from my shoulder and scarpered towards the stairs.

“You spoke to him!” Tilly exclaimed.

“No I didn’t.”

Technically, that wasn't a lie. My lips never moved.

"Yes you did," Tilly smiled. Almost triumphantly. "Not with words. But I could see something in your eyes..."

"Maybe you're right," I admitted. "But what of it? We all have secrets."

"I know that, Jack…" she whispered. She turned her eyes to one of the walls wistfully, and I felt a twinge of guilt.

I knew Tilly's secret.

There was a long, slightly awkward pause. The sort which is often experienced when two people are on the cusp of becoming friends. When they are in that formative period where they are intrigued by each other, but not yet comfortable.

"So..." I broke the silence and looked around the room for any forms of entertainment I might have stashed. I am not used to having guests. "Are you any good at chess?"

"I don't know how to play," she admitted.

"You don't know how to play *chess*?"

"I didn't even have friends until half a year ago. How would I?"

"Grab that box over there. I'll teach you."

She got the hang of the rules quickly. And she improved after a couple of games, but, as is the way with chess, she didn't learn enough tactics to offer me much of a challenge that first evening.

After we got bored of playing, she had a good nose through my collection of books and we discovered we both had passions for natural science and classical literature.

That got the conversation rolling, awkwardness dissolved, and, by the end of the night, Nuttles was curled up on Tilly's lap and the two of us were telling each other childhood stories.

When my eyelids began to feel heavy, I looked at the clock and discovered it was the early hours of the morning. I found her a sleeping bag and went to bed.

In the morning I walked back down the stairs to find Tilly sitting at the table playing chess with herself. The narrow-eyed concentration with which she carefully positioned one of the pieces into a new square, just before she carefully turned the board around to consider her counter-move, was quite charming to watch.

"Who's winning?" I asked.

She jumped at the sound of my voice and a misplaced hand knocked the board over and sent the pieces showering across the carpet.

"I'm sorry!" she squealed, and then bent down to gather them.

I laughed. "I'm the one who should be sorry," I said. "I ruined your game. Stop it! *I* will tidy it up. I insist."

"Are you sure?" she asked.

"Yes."

"I should go home, really," she said, reluctantly. "My grandmother will be wondering where I am. But thank you, Jack. For letting me stay."

"No problem," I said. And then, after a brief pause I found myself saying something else.

"You can come back whenever you want, you know. If you need to get away, or just hang out... my door's always open. Quite literally, actually. It doesn't even have a lock!"

No one was more surprised than me by the fact that I actually *meant* that.

I don't have many friends. Well, not close ones. I'm quite a private person. I know lots of people but I keep them at arm's distance. I'm not one to form tight bonds.

I guess the reason I was letting Tilly into my life was that I was secretly lonely. I used to have the band and that took up a lot of my time, but Faye's sudden exodus left a huge rift.

We did try to hold band practice last week, but Ellen was miserable and her heart just wasn't in it. It just didn't seem to work without Faye. When someone leaves a band, it is like a part of its soul is ripped away. Even if you replace them, it is never – for better or worse – quite the same.

We decided to take a few weeks off so we could recover our spirits before we began the process of finding a new flautist. Since then, most of my evenings had been spent jamming in my living room with my guitar, alone.

I didn't realise, until then, that the band was really the only anchor in my life. Without it I was adrift.

I guess Tilly was the same. Faye had let her down too.

Anyway... you've probably been wondering a little bit about me and how one lives the way I do. So I'll give you a rundown of my day.

After Tilly left, I ate a quick breakfast. It was cereal with UHT almond milk, and I ate it out of a plastic bowl.

I then went to the local gym to have a shower. Yeah, that's right. I go all the way to the gym just to wash. For a degenerate hippie I have fairly good personal hygiene standards, I'll have you know. I try to shower at least once every few days.

I do get some strange looks when I go there, but I am not of the ilk who cares. And I guess the price I pay is a total rip off when you consider that I fork out for a full membership when I never even have the slightest intention to pump any iron, but what else am I to do? No electricity = no shower. Grab a calculator. I bet that if you add up all the money *you* pay in rent, taxes and bills, I will still be winning fivefold.

I only work two days a week. And when I say 'work', it is in a second hand bookshop. I sit in a chair for a few hours and exchange money with the occasional customer. I get paid cash-in-hand weekly and it's enough to get me by. Sometimes if I need a bit of extra dough I will go out busking with my guitar, but that often leads to me getting harassed by the police. They're always bugging me about something called a 'permit'.

Today was one of my days off, though. So no work for me.

So what did I do with my time? Well, with the band being in hiatus, not much. I went to the library, took out a few books to read, and then I used one of their computers to catch up with what's going on in the world. It was pretty depressing, as usual. Deforestation. Corruption. War. Fracking. Climate change. Renewable energy was being suppressed again, and there was a lack in humanitarian aid. I was, however, very relieved to hear from polished intellectuals that 'the economy' was doing better... whatever that means.

I get most of my information from independent sources. I don't trust mainstream media. On the odd occasion I sneak a peek at a conventional newspaper, the obscene levels of wilful distraction and sophistry makes me angry. There's not much in those things for me.

I then went for a walk. Yesterville is conveniently close to some wonderful woodlands. I spotted some wild garlic and edible mushrooms along the way and I gathered them. I have a camping stove back in the house and I can actually rack up a fairly good meal when I can be bothered.

And, as the day began to come to a close, I made my way home.

When I walked up the stairs, I discovered that someone was waiting for me.

Jardair, my father.

Okay, change of plan. This is definitely not going to be a good example of an average day.

"What are you doing here?" I said, folding my arms over my chest.

He had made himself at home on one of my chairs and was smoking his pipe. It had been five years since I last saw him, yet he still looked exactly the same. He never seems to age.

"Is it strange for someone to want to call in on his offspring?" he asked, blowing a cloud of smoke into the middle of the room.

"I have heard that for most families it isn't," I said. "But I wouldn't know that, would I?"

Okay, so now I should probably tell you a little about my father.

There are many names for what he is. Most of the ones *I* would use are profanities, but people of certain persuasions would call him a Wildman. A woodwose. Wuduwasa. Whatever spelling you like is fine with me.

He's a bit on the fey side of human, basically. I guess that makes me a half-breed. Probably explains the weird connection I have with animals.

He flitted in and out of my life throughout my childhood.

He always came when least expected, and never stayed long. He's a bit fleeting and mysterious like that.

"I was just passing through town and thought I would come see you," he said, placing the pipe on the table and drawing to his feet. He looks a bit like me – a fact that I hate – but he's taller and his hair is darker.

"Well. You've seen me now," I said.

"What's all the sulkin' for?" he asked. "You not happy to see the man who sired you?" He surveyed my thrifty home and smiled. "You've turned out a bit like me, it seems."

I shook my head. "I'm just living off-grid. It's not like I'm in a den made of sticks or running into the woods with a spear whenever I'm hungry. Seriously, *Jardair*," I said, emphasising the name. He's always trying to get me to call him 'Father' but I refuse. "What do you want? I'm not going to ask again."

I heard a thud upstairs and looked up. At first I thought it might have been Nuttles, but what I was hearing was, in fact, footsteps. Several of them. All far too heavy to be a mere squirrel.

"Who's up there?" I asked. I began to hear voices, too.

"Just some of my friends," Jardair said, smiling. "Geez, Jackael. When did you become so uptight?"

"Come down you lot!" he called, tilting his head up to the ceiling. "It's my son! Come meet him!"

A few moments later a band of women and men entered the room. Some of them were fey, some were human. Most of them were of various shades between. I could tell which ones were which just by looking at them. The ones of feyer blood had something about them which is hard to describe. A slight sheen to their skin, a twinkling in their eyes, perhaps? It's like a kind of glamour. If you're a mundane you most likely wouldn't notice it – not consciously, anyway – but you would probably find yourself inexplicably drawn to them.

A girl came skipping towards me with a horn in her hands. She had such a sweet smile I couldn't resist trying the gleaming libation she was carrying. I drank from it. It was mead. Probably the best mead I've ever tasted. Calescent ecstasy trickled down my throat and rested warmly in my belly, like an old friend. She offered the cup to my father, and he laughed heartily.

A young man came to me next and offered me a pipe. I tried it. It was marijuana, as expected, although probably not quite like any strain you've ever tried. My father is a wild man of the forest, after all.

I forgot to mention earlier that, if there is one good thing about my father, it's that he sure knows how to start a party.

A few more horns of mead and some interesting mushrooms later, we were all on a hillside out of town, dancing our way hand-in-hand through the forest. Singing. I can't even remember what the words or melody were. The woods became alive. The moon was incredibly big and bright in the sky, and it washed everything with a glowing incandescence. The spirits of the forest made themselves visible, coaxed out of their hiding places by my father's presence, and I could see faces in the trees.

The woman in front of me – the one who carried the horn of mead which never seemed to go dry – pulled me aside. She pulled me into her soft lips. She pulled me to the ground, and we laughed as we tumbled onto the grass. She pulled my tunic over my head, and cast it aside. I pulled away her blouse, and began to shower her neck with kisses.

I awoke in the morning to birdsong and a blue sky. My skin was wet with mildew and, as I stirred, it woke her.

Our bodies were still entwined. We smiled at each other.

"I don't even know your name..." I said, apologetically. She was even more bewitching in the daylight, with her curly brown hair and dimpled cheeks.

"I'm Parmella."

"Well, Parmella, you are very beautiful," I said. "But I think we should get dressed. People walk their dogs here in the morning."

She giggled and planted her lips on my cheek.

"You aren't, by any chance, going to tell me why my father is here and what he wants from me, are you?"

She shook her head impishly.

"I thought not..."

"Ask him yourself," she said, touching my arm with one hand as the other reached for her blouse. "He's waiting for you."

We made our way back to discover that my house, which had once been so agreeably cloistered, had been transformed into a flurry of activity. A group of ladies dressed in flowery garments were lounging in the overgrown bed of weeds in my garden and I crossed paths with two young men when I entered the front door.

I found my father in the living room with six other people. They were all gathered around my dining table having, what appeared to be, a very serious and animated meeting.

"I think the best way to begin is to start here," a woman standing beside my father said. She was wearing a tattered old robe and had leaves and twigs caught in her tangled brown hair. She looked like a Disney witch, only she was real. Her finger was pressed to – what I guessed to be – a map of the city. It was covered in notes and asterisks, all done with a red pen. "Go for the banks and the–"

"But what about this factory over here," a man interrupted her. "I bet they're–"

What the fuck is going on? I wondered. If these people were wearing suits instead of a motley of vibrant colours, or in an office instead of my ramshackle abode, I could have almost mistaken them for some kind of officious committee.

"*Jardair*," I said, breaking the conversation. My voice was so firm that a few of them jumped. "I want to speak with you. *Now*."

They all stared at me with such surprise in their expressions I could tell they weren't used to hearing someone speak to my father that way.

Jardair drew a deep sigh. "Okay – fine! I'll be back in a few moments," he said to the others.

He left them and we both walked into the kitchen.

"Who the fuck are all these people?" I asked, once we were alone.

"You seemed to like them well enough last night," he grinned. "Especially *Parmella*."

"I was off my head!" I retorted. "And I would bet money

you got her to seduce me."

He neither confirmed nor denied it. He just looked at the window and changed the subject. "This is not what you think, Jackael. I am actually trying to do something good."

"I find that hard to believe."

"Have you ever heard of Taxus Baccata?"

"You're part of Taxus Baccata?" I asked. Taxus Baccata were a political movement. I first heard about them a couple of years ago when they became famous for forcing an oil refinery to shut down for a week due to numerous acts of sabotage. They have been involved in many other operations since then. Their methods can be a little guerrilla style and crude at times but a part of me has always rooted for them.

"I *am* Taxus Baccata," he replied.

I frowned. Could it really be that my father was at the head of it?

"Since when did you involve yourself with the petty affairs of the human world?" I asked flatly. "You never gave a shit about any of us before. You know, like my *mother*. Do you actually *remember* my mother?"

"I would love to go back to the forest, believe me," he said. "But there's not much left now, son. And it's getting even smaller. A few years ago I decided it was time to do something about it... Jackael, I came to you because I want you to help me. I'm spreading our wings. I want to start a revolution. You already know this town and you could save me a lot of time getting some roots planted here."

I stared at him for a long time.

"Why should I?" I asked.

"Because I think it's within your interests too," he replied. "Now that I have seen the way you live... Whether you like it or not, you're a chip off the old block."

"I am *nothing* like you," I said. "I never want to be, either!"

"You think you are doing fine now," he asked, waving a finger around my dingy kitchen. "'Living off-grid' you called it, huh. How long do you think you will get away with it for? The net is tightening, and you know it."

I hesitated. I couldn't argue with that point, because his words resonated with some of my fears.

I like the way I live, but I know that they will catch me

eventually. One day, some ambitious upstart from the authorities will turn up with a clipboard in their hands. *Oh,* they'll say, as they begin to compose officious notes upon it. They will pretend to be all procedural about it but, really, the decision to turf me out of here would have been made long before they even graced my doorstep.

You can't live here, they'll say.

'*Safety regulations'.*

'Planning permission'.

'Living conditions'.

They will probably be working for some promotion they've been dreaming about, and I will be one of the assignments they are hoping will earn them it. The people above them will have incentives and targets – and maybe even a future promotion on the cards for themselves, too. The ones at the top will give the order because it offends them that I am not part of the system. They want me to pay taxes. They want me to pay rent to the gentry. Pay it by getting some meaningless job. Eventually they'll have me working so hard I'll be miserable.

It is unavoidable.

It seems to me that this country is run by sociopaths with gloating expressions and oily hair. They wander around Westminster with their leather briefcases, selling off public assets to their pals from boarding school and members of their extended family who have vested interests. All the while, class war is waged through an ever-encroaching succession of draconian legislations. They will not rest until they have rounded up everyone into the rat race because they, by fortune of birth, are the big cats. And the more rats there are, the more they have to dig their paws into.

It makes me angry every time I think about it.

I tell myself that the only thing I can do is lie low and hope I will slip past them unnoticed.

But I know that it is very probable they will catch me eventually.

Is it really possible that my father, and others like him, can stop them? It seemed unlikely. It would rely upon the public to rise up too, and I am not sure I have that much faith in the general masses – the majority have proven themselves to be a little too complacent and docile if you ask me.

On the other hand, do I want to be one of those people who complains about the world but sits at home and does nothing about it?

It is very easy to be enraged about the passivity of the rest of the population from the comfort of your armchair.

"Fine," I said, between gritted teeth. In my mind, I knew it was a bad idea, but in my gut I felt compelled. "I'm in."

He smiled.

And thus began my sally with Taxus Baccata.

The very next day my father sent me out with some of his gang recruiting.

I began by taking them to Dinnusos. I figured that the patrons there were just the sort of individuals who could be inspired to fight for a cause of liberty. I then went on to some of my other favourite haunts. The record stores, the music venues, art galleries, squats, workshops, bookstalls, and even the library.

By the evening I had gathered quite a crowd. I felt a bit like the pied piper as they followed me through the deserted streets of Yesterville to meet my father. He addressed them from the balcony of a derelict house with a lengthy and passionate speech. He spoke scathingly of the government and the impact reckless industrialisation was having on our environment, and the rich elite who were pulling the strings. Even *I* was convinced (but that might have had something to do with the various narcotics and suspicious libations my father's crew were coaxing upon us as they mingled through the crowd).

Filled with ire and zeal, and that electrifying energy people feel when they become newly united with a common purpose – not to mention the mysterious intoxicants of the fey – he then sent us off on our first errand.

We broke into the tax office. We took their records. We carried them to the streets outside and burnt them. We danced around the flames. We cheered.

We replaced their documents with some of our own.

Statistics. How much tax powerful corporations have avoided by abusing loopholes. The amount of money which was lost bailing out corrupt bankers. The billions which were spent on public services only to be siphoned by privateers who walked away with the profits.

And when I say we 'replaced' them, that is not strictly true. These new documents were not conveniently filed away into cabinets and drawers. They were plastered to the windows and walls, and painted over with industrial grade varnish.

When we heard the sirens we scrammed. It took us a while to dodge the rozzers – we had to split up several times during the process – but, shortly after, we found each other again and stumbled upon a rave. We were still on a high, so we went inside and bragged about our exploits to the revellers. Many of them showed an interest in joining us.

The rest of the night was a hazy affair... I somehow made it back to my bed, but I couldn't even remember how I got home.

When I got dressed and walked downstairs the next morning, I found my father and his inner circle sitting around the table plotting again. I was a bit incensed to notice that my home had been tidied and some of the furniture had been replaced.

They weren't the only things which had changed. When I wandered back up the stairs to use the bathroom I discovered that one of the upper rooms had been taken over by a team of tech nerds who had each made a little cosy little nest of computer screens and hard drives around themselves. They were so busy tapping away upon their keyboards they didn't even notice me.

I couldn't be bothered to begin asking any of the numerous questions which were forming in my mind – such as how they were generating electricity, or even an internet connection – so I left them to their cyber-world and shut the door behind me.

My home had turned into a hive, and my father's drones were buzzing around and in and out of the place, running errands and performing tasks. It made me claustrophobic. It wasn't the fact that my father seemed to have taken over which bothered me – because it wasn't really my house anyway, and I didn't own anything of value – I was just not used to being surrounded by so many people.

I shrugged – I guess this was one of the sacrifices I was going to have to make for the revolution.

And, besides, last night had been one of the most thrilling nights of my life.

I then realised that I had not seen Nuttles for a couple of days – well since my father and his crew had arrived, to be exact – so I climbed the ladder to see if I could find him.

When I reached the loft, I found Nuttles sitting on the windowsill. He seemed a little unhinged.

"It's okay," I cooed, as I stroked his head. It was really for my own comfort rather than his that I was verbalising. When I communicate with animals it is not in a language, as such. It is mostly through the sharing of mental images and impressions. The brains of most creatures are not very coherent by human standards.

He related to me strange smells and sounds, and a sense of unease. I refilled his bowl of nuts and spent a while soothing him.

When I walked back down the stairs again, Tilly was there.

"Jack?" she said. She had obviously only just stepped in, and her eyes widened at the sight of all the people. "What..."

"Hello," my father said as he walked over to greet her. "What is your name?"

"Tilly..." she mumbled, looking up at him as he shook her hand. "I'm–"

"A friend of Jack's?" he finished for her. "Good. I'm his father, and any friend of Jack's is a friend of mine. Me and some of my friends are just staying here for a while."

He gave her one of his most bewitching smiles and she blushed. My father tends to have that effect on people. It's a bit like my gift with animals.

"Tilly!" I called, waving at her from the landing. "Come up."

"Okay," she said, turning around to stare at my father and his crew one more time before she walked up the stairs. I led her to my bedroom – one of the only ones which had not been taken over by my father's gang – and shut the door behind us.

"What's going on, Jack?" she asked. "Your father, he–"

"He's an activist," I said. It was a bit of an understatement, but I wasn't sure how much I wanted Tilly to know. It wasn't because I didn't trust her, it was more that I felt protective. Tilly has enough problems of her own without getting mixed in something like this.

"An activist?" her face lit up. "What kind?"

"Just this thing called Taxus Baccata. They're–"

"*Taxus Baccata*?" she exclaimed. "I *know* them!"

"How do *you* know about them?" I asked. Tilly was just a kid.

"I'm vegetarian and they're into animal rights!" she replied. "I heard about them on the net. Did you know that Taxus Baccata is the scientific name for the yew tree? They call themselves that because it is–"

"My father isn't all he's cracked up to be, trust me," I interrupted her.

"He must be pretty awesome if he's part of Taxus Baccata!" she said excitedly. "I didn't realise they were active in this town..." her eyes then brightened. "What are they planning at the moment?"

"*No*," I said. "Tilly, you shouldn't get involved... You–"

"What's the problem?" she asked. Her black eyebrows drew together into one line. "You aren't my father, Jack. Let me go down and talk to them."

She made for the door.

"Tilly," I said. I tried to think of another protest but, before one came to me, she was already racing down the stairs.

I chased after her but I was too late.

"Hi," she said, as she approached the table, disturbing their meeting. Jardair and his advisors all turned and stared at her.

"You're Taxus Baccata?" she said, ogling them. "Sorry!" she added, quickly turning to me. "Jack tried to hide it, but I guessed. And you don't have to worry. I will keep it secret. I want to help you."

"I am sure I can think of something you can do..." Jardair said, guardedly.

Tilly peered at all the pieces of paper which were scattered across the table and began to leaf through them. One of the women opened her mouth to make an objection, but Jardair raised his hand in a pardoning gesture.

"Is this what you're planning today?" Tilly asked, as she lifted one of the sheets of paper and held it up to her face. In her excitement, she seemed completely oblivious to the incredulous expressions on the faces of the people around her.

I watched her eyes move from side to side as she read a few lines, and then she giggled. "Oh, that's a really good idea. Oh, and that, too!" she then exclaimed, breaking into a cackle.

She then looked at my father. "I think I can help you."

That day we sabotaged one of the supermarkets.

It was actually a pretty good idea. We spent the morning putting up fake posters around the town which promised a wide range of extremely generous deals.

'Buy 1 get 2 free!'

'75% off **ALL** electrical goods!'

'Economy Eggs, 20p a dozen!'

My father's graphic designer did a fantastic job. The faking of the logo was perfect, and they were actually pretty convincing.

You may think that this sounds like a mere juvenile prank – and I guess it was, in a way – but if you thought it wouldn't be effective, then you have obviously never seen the chaos which ensues as the doors open on Boxing Day when the 'January' Sales begin, or the disorder which erupts on Black Friday in countries overseas. Times that by ten, at least, and you'll get a pretty good idea what happened.

As soon as the store opened it was swarmed with people, and they began to fill their trolleys. They pushed and shoved at each other to be the first to reach the most desirable aisles, and bottles of liquor and electrical hardware were smashed in the stampede as people rushed to snatch the finest wares. Eventually, there were only a few flat-screen televisions left, and people began to wrestle over the last ones. Others merely sprinted around the grocery section, filling their trolleys as if their lives depended on it.

A sweaty, balding manager hobbled onto the shop floor,

and his face turned increasingly purple as he realised what was going on.

When the customers found out that they had been duped, it didn't take them long to get riled. Within minutes, the store had a riot on their hands.

Tilly and I laughed and laughed and laughed, until tears were streaming from our eyes, as we watched the store break into mayhem.

I have to give Tilly credit where it is due. It was her idea to make many of the promotional items morally questionable produce, such as net-caught tuna, battery farmed eggs, and unfairly traded tea.

But why, you are probably wondering? Simple; it was a way to trick even the most short-sighted of societies' consumers – the ones who willingly close their eyes to, or simply do not care, that the goods they buy are cruel to other living beings or environmentally damaging – suddenly become impassioned. Enflamed. Motivated. Righteous.

All because we had crushed their dreams of buying implausibly cheap bacon.

We went back to mine to celebrate and, that night, Tilly smoked her first joint.

I did *try* to stop her. Briefly. But there was only so much I could do. A teenager trying out marijuana isn't exactly something to get hysterical about.

And, even if it was, Tilly had the right to indulge, enjoy herself, make her own mistakes, and learn from them, just like everyone else does.

I guess the reason it bothered me so much was that Tilly was one of the few members of my social circle who never drank or took drugs. She was the youngest, too, so we all had a soft spot for her. It felt like her innocence had been tainted, and that made me a little sad.

I couldn't say much, though. Not when I had spent half of the night with a rolled note up my nose, hoovering up lines of cocaine with Parmella.

She was exquisitely lovely that evening. At the end of the night I invited her up to my room and she said yes.

The next few weeks slipped into a sequence which could almost be deemed a routine, despite the trail of chaos we left in our wake.

We mostly used conventional forms of protest during the daylight hours. We marched through the streets with placards to try to raise awareness about the issues which were affecting our world but most of the passers-by ignored us and walked on. The few who *did* listen, however, usually ended up getting involved, and our numbers grew a little each day.

Once we had gathered enough people, we began to take more direct action.

The first high street venue we targeted as a large group was a clothes store. We found out that it was part of an international chain which quietly endorses the use of sweat shops and child labour, so they were high up on our list.

They opened the doors one morning, and we entered the premises like lemmings – dozens and dozens of us – and sat on the floor so that there was no room in the aisles for shoppers. The police came and tried to intimidate us, but we drowned out their voices with various chants. We stayed there till late in afternoon, just before closing time.

The store hired extra security staff the following day, and an imposing squad of stalwart men were waiting for us at the entrance with their arms crossed over their chests in anticipation of our return. But it was a waste of money. We were camped outside one of the banks that morning.

We hit a different location each time to maximise the element of surprise. It wasn't random though. We always had a reason. Coffee shops which exploited South American farmers. Fast-food cafes which were cutting down rainforests for cheap land to graze cattle. A department store which was lobbying for the minimum wage to be scrapped.

We also partied. A lot. The partying felt almost as important as all the rest of the stuff we did because it kept people (with some, quite literally) on a high, and it was good for morale.

Over time people slipped into roles, too.

My father and his inner circle spent most of their time standing around my dining table, plotting and scheming. Deciding which places we were going to target and when.

The geeks tapped away at their computers. They were all accomplished hackers, and they spent most of their time leaking information about malevolent deeds of the government and military.

Parmella and a few others left each morning, dressed up all smart, to attend jobs they had acquired in offices around town. They hadn't actually done anything particularly damaging yet – they were all just steadily building up their reputations, gaining trust among their bosses and peers, using a bit of their fey glamour along the way to make themselves that little bit more persuasive. No doubt my father had big plans for them at some point in the future but, for now, they were sleeper agents.

Even Tilly took on a role. Many young people wanted to join our cause, and she acted as an ambassador between us and them. I perceived quite early that it was morally questionable to let youngsters get involved in a revolution, so I made both her and my father promise to only invite them to the more conventional forms of protest. The acts of sabotage were events I tried to restrict to adults only, but I was not always successful in that endeavour.

And, finally, a handful of my father's team focussed their attention on the media.

It was needed because the news channels and tabloids were doing their utmost to demonise us. Footage and photos were being carefully selected, and it seemed their cameras only had spare film for the more outrageous members of the movement – they particularly favoured individuals with lots of tattoos or piercings. The causes we were fighting for were glossed over. They never told the public *why* we were doing the things we were doing. They made us seem like rebels without a cause.

My father's publicity team managed to get some articles about our true motivations published in independent news sources, and they made a presence for us on social networks. It didn't fully make up for the smear campaign being made, but it was a start.

They also pulled off some pretty nifty PR pranks.

One of my favourites was when they convinced the newspapers that a big multinational oil company (which was infamous at the time for poisoning the water supply of a large area during fracking operations) was going to donate large sums of money to environmental charities to atone for the damage it had caused.

It was ingeniously clever, because it put them in a very difficult decision. Do they:

a) Cough up the money to save face

or:

b) Risk making themselves look very bad by issuing a counter-announcement that they were, in fact, doing nothing to correct the wrong they had done?

Do you know what was *really* fucked up though? As soon as the announcement of their gesture of goodwill was made, their stock value dived and there were reports of mass offloading of bonds by shareholders...

... apparently investors do not want anything to do with companies who appear to have a conscience.

This unexpected (but, in hindsight, predictable) revelation sickened me, and strengthened my resolve. It made me realise just how deep the sickness in our society had taken root. It made me even more dedicated to my father's cause.

I also realised that *I* needed to craft for myself a role in all of this.

I *am* the son of Jardair the Wildman, after all. And I had a legacy to live up to.

So I began plotting...

A couple of weeks later I was driving a lorry into the headquarters of Sonmatis.

Sonmatis are an international agricultural biotech company. They specialise in genetic manipulation, chemicals, and pesticides. If you look up their website you'll see pictures of golden fields, smiling farmers, and heart-warming scenes of children spooning food into their mouths. They claim that they are performing the world a service by creating a sustainable future. Their slogan is 'Progress. Habitat. Harmony."

That is what they say. The real story is that they are

biopirates and, as far as the monsters which have emerged from the decayed modern era of capitalism go, they are among the worst.

The real secret to Sonmatis's commercial success relies upon abusing a certain rule of nature: cross pollination.

You see, if you're a farmer and one of your neighbours is growing Sonmatis's patented crops, you have no other choice but to convert to their style of farming too. Sonmatis will send their rodenty agents out to scurry around your fields at night and take samples. If they find any strains of their patented species, you will soon find an aggressive tirade of lawsuits and litigations being pushed through your door.

Of course, everyone knows that what is *really* happening is Sonmatis are crushing the world's biodiversity and those poor farmers are not at fault for a simple rule of nature, but Sonmatis have multiple connections to the Supreme Courts, governments, and international trading syndicates. They have a rather substantial and aggressive legal team who are well practised in the arts of fallacy.

We don't live in a world where common sense has any mandate anymore. We live in a corporatocracy. Laws are drafted by big business, and lobbyists are the winged messengers who deliver them to the governments. The person who wins the battle is not the one who is right, merely the one who has more money and uses the fanciest rhetoric. And a multi-national like Sonmatis can afford much savvier lawyers than a poor farmer who's just trying to feed his family.

Sonmatis have been trying to get their seeds planted in this country for decades. And now, thanks to an international trade deal currently being fast-tracked by our government, they are due to begin next year.

Not if I can do something about it.

The whole place was fenced off. I came across a barred gate, but it was no problem – not with the fake ID my father's nerds managed to fabricate for me. I flashed it at the guard and he let me through.

I drove into the complex and what I found when I got further inside was, quite frankly, a bit of a disappointment.

Considering the massive levels of security it was surrounded by, it was nothing grand. Just a dingy and characterless warehouse.

Someone appeared outside the entrance and communicated to me by waving their arms that they wished me to drive inside. I revved the engine and steered the lorry in.

It was dark at first, but then my eyes adjusted. The warehouse was filled with crates of *MusterIt* – their bestselling pesticide – and there were dozens of large skips filled with seeds.

"Hi," a suited, booted, slicked-back-hair-shiny-forehead man said, as he walked over to shake my hand. "I'm Mr Turpin, managing director. You have a delivery for us?"

"Yes," I said. "Were you not expecting us? I *did* send an email..."

"I'm terribly sorry," he said, looking me up and down. My father's team had scrubbed me up pretty well: I was clean-shaven, in a shirt and tie, and my hair had been finely combed back into a ponytail. "We've been very busy. Some damn nature-lovers have been pressing the MPs," he shook his head. "We had to send powerbrokers over to Westminster. *Again!* It's proving quite expensive..."

I feigned a sigh. "Sorry to hear about that... you *did* manage to get that research at the university shut down though, I hear?"

That piece of information had mysteriously not made it to the papers, but the nerds in my attic had found out about it somehow.

Mr Turpin's face lit up. With information like that I could only be an insider in his eyes.

Any suspicion he might have had about me immediately evaporated.

"Aye. But that'll probably cause a shockwave in itself. Soon we'll have people screaming about it being some kind of conspiracy," he shook his head. "Nothing but trouble..."

"I have some brand new produce for you," I said.

His eyes went to the lorry behind me. "What is it?"

I smiled. "It's been shipped here all the way from the States," I said. "It greatly increases yields and it fertilises soil."

"But what about pollination? Does it help the crops spread?" he asked, rubbing his chubby hands together eagerly. "I have been promised bonuses..."

"I am sure it will give you plenty of cause to make litigation claims," I reassured. "Anyway, if you don't mind, I'll get my assistant here to open up the cargo so you can see."

"Of course," he said. "Open it up."

I gave Parmella the signal and she got out from the passenger's seat. She was dressed in a white lab-coat – it just seemed appropriate, for some reason – and she smiled at us bashfully before whisking over to the back of the lorry. Mr Turpin and some of his associates formed a little circle around it, their eyes all bright and excited.

Parmella lowered the ramp and pressed the button. The door began to open and a strange buzzing sound echoed from the widening gap.

"What is that?" Mr Turpin asked, turning to me.

I smiled as a black cloud emerged from the opening. Some of Mr Turpin's colleagues backed away, their eyes widening.

"What have you *done*?" Mr Turpin croaked, turning to me. He opened his mouth to say something else, but he was forced to make a sudden dive and he planted his body face-down to the ground as the swarm flew towards him.

"Locusts," I said, grinning.

"Close that door!" he yelled. He lifted his head briefly to look for his colleagues, but they had all fled, so he was forced to attempt it himself. He began to crawl towards the lorry, but the flocks of locusts kept flying into him.

Of course they were flying into him. I was plugged into their collective unconscious, triggering the impetus of their flight patterns.

Parmella giggled.

"What is the meaning of this!" he screamed, his face now red with rage. He looked at me. The locusts were everywhere by this point, but around Parmella and I. We seemed to have a bubble of airspace around ourselves they were avoiding.

His eyes widened.

"Don't you understand?" I said, looking down at him. "Their bodies are abundant in proteins and minerals! When they die they will enrich the soil!"

"They're eating the seeds!" he screamed, his eyes turning to the skips. "They're eating the *seeds*! You'll pay for this!" he yelled. He tried to pull himself back to his feet again but was knocked over by another swarm.

I walked back to the door of the lorry, smiling.

"You're a genius!" my father exclaimed, patting my shoulder. "*Genius*!"

"I couldn't have done it without you," I said, feeling embarrassed. I never thought I craved my father's approval but, during that moment, as he was patting me on the back with a big grin on his face, I found myself experiencing something which was strangely gratifying. "Getting those locusts and all."

Gods know where he got them from, I thought. *And the lorry.*

I probably didn't want to know.

"But you were the brains behind that operation. That was not just a good stunt, son. It had *style*! A bit of panache. You'll go far in my team. Got any ideas for the next one?"

"I haven't thought about it yet, to be honest," I said.

"Well I'll give you some time to think about it!" he said. "Anywhere you like. There must be *somewhere* in this town you want to see go down?"

And it was then that I had a thought.

"What is it?" my father said, frowning at me. He must have noticed a change in my expression.

"Well... there is somewhere I can think of..." I admitted. "But it..."

I shuddered involuntarily.

There is this place on the other side of the city...

I am not sure what goes on there, exactly. I just know it is something evil.

Whenever I go near it, a terrible feeling twists inside me. It feels like a dark, ghostly hand has worked its way into my abdomen and coiled its fingers around my guts.

It hurts so much I find it hard to breathe. I have to walk away. I have never been able to make myself get close enough to the place to find out what is going on in there.

It has something to do with the connection I have with animals, I understand that much. I can feel that part of myself being tugged upon.

That is all I know.

I guided my father there that night. To the outskirts on the other side of the town which was near all the industrial parks and factories. We walked there silently, under the dull haze of streetlamps.

"There," I said, stopping in the middle of the street and pointing to a large multi-storey building.

There was no sign on the outside of it to indicate what its purpose was, and the windows were boarded up. It had the appearance of somewhere which had been abandoned.

It was almost as if the place was trying to make itself invisible.

But *I* knew there was something odd going on in there.

"I sense it too..." Jardair said. "Go home. I will see to this... you will never have to worry about this place again."

The energy of that place really affected me – it always does – so it was in a solemn disposition that I returned home that evening.

And maybe that was the reason I fell out with Tilly.

I found her in my living room. Sitting with a rabble of my father's friends and, at the precise moment I stepped through the door, she was in the process of leaning over the coffee table with a rolled up note held into her nose, snorting up a trail of white powder.

I don't know if it was just my mind exaggerating it – because I was feeling a little bit melancholy that evening – but, it was during that moment, that I became aware of just how small she was. How vulnerable. Even for a fifteen-year-old, Tilly looked very young.

And I know there is hardly a *right* way to do drugs. There isn't a right way to do many of the things that people do for pleasure, but they still oblige them. If you cut everything out of your life which was bad for you, existence would be pretty dull. I like to indulge in drugs occasionally, but I would like to think that I am a 'sensible' user. Whatever that is.

But have you ever witnessed someone taking drugs, or recklessly drinking, and felt something unsettling about it? Sensed an air about them. Sensed that they are not simply caught in a moment – swept into the ebb and tide of a social occasion and riding the current while everyone is having a good time, on a journey together, bonding while they are tuned into the same wavelength – and just enjoying being a part of it. They are not enjoying themselves. They're seeking annihilation. They are drifting and they don't care where they are being swept to, or even know if they have the strength to ride the current, because anything is better than where they are now and they are trying to escape. They are not comfortable in their own skin. They don't value themselves.

That was the vibe I was getting from Tilly that evening, when I caught her snorting cocaine in my living room.

When she was done, her eyes rolled into the back of her head, as oblivion, peace, for a few moments, took her. She closed her eyes, and then she opened them again. And she seemed sad. But she seemed conscious of the fact that she was sad, so she smiled. But it seemed empty. She giggled, but that sounded empty, too. For a brief moment – between all the laughing and chit-chatter as the person next to her racked up the next set of lines – she turned her eyes to the window, and I witnessed her bite her teeth down upon her lower lip. But then someone said something and she turned to them and giggled again. Emptily.

And then her glassy eyes were drawn to my side of the room and they settled upon me, wide and staring.

"What the fuck are you doing, Tilly?"

I think everyone must have sensed something in the tone of my voice, because they suddenly went quiet.

"Jack!" she said, not even able to hide her surprise or unease. She tried to feign a giggle, but it came out as more of a squeak. "I was just–"

"Leave!" I said to the people around her. I didn't even know any of their names but I recognised their faces. They were my father's underlings. "Leave. *Now*!"

They got up without a word of protest. They all knew I was Jardair's son, and that seemed to make me somewhat a prince – something which had always made me feel a little uncomfortable, but this was one occasion where I was not going to be sore about it.

"No, not you," I said, as Tilly began to raise herself. "You stay."

A few moments later, we were alone. Tilly placed her elbows on the table and let her face drop into her hands. Ran her fingers through her hair.

She was a mess. Even worse than when I found her on that bench all those weeks back. That felt like a long time ago now, but it had been a few months at the very most. Back then, she was sad and vulnerable, but innocent. Now some of that innocence had gone, but she was, if anything, even more damaged.

"What the hell are you doing, Tilly?" I asked.

"What?" she asked me. "Am I not allowed to have fun?"

"You're not having fun. I can tell that much."

"You embarrassed me!" she said. "In front of everyone..."

"What's the matter?" I said. "What's going on with you? Just tell me."

"Oh, so you think that if we all just sit down together and talk about our feelings then it will make everything better?" she said, mockingly pitching her voice high. She shook her head. "Trust me, Jack. You will *never* understand what it is like to be me."

She was right, of course. I'm barely even human. How could I possibly ever understand her?

"No," I admitted. "But just because I can't completely understand doesn't mean I can't be there for you. Talking isn't going to solve everything, but it can help..."

She laughed – cackled, bitterly – and turned her face up to the ceiling. "You are so *fucking* oblivious, Jack. You are the *last* person I can talk to…"

I didn't know what she meant by that, but it hurt me. I know that Tilly and I had not known each other for all that long – and I didn't even really know that much about her, really – but I had thought we had a connection. A bond.

Something I rarely allow myself to have with anyone.

"Tilly..." I said, and then I hesitated. I tried to think of a different angle I could use to get through to her. "You are too young for all of this. Can't you see that? I should never have let my father–"

"Oh, *fuck off*!" Tilly cut me off. She rose to her feet, her face red with anger. "Too young!" she repeated. "Too fucking *young*! Seriously, Jack? That just goes to show how little you know about me!"

She got up. "I never got to be a child! I am too fucking young for a lot of things, but they still all happened to me. Fuck this, I'm leaving! I am not going to let you or *anyone else* treat me like a child!"

She grabbed her bag and marched towards the door, turning around to say one last thing.

"Don't you *ever* try to tell me what I am too fucking young for!"

When she left, I kicked the table over, scattering a load of cups, bottles and remnants of narcotic dust. I was too hurt by our exchange to feel like I could follow her.

I slumped onto my couch. I vaguely remember hearing Tilly's voice outside my house shortly after she left – and other voices, too – so I guess she must have regrouped with my father's wreckheads and gone elsewhere.

Humans. They have a certain magnetic quality, but it is at moments like these that I remember why it is best to keep them at a distance. Occasionally I forget. I let someone like Tilly get too close. It always ends up the same.

People baffle me. They all seem to be programmed by these peculiar neuroses which were imbued into them by events during childhood. They're victims of their past. They spend their formative years accumulating wounds and their adult lives picking at the scabs. They are always worrying about the future. They forget to live in the present. Many of them end up working themselves to death – saving, investing, hoarding – and, by the time they reach 'retirement', they are worn out and they have all this crap that they don't even use nor need. Their youth is gone. They spend the rest of their days regretting.

Everyone has so much baggage. But only because they choose to carry it. My life has had its ups and downs. I have had some shit times. Whenever I have felt like I don't favour the situation I'm in it has always been in my nature to drop everything and move on. I don't look back.

I guess that, whether I like it or not, I *am* a bit like my father. His DNA has imprinted upon me more than I would ever admit. Numbed me to much of the human experience.

Even my mother. I try to take the moral high ground and give Jardair a hard time over the way he treated her, but is it really all that different to what I did? When she finished raising me I realised that I didn't belong. I left.

I visit her once every couple of years, usually around Christmas, and she always makes a big deal about it. She decorates the house, makes a huge meal, dotes upon me the whole time I am there. She tells me that she thinks about me all the time. I don't think about her that often at all, to be honest. It makes me feel guilty, but, the truth is, I am usually relieved when I leave. I love her, in my own way, but I don't understand her.

My thoughts were disturbed by Nuttles leaping onto my shoulder. I turned my head and looked at him, realising that it was the first time he had dared come downstairs for weeks. My father had still not returned, and the rest of his crew were suspiciously absent. It had been a long time since Nuttles and I had the house to ourselves.

It was a relief. I have always felt much more at ease in the company of animals. They're not so convoluted. They *do* love, but it is simple, pure, in the moment.

I stroked the back of his head. He was worried about me. He could sense I was upset and he couldn't understand why – I had warmth, food and company, didn't I? What else could I possibly need?

Maybe I am a little more human than I think...

I began to worry about Tilly. I wondered where she was and what kind of state she was in.

I realised that I shouldn't have let her go off with all of those idiots. She was probably even *more* out of her mind by now.

What the hell was I thinking? I let her outburst affect me so much that I forgot my duty as her friend to keep her safe.

Nuttles picked up on some of my thoughts. He remembered Tilly. He had liked her – which was unusual for him because humans usually frightened him. He didn't know why.

"Do you know where Tilly is?" I asked him.

He sniffed the air. I was tuned into his mind, so I could sense much of what he was experiencing.

There were a few traces of her scent around my flat, but that was to be expected. She had been here a lot over the last couple of months.

He didn't detect any sources which were acute enough for him to think it was actually *her*, though.

"Come on Nuttles," I said, getting up. "Let's go for a walk."

I walked around the city aimlessly. Well, not completely aimlessly. I was hoping Nuttles would find Tilly's scent and that walking would help all the thoughts swarming through my consciousness disperse.

I wondered as I wandered. A drunken man was being guided home by his friend. Three girls in high heels stepped out of a bar, their arms linked, giggling. A few cars passed. Even an ambulance, sirens screaming and lights flashing. Each time one of these events happened, Nuttles climbed into the inside of my coat to hide before anyone could see him, and only emerged when we were alone again. The two of us often walk around like this at night, so he has become well practised in the procedure.

I pondered whether I should just move on again. I had lived in this city for a fair few years now. I had made a home for myself. I had been content, but now I wasn't so sure. Sunset Haze were still in hiatus, and I wasn't sure if we were ever going to be able to reform. I bumped into Ellen a few weeks ago, and she still seemed broken. Without her, the whole thing was over. She was the nucleus.

My father and his rabble had taken over my home. It was fun, at first, playing the insurgent. I felt like I was doing something good for the world, but now it was all getting a bit too much.

The streets began to illuminate gently. I heard birds

singing. The sky went from azure, to grey, to light blue. I carried on walking.

I still couldn't decide what to do. It made complete sense to just up and leave. Move on to another town. I had done it before, so why was I so reluctant *this* time?

Nuttles suddenly crawled from one shoulder to the other. His tail tickling my neck, pulling me out of my thoughts.

He had caught Tilly's scent.

Nuttles led me to Dinnusos. Which seemed strange, as it was way too early for the place to be open, but when I got there the door was ajar so I ran inside. Nuttles leapt from my shoulder and climbed up the drain pipe to hide on his usual spot on the roof.

I found Tilly lying upon one of the benches in the back room. Her arms and legs were drawn to her chest and her eyes were closed.

"Tilly," I said, gently, as I knelt beside her. I prodded her shoulder and she groaned.

"I found her outside," a voice behind me said.

I turned around. Neal was in the doorway with his arms crossed over his chest. "Great image, that," he uttered. "Drugged up underage girl on my doorstep. Great image…"

He was angry. I had never seen Neal angry before, but I could tell. The lines on his forehead were tensed tightly together and there was a flame in his eyes.

"Can I have a word with you, Jack?" he said.

I got up and followed him into the main bar, closing the door behind me.

"What the hell do you think you're *doing* letting her get in a state like that!" he screamed, once we were alone.

"I didn't," I said. "I tried to stop her. She–"

"They're your mates she's been loitering with recently, aren't they? In that bloody squat of yours!" Neal slammed his fist onto the bar counter and all the glasses around it rattled. "I have a mind to break your fucking jaw. Letting her get involved in a rabble like that. She's just a girl!"

"Neal, I'm sorry," I said. "I just–"

"Tilly deserves much better friends than you lot," Neal said. "I just tried to call Faye but she wouldn't even answer her phone! What's been getting into everyone recently?" he shook his head. "It's like the whole town's gone crazy. *Everyone's* high! Riots! Bombs going off! What the–"

"Bombs?" I repeated. "What bombs?"

"Haven't you heard?" he exclaimed. "What planet do you live on? Some bloody farm got blown up. It's all over the news!"

Oh no... I thought, as a terrible feeling bloomed in my chest. *Oh no...*

I ran home as fast as I could and, when I arrived, I found Jardair sitting on an armchair in my living room. He was alone.

"What the hell have you done!" I screamed.

"I am guessing word has trickled down the grapevine..." he said calmly as he drew his pipe to his mouth. A cloud of smoke burst from the embers, obscuring his face.

"You blew it up?!" I exclaimed. I paced towards the window and then back to the door. I couldn't keep still. "Shit! Shit, shit, shit, shit, shit!"

"Oh calm down," my father said. "No one was hurt. I made sure of that. The building was empty."

"Really?" I asked, looking at him.

He nodded.

"What about the animals?" I asked. "There were animals in there, weren't there? I could sense something..."

He grimaced. My father doesn't let tender emotion show very often, but this was one of those occasions where I could tell that even *he* had been affected by something.

"Yes, there were animals in there..." he said. "In a sense."

"What were they doing to them?" I asked, recalling the terrible feeling I used to get whenever I went anywhere near that building.

"They were chickens, Jack. Birds. But you don't want to know what had been done to them."

"Tell me," I said.

He looked for a few moments "Their beaks and claws had been snipped away when they were just chicks, and they had never seen the light of day. They were packed in cages so tight they were all squished together, and they had never even stretched their wings..." he shuddered and shook his head. "What was going on in that building was evil, Jack. There's no excuse... in my mind anyone who could even bring themselves to be involved in something like that has something wrong with 'em... I mean imagine *working* there. Walking around that building every day... No amount of damned money is worth that depravity. You say I am heartless, Jack. But people like that have something... missing. I had half a mind to kill them too, but... well, I had a feeling you wouldn't have liked that, so I spared them."

"Neal said it was a farm..." I said.

"I wouldn't call it that," he scowled. "It was a factory. Filled with grey machines, and creatures with more chemicals in their blood than food. Don't give it the credit of calling it a 'farm'."

"You still shouldn't have bloody blown it up!" I said. "The police are going to be after us now!"

He shook his head. "No. They will never be able to connect it to Taxus Baccata. I made sure of that. They will have *suspicions*, sure. But I have covered all tracks."

I crossed my arms over my chest. The situation was, admittedly, not quite as bad as I anticipated. When Neal mentioned bombs, I assumed the worst.

Nobody had died. And, on the scale of things, I could see my father had done what seemed right. He had just put an end to the suffering of thousands of animals. Whatever flaws he had, there were certain things my father held in the utmost value, and the right for all living creatures to live free and how nature intended them to was one of them. He had spent most of his life – however old he was – in the forest, so many things about modern society must seem barbaric to him.

But I still couldn't help but feel unsettled by it all. Like a line had been crossed.

"Things are going to have to change..." I said.

He frowned at me.

"I mean it. Things are going to have to change. Or I'm out."

"What things?" he asked.

"No more bombs, for a start," I said, as I sat down opposite him. "I know you didn't kill anyone, but bombs just have a way of freaking people out... and, don't take this the wrong way, but I can't live with all this around me anymore," I said, waving my arm across the house.

"You want us to change quarters?" he asked, scratching his chin thoughtfully.

"No," I shook my head. "Too many people know this as the base for Taxus Baccata now. It's more your place than mine. *I'll* move. There's plenty of empty houses in Yesterville. This is one of the more... preserved places, but I'm sure I'll find something."

"Okay," he said. "But you are still going to stay involved, right? You're great for the movement, kid. You understand people better than I do, and you have good ideas."

And I think I am the only person who can reign you in, I thought, but I didn't say it out loud.

"There's one more condition..." I said.

"I'm listening."

"Don't give Tilly any more drugs," I said.

He frowned. "I never gave the lass any drugs, Jackael."

"I know *you* didn't, but your crew have been. If you put an order out there I am sure they'll oblige. They listen to you. And I want Tilly to be... distanced a little. Not fully, because I think causes give her life some meaning, but at the moment she's too involved. I just want her safe. If you can agree to that, I will stay in Taxus Baccata."

After my father and I had shaken hands and sealed the deal, I walked back to Dinnusos. It wasn't far.

When I reached there, Tilly was still curled up on the bench. I picked her up and cradled her in my arms. She was so light.

"Jack..." she whispered vaguely. Like she wasn't even sure if it was me and she was truly awake or not. She draped her arms around my neck.

"Hello Tilly," I said. "It's okay... Just go back to sleep."

"Don't... take me to my grandmother..." she groaned. "She–"

"I'm not taking you to your grandmother, Tilly. Don't worry."

I carried her out of Dinnusos. Neal nodded grudgingly as I

stepped out of the door. He was still a little mad but I hoped that, given time, he would forgive me. Which was a surprise; there are very few people in this world of whom I care all that much what they think of me, but that number seemed to be growing. I wasn't sure if that was a good thing or a bad thing. Probably both.

I carried Tilly out of Yesterville. Away from its lawless, wayward streets. Away from my father, his minions, and their mindless revelry. Away from this episode of her life where she got carried away.

But I knew that there was only so much I could do. I couldn't carry her away from her demons. Or from herself. I wasn't quite sure there was anything I *could* do to help her with those things. I just knew that, in this moment, here, now, I could do this for her.

I carried her across town to Faye's house. I knew where it was, as I had walked her home from band practice a few times before, and it just seemed like a good idea. Faye had one of those liberal mothers. The sort who would probably know how to deal with a situation like this. I could trust her not to do the 'sensible thing' – freak out, ring Tilly's grandmother, or the police. She was one of those wiser, worldlier parents. One of those mothers who knew that, sometimes, the 'sensible thing', was not so sensible.

It was Faye who answered the door. She looked at me and then down at Tilly, and gasped.

"Jack!" she squeaked. "What–"

I carefully placed Tilly on the doorstep.

"I don't know what's going on with you at the moment, Faye," I said, just before I turned away. "But you need to pay more attention to your friends."

3
Barking at the Moon

Meet me at Dinnusos.
Tonight at 7.

The note said.

Typical Frelia. She could have sent me a text message. She could have emailed. She could have even rung – although that might have been a little awkward, considering we haven't spoken for over six months.

No, not Frelia. She just simply *had* to write me a note and push it through my door.

There was no signature, but I *knew* it was her. I recognised the shape of the letters. The loops and curves were, as usual, so irregular it almost seemed deliberate.

The envelope was not even stamped, so I can only assume that she came here and delivered it herself.

Why couldn't she have just dinged the bell? I thought. I would have invited her in and we could have chatted in my living room over a cup of tea.

No, I realised. *She wants us to meet on* ***her*** *grounds. That way she will have that edge over me.*

She was going to make this reunion as uncomfortable for me as she possibly could.

But I guess I deserved no better.

I found it difficult to concentrate at work that day. I agonised over my impending reunion with Frelia. I rehearsed in my mind all of the things I wanted to say, but none of them quite cut it. I have never been very good at apologies. I'm far too proud.

You don't ***have*** *to go*, I kept telling myself.

But I knew I would.

I spent almost an hour simply staring at the letter. At her handwriting. Trying to figure out if it was the scrawl of someone angry, vengeful, or seeking reconciliation.

The door opened and I almost jumped.

It was Mr Watts.

I stuffed the note back into my pocket.

Mr Watts is my boss. Part man, part petroleum jelly.

I call him that because it is my belief he immerses himself in a vat of Vaseline every morning. It really is the only explanation for the slickness of his swept-back hair and that shiny forehead of his. Even his (implausibly white) teeth are always gleaming.

Another theory I have is that this practice leaves him so well lubricated that he just spends his days slipping and sliding around the corridors of the building, occasionally managing to grasp hold of a door long enough to pull himself into one of the rooms. *That* explains why he is always flitting around other people's offices, rather than in his own. I am not quite sure what exactly it is that he *does*, as he seems to have no other purpose but do the rounds and check-up upon others. He has reached that golden apex of his career where he is considered so good at his job – whatever it is – that he no longer needs to actually do it.

His face emerged from a gap in the door and he cocked his head, like a snake which had just spotted its prey.

"Pandora," he hissed as he slithered into the room. He shut the door and we were alone.

"Hello..." I said.

He slicked towards me. There is a chair in my office which appears to be his – don't ask me how *that* happened, it just appeared one day and he always makes himself at home upon it. "How is the Equeld proposal going?" he asked.

I took a deep breath. How could I have forgotten about the Equeld proposal?

One word. *Frelia*.

"I don't think we should invest in them," I said.

"Why not?" he frowned. The nearest thing to what one

could call an emotion which can ever be prompted out of Mr Watts manifested itself in a tightening of his voice, though it was not quite the sentiment one would expect. It was frustration he was expressing. Like I was a machine which wasn't working properly and he couldn't figure out why.

I paused. "During my research I came across some... problems with their business."

"Problems?" he repeated. "*Problems!* What kind of *problems*? I've seen their figures. Their profits are through the roof! They're a sure thing! What kind of *problems* have you found?"

"Well..." I began. "In the last five years they have been heavily involved in the palm oil trade. You see, in Sumatra, they're–"

"That's in Sumatra. What else?"

"Last month, in India, dozens of workers died in–"

"That's in *India*," he shrugged dismissively. "I am more interested in what they can do for *us*. *Here*."

"There were children in that fire..." I said, softly. Hoping that maybe, just *maybe*, I could elicit some empathy out of him.

I'd sooner draw blood from a stone.

"Oh Pandora," he shook his head. He smiled. "Pandora... I understand what you are saying. I *really* do," he said. But his dead, lizard-like eyes, said otherwise. "But, Pandora," he put his hand on my shoulder. I hate it when he does that. "You already know what you are supposed to do when you have concerns like this, don't you?"

"But I did that last time–"

He raised the volume of his voice and adopted that tired patriarchal tone that I have grown all too familiar with. "What-does-company-procedure-say-you-should-do-if-you-have-a-comment-to-make-on-practice?"

"Fill out a 'Comment Caroline' form," I said.

He nodded. "So do that," he said. "Fibertine Investment Bank has a dedicated Ethical Practices Officer now. It is *their* job to worry about such things."

I knew that. All too well. I submitted an application for the role when it was created a few months ago but was turned down. They gave it to a woman called Germaine.

She is a bit like Mr Watts, only she has a vagina.

And she didn't apply for the position because she was passionate, or felt a calling. She's a careerist and saw it as an opportunity to elevate herself.

She was perfect, because Fibertine were never interested in becoming ethical. They wanted a thinly veiled PR officer. A drone, who was charming enough to keep up appearances, knew how to smile at the right moments, and possessed enough faculties to be able to spin plutocratic rhetoric.

"I'm sure they will take it on board," Mr Watts lied. "*But*, in the *meantime*. I want that proposal finished. The board want *you* to present it. Tomorrow morning. Isn't that exciting?" his voice changed, becoming higher, and his hand ventured down my back a little. And then it settled on my waist.

I really wish he would stop touching me.

He put his mouth close to my ear. "They want you to do it," he whispered.

Like it was the highest honour I could have ever dreamed.

"You could get a promotion out of this," he added with a wink.

He then got up, and his greasy hand returned to pat me on the shoulder.

"Remember what I always say to you, Pandora?" he said.

I nodded.

"What is it?"

"Business is blameless," I uttered. It was his mantra.

It basically means that, when you are in this building, everything you do is in the name of the company, not your own. So there is no need to feel guilt, or worry about facing consequences.

The consequences part is mostly true. Some of the employees here get away with murder – not literally, but effectively – and all that happens is that the company gets involved in an occasional legal battle and ends up paying a fine. No one has been given any jail time. Fibertine Investment Bank's profits are so high we're almost untouchable.

I'm still working on the guilt part.

At 5pm, I made my way home and got ready for my showdown with Frelia.

I turned the TV on simply for a bit of background noise. It had been over three months now since Stephan left me, but I still wasn't quite used to living alone and I found the voices comforting. It made the house seem less empty.

By the time I emerged from the shower they were reporting the local news. I listened as I dressed.

"The dissident movement, Taxus Baccata, continues to wreak havoc upon the city, today causing riots in a high street shop and disrupting the lives of civilians. We are now going to hear some words from Miss Tara Lisbon, the store manager, who is speaking from the scene of the incident about her thoughts on today's events."

The voice then changed and I looked up at the screen as I fastened the buttons of my blouse. "The real victims of the vicious crime which was committed today, are my employees," she stated. "Innocent workers who are just trying to make an honest living... we were put into a position where we had no other alternative but send them home because it was impossible for them to carry out their jobs. What we have seen today is nothing more than, yet *another*, reckless, thoughtless, and unprecedented attack, by a group of individuals who themselves do not wish to work, but choose to affect the lives of those who *do*."

Despite the slightly flat delivery – which made me suspect that the statement had been well rehearsed and, most likely, committee drafted – the content resonated with me. It made me feel angry that, while I had been working all day, a bunch of hooligans had nothing better to do than cause mayhem. Sure, there were problems with 'the system' (as they probably call it, in their youthful, reductionist way) but there were much more civilised ways to go about bringing change.

Though, I also couldn't help but think that the woman – who had just spoken so compellingly about the plight of her poor downtrodden employees – was not all that qualified to speak of their circumstances. *She* had obviously not been sent home early that day and, even if she had, it probably wouldn't have affected her salary. She likely earned a figure at least four times the amount the workers on the shop floor were paid.

And there was something about her which reminded me of Germaine.

The news then cut to footage of the protestors themselves. “It has been over two months now since the plague of the Taxus Baccata movement spread to this city,” someone narrated. “But it seems that, despite endless efforts by the police to keep the revellers in order, the party is still going strong and the mobsters have no inclination to curb the festivities.”

Footage of a group of teenagers dancing, in what appeared to be an abandoned warehouse, came up on the screen. Most of them had multiple face piercings and fluorescent hair – and I was pretty sure from the size of their enlarged pupils and the uninhibited way many of them were dancing they were high, too.

“Later on we will be interviewing MP, Mr Ben Fitzgerald, to see if he can shed any light upon rumours Westminster is considering bringing in new legislation which will grant authorities more power to dismantle anti-social behaviour. But first, we have more local headlines.” There was a brief pause. “It has now been confirmed that two men died in the explosion which occurred two nights ago on a family farm on the outskirts of–”

I shuddered. Things did seem to be getting rough in this town.

It was a strange place to be bombed, a farm. Usually terrorists target zones like transport hubs and centres of trade, but now it seemed that even innocuous locations were not safe.

If they were happy to blow up the grounds of a farmstead, they wouldn’t think twice about targeting a place like where I work... I thought with a shudder.

“No groups have come forward to claim responsibility for this brutal act of terrorism yet, but there are rumours that it could be related to an auxiliary branch of Taxus Baccata. The police are investigating all leads and are asking for anyone who thinks they might know something to come forward.”

I grabbed the remote and changed the channel. That was quite enough of that. I was a nervous wreck that day as it was without more to fret over.

Usually when you watch tragic events on the news you feel *something*, but it is numbed because the bad things are happening to people far away who you don't even know. All of this was a little too close to home.

I settled upon a radio station which was playing classical music.

I then walked over to the mirror and began to apply eye shadow and other touches to my face. I am not usually one for wearing much makeup, but I felt like I needed it tonight.

I was meeting Frelia. It was time to apply my war paint.

When I was ready, I searched for 'Dinnusos' on my smartphone but none of my apps were able to pinpoint its location. I couldn't find a postcode for it either. I eventually got frustrated and went to my computer and typed it into a search engine.

I found some directions for it in a somewhat obscure forum on the internet. It was in Yesterville. Oh, great. Yesterville. Best keep an eye on my purse and not take too many valuables with me then.

I turned to the window. At least it was still light outside.

There was no way I would *ever* walk to Yesterville alone in the dark.

A few minutes later I was walking out of my house, destined for Dinnusos.

It took me a while to find it but, admittedly, the venue Frelia picked for our rendezvous was not as bad as I was expecting it to be. In fact, it even had a certain charm about it. It reminded me a little of that Janus place she took me to once, only it was brighter and had more character. The walls were covered in paintings and there were slightly wonky shelves on the walls filled with kitschy memorabilia.

The barman was rather charming, too. A handsome man who talked to me as he poured my drink. He made me feel welcome and put me at ease.

I checked the time. It was 6:53 PM, so it seemed I was early. There were a few small groups sitting around the bar, but none of them were Frelia.

I claimed a table in the corner and sipped upon my wine spritzer as I waited.

Where the hell is she? I thought when I checked the time a few minutes later. It was 7:02. I looked around. The barman caught my eye and he smiled. Was it a sympathetic smile? I couldn't tell. He probably thought I was waiting for a date and been stood up. How embarrassing. I looked away, breaking eye contact.

It was just when I had finally had enough and was about to leave – I was literally in the process of grabbing my handbag and raising myself from my chair – that she burst in through the door. And when I say she burst in, it was not because she seemed like she had rushed here, conscious of the fact that she was late, at all. The door simply swung open and slammed shut again, in that loud and careless grace which Frelia seems to do *everything*.

Our eyes met, and we both grimaced. The last time we had seen each other was not a pleasant affair – it made me cringe just thinking about it. The sight of her face brought back awful memories.

She crossed the lounge to meet me.

"Sorry," she said, in a very un-sorry kind of way. They were just words. A formality. "I bumped into someone on the way here and I hadn't seen her for a while so we got chatting. Do you want a drink?" she asked, looking at the glass in front of me which was almost empty.

"Yes..." I tried to say, but it came out as an incoherent mumble. "Yes," I then repeated, after clearing my throat. "Please."

"What would you like?" she asked.

"White wine spritzer," I said. "Thank you."

Frelia wandered over to the bar and, as the landlord made the drinks, she leant over the counter and chatted with him. I couldn't hear what either of them were saying, but they both giggled a couple of times so I got the impression that they were familiar with each other. Or, knowing her, she was probably flirting with him.

When she returned, she had a pint of beer in one hand and a glass of wine in the other. She had forgotten the spritzer part, but I decided to let that slide. Only a few moments within her company, and I was already craving something a little stronger.

She sat down opposite me and, for a few moments, we

stared at each other. It was awkward.

We must have looked like a right pair. We couldn't be more different. She, with three rings dangling from her eyebrow, her messy hair, and torn jeans. Myself, the way I am. You're probably beginning to wonder how we even know each other.

Well, *that* is a long story...

"So..." she said. Of course, she would have to be the one to break the silence. "It's been a while..."

I nodded. "Yes," I said. "It has..."

"A few months, at least."

"Ten," I clarified.

She drank.

"Do you have anything you would like to say to me then?" she asked.

We stared at each other for a few more moments and I swallowed a lump in my throat.

"I'm sorry," I said.

She raised one of her eyebrows. "Sorry for what, exactly?"

"You know what..." I said, looking down at the table.

"Yes, I do," she replied. "But I want you to say it."

I drew a deep breath. "I'm sorry for what happened," I said. "With Stephan."

"And what *did* happen with Stephan?" she asked, placing her elbows on the table. I made the mistake of looking up at her briefly and saw that she was smiling. *Smiling!*

She was enjoying watching me squirm.

"Go on. Just say it," she said. "You fucked him."

"*Frelia!*" I exclaimed. I looked around us, worried that someone might have overheard but, to my relief, it appeared everyone around us was caught up in their own little worlds.

"What's the matter?" Frelia asked. "You weren't so prim and proper when I caught you bouncing away on his–"

"Stop it!" I exclaimed, feeling heat rising into my cheeks. "I'm sorry – okay! You know I am. What do you want from me, anyway?" I asked. "Why have you brought me here?"

She shrugged. "I just thought it was time to bury the hatchet, you know. We've known each other a long time, Pandy."

I flinched when she said that name. She knew I didn't like

being called Pandy anymore because it reminded me of who I used to be.

She was just trying to get a rise out of me.

I sipped my wine, denying her that satisfaction.

"We shouldn't let someone like him come between us," Frelia finished. She drank again. "He ain't worth it."

I nodded. Frelia and I used to be close once, in a weird way, but I'm not quite sure if we were friends. She is kind of like my sister, and yet she isn't. We're not even related.

We were both raised in foster care. I am an orphan – my parents died in a car crash when I was eight years old – and Frelia, well, her mother is a little crazy, and her father... I'm not even sure she knows who he is. For a part of our childhood and some of our early teens, we dwelt in the same institution. We even shared a room.

Until we were separated.

"He's gone now," I said.

She shrugged. "Tell me something I don't know. I figured he wouldn't stick around long. The only reason I'm even speaking to you is because, to be honest, I think you did me a favour."

"So I'm forgiven then?" I asked.

She looked at me thoughtfully and, during that moment, I was surprised how much I craved her to accept my apology.

"Not quite," she said. "Some of the trust is gone. I can't help that…"

I nodded gently. It was understandable.

"So where did he hike off to, anyway?" she asked.

Oh, so you're assuming that he left ***me****!* I thought sourly.

But it was true.

"He joined the Hari Krishnas."

Frelia laughed heartily, raising her head up to the ceiling. "Yes," she chuckled. "That certainly sounds like the sort of thing he would do. And no doubt, since then, he's moved on to join the travelling circus too."

I stroked my wine glass, making a line through the layer of condensation which had formed around it. "I came home one day, and he was just packing his bags," I said. "Two hours later he was gone. He didn't even..."

I think about that day often. It wasn't the fact that he left which upset me. It was the fashion. It was the realisation I had been used.

When I took him in, he had just been kicked out of a monastery for breaking his vows. He had nowhere to go and he owned nothing but the tattered old robes on his back. I gave him a home. I fed him. Helped him find a new job and bought him a lovely suit so that he could turn up to the interview looking respectable.

I created a whole new life for him, and he never properly thanked me. Or even acknowledged all the things I did.

But, looking back now, I think I used him too in a way. The truth is, I didn't even *like* him that much. I was just lonely and he was convenient. He was like a puppy. Simply pleased. One dimensional. Completely fixated by whatever passing fancy was his 'thing' at the time. Easily distracted by something new. Totally oblivious to anything which was not his current furore. It was quite charming.

It was the *way* he left which hurt.

When I came home that day I walked up the stairs and found him packing his bags. He had a big smile on his face. He was giddy. Excited. He had found something new. He was moving on. He didn't care to think about what he was leaving behind, or the effect his departure may have upon anyone else.

If he had a tail, it would have been wagging.

He had that big smile on his face all the way up to the moment that he stepped out of my door.

And, just before he left, he waved.

Like I was a receptionist.

A receptionist he had become rather fond of, during his stay.

But still a receptionist.

He walked away from me as easily as if he was checking out of a hotel.

And he didn't say goodbye.

He didn't validate me with any kind of closure.

I didn't let myself cry until he closed the door and his shadow had left my driveway.

"Still," Frelia said, tilting her glass and staring into the last dregs of her drink. "At least he had a big dick."

She winked at me. I tried really hard not to giggle, but I couldn't help myself. I was secretly glad I did in the end because she laughed too and it dissolved some of the tension. She downed the rest of her drink.

"And now I believe it is *your* round," she said, as she slammed her empty glass on the table.

I came back with a bottle of wine to share. We caught up. Well, in all honesty, I diverted most of the questions she asked about me because my life had been a little depressing of late and I didn't want her to know. I distracted her with questions about herself. She was doing well at college and been predicted good results at the end of the year. She had a new boyfriend. Her mother's mental health was improving and she had been moved to a less secure ward – Frelia even seemed to believe that it was possible she was going to be released sometime in the next year.

It was all music to my ears. Frelia had a rough childhood, and during her teenage years she spiralled into a rather destructive episode. She seemed much more balanced now. Which was good. She deserved to be happy.

I only wish she could work on the way she dressed. And her manner! I worried about her job prospects.

We were suddenly disturbed by a young man who approached the table.

"Frelia!" he exclaimed, grabbing her shoulder. He was skinny and tall, with scruffy hair and a lazy shadow of facial hair around his chin and mouth. Probably in his mid-twenties by the look of him. "I *knew* it was you."

"Kev!" she yelled, matching the pitch of her voice to his own raised volume and getting up from her chair to embrace him.

It seemed our quiet get together was over.

"How are you?" she asked. "You weren't at the rally today?"

"Oh yeah, sorry," he said, scratching his head. "Went and got a job, didn't I. I'm a working man now!"

I stared at them. A rally? Today?

He then looked at me, as if only just noticing I was there, and his eyes widened. "Hello..." he said. "Sorry for crashing on your... I just–"

"Oh, don't worry, you fool!" Frelia said, patting his chest fondly. "This is my friend, Pandora. Pandora, this is K-Hole-Kev–"

"I'm not K-Hole-Kev anymore!" he said indignantly. "I've cleaned up now, remember?"

"Fine," Frelia smiled. She then turned back to me. "Pandora, this is *Kevin*. Kevin, Pandora."

He made his way around the table to shake my hand – he managed to kick a chair on his way and sent it skidding across the bar, but he didn't seem to notice. His palm was a little sweaty but I went through with the gesture, forcing a smile.

"You best come to the next one," Frelia said to him.

"Of course!" Kevin said, turning back to her. "I'm only working part time. Have you heard about the mushrooms they've got upstairs?"

Frelia shook her head.

"*Really?*" he exclaimed. "It's the reason I *came* here! Oh my God, Frelia. You've *got* to try them! Pag did them last night and he made contact with *trans-dimensional beings*! It's *changed* him. He can read Latin now! And Hebrew! He couldn't even read English proper before..."

"I thought you'd 'cleaned up'?" Frelia raised one of her eyebrows.

He nodded. "I have. I've gone organic. Even my shoes. Look!" he said, pointing to the brown and slightly flimsy looking things around his feet. "No more chemicals. This stuff's all natural, Frelia. You know that woman, Kendra? You know, the witchy one who's always standing behind Jardair when he's giving his speeches? She knows about all these crazy plants and things which can expand your mind. And they're not even illegal because the authorities don't know about them. These mushrooms are one of her secrets. Only *she* knows where to get them. She's upstairs, now! *Giving* them away!"

"I am just having a quiet drink with Pandora tonight, Kev," Frelia said. "Sorry. Maybe some other time..."

Kev shook his head. "It's now or never, mate. Apparently they only grow two nights of the year – it's to do with the spores, or something – and they have to be eaten within a few hours of picking, too. This is the last batch."

Frelia paused. For a brief moment, I caught that mischievous glint in her eye – the one which I knew all too well.

She was tempted.

"I'll think about it, okay..." she said.

*Not if **I** have anything to do with it.*

"Alright..." Kev nodded. "Anyway, I'm going to get mine before they're all gone. See you later. Nice to meet you, Pandora!"

He then bumbled off towards the stairs.

Frelia looked at me. "Kev's a friend of–"

"Are you involved with Taxus Baccata?" I interrupted her.

She hesitated.

"*Frelia!*" I hissed. "You don't want to be getting muddled with them. Even *you* should have better sense than that. They were all over the news earlier."

She chuckled. "Oh yeah, I saw that one. It was hilarious, wasn't it? They–"

"This is no laughing matter!"

"Please don't tell me that you actually *believe* the news?" Frelia asked me, her voice turning flat. "What did they call it again? A '*riot*'?" she rolled her eyes. "It was a peaceful protest. No one was harmed.

"Tell that to the poor workers who went home to their families without being paid today," I said.

"It was the company's choice to not pay them. Not ours," Frelia shrugged. "Personally, I feel much more sympathy for the children working in their sweatshops in Bangladesh. *That* was the reason we targeted that store, Pandora. But, as expected, the media completely blacked out *that* part of the story."

I couldn't think of any counter argument off the top of my head. "I don't like the idea of you hanging out with junkies," I eventually went with.

"Are you referring to that little montage they made with all the flashy lights?" she asked. "The Taxus Baccata ravers, and their sinful, debauched ways," she said, adopting a sardonic tone. "That was some fairly standard propaganda, Pandora, and if you fell for it then you're obviously not as clever as I thought you were. There are a few members of the movement who like to party every now and then, and so what if they do?" she shrugged. "If they're not harming anyone. Most of the people in this bar now were at the protest today. Do *they* look like the hooligans and thugs Murdoch's minions have made them out to be?"

I glanced across the room. It was evening now, and the place was getting busier. Sure, some of them looked a little bit eccentric, but they all seemed like harmless artists and bohemians to me. The atmosphere was pleasant.

I found it difficult to assimilate this scene with all the things I had heard about Taxus Baccata.

"Even some of *your* kind have got involved recently," Frelia said, winking at me. "Although most of them are doing it on the down low. Anyway, Pandora, are we going to take those mushrooms or what?"

I was so shocked – both by the sudden turn in the conversation, and the new topic itself – that all I could do at first was mumble incoherently. "No... No! Frelia, we can't. It's–"

"*Why?*" she asked, leaning towards me. "They're not illegal."

"I'm a Christian," I said.

I know that sounded like a rather pathetic excuse, but it was just the first thing which popped into my head.

"Aww, go on..." Frelia pleaded. "Let's do it! It'll be fun. You can just go to confession on Sunday and be forgiven anyway."

"That's Catholics..." I said. "I'm an Evangelist."

"Be a Catholic tonight," she shrugged. "You can go to confession on Sunday and be forgiven. And *then*, after that, you can be Born Again, *again*, as an Evangelist. Next week, or whenever. Then you'll be forgiven twice. I think that covers all clauses for your spiritual salvation..."

"It doesn't work like that."

In truth, I haven't actually been to church for a while. But I didn't want to tell Frelia that. She was an atheist and would only get all smug about it.

I just couldn't face any of the congregation since I started sleeping with Stephan...

The weirdest thing was realising that I didn't feel guilty. I didn't even feel like what we were doing was wrong. And, once I started to question that, I began to question everything. Every niggling thought and theological paradox which had ever formed in my mind but I swiftly repressed, began to wriggle around in my mind. Squirming and growing.

It's not that I don't believe in God anymore. This world, to me, has always seemed too miraculous and wonderful for it to be explained by purely materialistic terms. I just couldn't imagine that something *this* extraordinary could simply explode into existence without some kind of instigator. A demiurge.

I still believe in *something*. It's more that I am stuck on the details...

"How about if I said that, if you do this with me, I will forgive you..." Frelia said, interrupting my train of thought.

I looked back up at her. I am not sure how long it had been for, but I had been staring into my wine glass for a while.

No one was more surprised than me when I found myself saying, "Fine. Let's do it."

The next sequence of events was all a blur. Frelia led me up the stairs. Through a chamber, and then along an eerie corridor which was framed by a series of parabolic wooden beams. This part of Dinnusos was unsettlingly quiet. Even a little spooky.

Frelia then opened a final door and we walked into a room where Kendra was waiting for us.

'The Witchy One' was a fair description. I couldn't see much because the room was lit by only a single candle, but Kendra appeared to be wearing some kind of tattered robe and she had one of those faces where it was impossible to tell how old she was. Someone could have told me she was in her twenties or seventies and, in either case, I could have believed them. Her hair was like a bird nest. Quite literally. All brown and messy, and there were twigs and leaves caught within the tangles.

And this is the woman I am supposed to trust with the state of my mind this evening, I thought. But I knew it was too late. I had just consented to Frelia, of all people. There was no going back now.

Frelia approached the table first. Kendra looked her up and down. And then she smiled and dug a handful of little mushrooms with long black stipes out of a pouch and dropped them into Frelia's hand.

She looked at me next and narrowed her eyes. She muttered something under her breath, but I never quite caught what it was that she said. She seemed to stare at me for a bit longer than she did at Frelia though and, when she dug into that pouch of hers again, it was a much larger handful of the mushrooms she tipped into my palm.

I looked at them, and then turned to Frelia. "I've got more than her," I said.

I tried to give some of the excess ones back, but Kendra hissed and made several hand gestures. She didn't like that at all.

It appeared that dose had been specifically chosen for me.

"Bottoms up, Pandora," Frelia said, grinning as she raised her balled fist up to her mouth and then waited for me.

That expression doesn't even make any sense! We're not drinking from glasses... I thought as I mimicked her. *I can't believe I am doing this. I only slept with* ***one*** *of your boyfriends, Frelia.* ***This*** *has got to be worth five, at least!*

Nevertheless, I dropped them into my mouth. I chewed a few times, expecting them to be foul, but they weren't too bad actually. In fact, they were quite sweet.

"I think tonight is going to be fun," Frelia then said, as she grabbed my hand and led me away.

We walked back down to the bar together. I was nervous. Frelia bought the next round of drinks. Wine again. That calmed me down a little. She began to talk, but I wasn't really listening to what she was saying. Anxiety crawled into my chest. I looked at the walls. The window. The ceiling. Watched the motion of her lips as she spoke. Waiting to see if anything changed.

"When do you think it's going to kick in?" I eventually interrupted her.

"I don't know," she shrugged. "This one's going to be entirely new to me as well... probably about the same time as other shrooms, I guess."

"And how long is that?"

"Oh, don't go acting like you're all clueless with me," Frelia droned, irritably. "This is hardly the first time you've done this, *Pandy*. That act you put on when you go to church and swish around that fancy job of yours doesn't fool me. You seem to forget how long I've known you..."

I hesitated.

I couldn't think of a retort. And I didn't tell her off for calling me Pandy, either, like I usually do.

Because I realised what she had just said was true.

I *am* turning into Pandy again...

Want to know what Pandy was like?

High on a school night, her eyes rolling into the back of her head. That was what Pandy was like. Lost her virginity at the age of thirteen while drunk on a cheap bottle of vodka. That was what Pandy was like. Wandering around raves wearing a skirt which was so short and tight that everyone could see her knickers, *and* being happy about it because she enjoyed the attention. That was what Pandy was like. Not even knowing the names of any the men she made out with, but remembering that most of them were at least twice her age (because that was the sort of parties *she* went to).

Pandy.

Let her foster-sister take the rap for *her* drugs during a police raid, and then, as she is dragged off to juvenile detention, say nothing.

That was what Pandy was like.

"Are you alright?" Frelia asked. Her expression softened and she took one of my hands. "I'm sorry," she said. "I know I am a little blunt at times... don't worry. You'll be fine. We're in this together, okay? I'll look after you. Just try to enjoy yourself. When was the last time you actually let yourself loose a little?" she asked.

Just before that night you were taken away from me...

I drank more wine.

"Don't worry," I said. "I'm fine."

The truth was, it wasn't just anxiety I was feeling. I was excited too. It had been a long time since I had experienced this. That feeling when you have just taken the plunge on a substance you have never tried before and you're waiting for something to happen. The anticipation. Your heart rate starts to quicken, and you're not quite sure if it is the drug or just adrenaline. You're worried. Exhilarated. You keep thinking; *well, it's too late now...*

My eyes were drawn to something on the wall. It was blue. Very blue. Almost neon in its radiance. And the lines were all wavy. They were moving, too. I became fascinated by it and walked over so that I could see it better.

It was a landscape painting. Of a river surrounded by fields and hills.

"It's Tristan's," Frelia said, standing beside me. "You remember him? You met him that time I took you to Janus."

I nodded. "It's beautiful..." I said.

I experienced a peculiar compulsion to touch it. So that I could feel the textures – so that I could *know* it – but I reconsidered.

There's my inhibitions going... I thought, wistfully.

I stared at the river for a while. The patterns of blues and whites began to mingle and swirl. The river was moving.

"Look at that!" Frelia exclaimed, with a childish grin on her face. She was pointing at something. I narrowed my eyes to get them to focus and saw a piece of driftwood floating downstream. It had been swept into the current and was moving across the canvas. Frelia and I watched as it made its way to the other side of the frame, laughing, dimly aware that other people in the bar were staring at us, but not caring. Those people didn't matter. They didn't understand.

Frelia and I looked at each other in shared glee and, for a fleeting moment, I experienced anamnesis of the closeness the two of us used to have.

I looked back at the painting again. The driftwood had vanished now, but there were other things there which I couldn't remember seeing before. The picture had changed.

There were now several rows of grey buildings clustered along the side of the river. They were bleak looking, and all had chimneys which were billowing clouds of black smog into the sky. The hills in the background had been obscured from view. There were no fields now.

"What the–" I began to say, but Frelia grabbed my hand.

"Come, Pandora. Let's go outside and get some air," Frelia said. "People are staring at us."

We walked across the lounge. Side by side. Both grinning. I couldn't remember being this happy for a long time.

It can be a very intimate thing, taking a mind-altering substance with someone. You embark upon a journey together. From the moment it makes its way down your throat or nasal passages you know that, for the next few hours of your life nobody will ever quite understand you like the person who took it with you, and the same goes for them. You are tuned in to the same frequency.

Frelia opened the door and cool air caressed my face and neck. It was refreshing and invigorating. There was a body of water in front of us, softly undulating. Luminescent. I looked up at the sky, and the moon was shining. Full and blue.

"Where are we?" I asked, turning to Frelia. We had just stepped out of the bar but yet it seemed like we had entered a completely different plane. A different time. There were buildings all around us but they all looked a bit dishevelled and old. "Am I hallucinating, or is that a river in front of us?"

"It's just the canal which runs through Yesterville," Frelia said, as she walked towards the edge of it. "It's always been here."

"Ahoy there!" someone called.

Frelia and I both looked around, searching for the source of the voice, and the water rippled. Disturbed by something.

It was Kev, in a rowboat.

"Ahoy!" he said again, as he sank his oar into the body of the canal and steered the vessel towards us.

"Kev!" Frelia exclaimed, bursting into a fit of giggles. "What are you *doing*?!"

He looked up. "It's a boat!" he said, innocently. He had a big smile on his face.

I must have been high, because in that moment he looked

rather charming. And handsome.

"I know that, but what are *you* doing in it?!" Frelia asked.

"Come aboard!" he said, offering his hand.

Frelia and I both looked at each other.

I know that getting into a boat in the dark of night with a guy you have only just met, while high, sounds like it might be possibly one of the stupidest ideas in the world.

But, in that moment, it seemed like *exactly* the sort of thing I wanted to do.

Frelia clambered on first. And then, as she settled herself down onto one of the wooden benches, Kev turned to me and extended his hand.

There was a moment of hesitation. But then I looked at him, into those guileless and sincere brown eyes of his, and, somehow, I just simply *knew* that he was one of the good ones. A man I could trust.

I gripped his palm and he pulled me in. My feet left concrete and I stepped into the berth and the boat rocked. I grabbed Kev's shoulder to steady myself.

"All aboard?" Kev asked, once I had sat myself down on one of the benches.

"All aboard!" Frelia and I said, in unison.

He immersed the oar into the depths of the water and the boat sleeked into the middle of a thalassic plane. The starlight reflecting on the surface glimmered, and then flittered from the swell we caused. I reached out to touch it. Experienced a sense of elation, as my fingers ran through cool wet stars.

We were embarking on an adventure. And I had not felt this alive for years.

Kev rowed. Frelia kept talking. And laughing. I was only listening to her half of the time.

I lay back and looked up at the sky. The buildings on either side of me began to look a little older. We went under a bridge and everything turned black. I screamed. Frelia laughed. When we emerged on the other side, I realised that I was silly to be scared and chuckled too. I sat up. There were trees now, and the walkway had turned into a towpath.

And then, for a brief moment, something peculiar happened.

It was daylight. The boat was no longer floating upon water – we were suspended in mid-air – and there were men all around us, hacking at the sides of the bank with pickaxes. One of them was standing in the middle of the trench with a wheelbarrow in his hands and he looked up at me. His eyes widened.

Everything went dark again.

I shook my head and closed my eyes to see if I could ground myself with a reprieve of sanity, but shapes and colours danced behind my eyelids. A flower. The petals were spinning. Each one was a person dancing. Whirling around each other in perfect harmony. And then it opened up, blossoming, spiralling outwards, blooming in perfect Fibonacci concatenation.

My ears picked up the sound of someone crying, and I opened my eyes and remembered where I was. I had got so involved in the vision I had lost myself. I was in a boat. On a canal.

I could still hear the crying though.

Frelia and Kev seemed to hear it too, because their heads were moving from side to side and their eyes were searching.

"What is that?" I asked.

"Over there!" Frelia said, pointing to something on the bank. Kev began to row towards it, and the shape in the shadows began to become clearer. It was quivering.

It was a child. I couldn't see their face at first because it was covered by their hands but, as we got closer, I could make out that it was a girl.

The boat suddenly jerked when it hit the edge of the bank, and Frelia and I had to grab the sides to steady ourselves.

"Sorry..." Kev mumbled.

I climbed out of the vessel and the girl looked up at me as I approached her.

"Hello..." I said. Her face was dirty and her eyes widened at the sight of me. She seemed to be particularly intrigued by my clothes for some reason. "What's your name?"

"Lenora..." she said, hugging herself protectively.

"Where's your mother, Lenora?" I asked her.

"She's working," she sniffed. "I am betimes."

*At **this** time of the night?* I thought.

"Come with me," I said, offering her my hand. "It's okay. We will look after you. My name is Pandora, and this is Frelia and Kevin," I then added, motioning to the two figures sitting in the boat behind me. "They are my friends. Don't worry, you'll be safe with us."

She stared at me for a few moments and then looked at the boat. "Are you boat people?" she asked.

"No," I said. "We're just... people."

She seemed satisfied with my answer and got up, drawing herself to her feet unaided. She didn't take my hand.

It was only as she was walking towards the boat that I noticed her clothes were all brown and ragged. They looked a little coarse too, and were covered in dirty marks. It was not the sort of attire a girl of any age should be forced to wear.

I am going to have a word with that bloody mother of yours when I find her! I promised myself.

Kev stared at her with his jaw hanging open as Lenora stepped on board.

"Where does your mother work?" Frelia asked, putting her hand on her shoulder.

"At the mill," Lenora responded.

"The Mill," I repeated, thinking it must be the name of some pub or something. It seemed we were a little out of the city now as I couldn't see any buildings. "Kev, row us back to town," I said, turning to him.

"It's only over there!" Lenora said, pointing to the bank behind me.

"I'll go check it out," Frelia said, climbing out of the boat.

"No!" Lenora squealed. "Don't go inside! Most not fit to hold a candle to Mr Morgan. I went in once and he chalked me!"

"Don't worry, I won't go in," Frelia reassured, running a hand through Lenora's greasy hair. "I'm just going to have a look, okay?"

Lenora nodded.

"Pandora, look after her," Frelia said as she left.

"How?" I said, feeling panicky. It was instinct which made me get up and see a distressed girl into the safety of our boat, but now I was faced with the prospect of actually looking after her while Frelia went off on an escapade, I felt ruffled.

She was a child and, more importantly, she had not taken any of the mushrooms. She might as well have been an alien.

"Just tell her a story or something," Frelia shrugged.

Lenora stared at my feet as I clambered back into the boat, and then her eyes slowly wandered up to my face. She still seemed fascinated by what I was wearing for some reason.

I sat down next to her. "So, there once was this..." I began, but then my mind went blank. I tried to remember some children's stories, but my brain was refusing to coordinate with that need. "Kev," I eventually turned to him, hoping he would come to my rescue. "Do you remember any stories?"

He stared at us with his mouth hanging wide open.

Great, great, great, great, great! I thought, turning back to Lenora.

"How about *you* tell *me* a story," I suggested. *Kids like talking, don't they?* "Tell me about yourself."

She opened her mouth and began to speak.

Lenora's Story

I didn't always live here. I used to live in the country. The fields around my house were green. The trees were green – and they were also brown too, especially in autumn, but mostly they were green. My smocks were white, my petticoat was brown, and my gown was red.

My house was brown. My Mummy grew vegetables, and they were all kinds of colours. I used to help her milk the cows every morning, and their udders were pink and the milk was creamy.

My Daddy worked the loom. Mummy worked the loom too, but mostly Daddy worked the loom. It was a noisy thing. It weaved white cloth, and Daddy used to sell it to a man who came to see us every Thursday. He wore brown.

At night, the loom would stop being noisy. Me, Mummy and Daddy would sit around the fire. Mummy would tell me stories, but she was better at it than you.

One Thursday the man came to collect the cloth, and he and Daddy had bandy words because he would only give Daddy a fiddlers' money. Daddy went to other men to see if they would pay fair penny, but he was barking at the moon.

Daddy became sad. He said that, in the city, there was a new loom. One which was bigger and faster than the one we had. One which, if you had one, would make you rich. But you could only afford one if you were rich anyway, so it didn't make anyone rich. The people who were already rich got richer. And the poor... well, we became poorer.

Daddy moved away. Me and Mummy moved away too, but we moved to a different place to where Daddy moved. We moved to the city and it was grey and brown and dirty and smelly. And our home was grey and small, and lots of other people lived in it with us, too. The chimney was black, and the sky went grey from all the smog. The houses became greyer over time. The water went grey. My clothes went grey. My feet went grey.

Daddy still comes to see us sometimes, but his clothes are black now and they smell like our chimney. His hands are black too, but not completely black. When he comes, Mummy is happy and we eat nice food because he has money. But then he goes away again and Mummy becomes sad.

"What's the matter?" she asked, narrowing her eyes at me.

I'm not sure you're even real. And if you ***are*** *real I'm in no state to be looking after you. That's what is the matter.*

"Your clothes have lots of colours," she said, matter-of-factly as she pinched the hem of my skirt. "Where did you get them from?"

I heard footsteps behind me and turned around. Frelia was back. *Thank God.*

"Stay there!" I said to the girl as I climbed out of the boat.

"Frelia," I called as I ran to her. "Please tell me you found her Mum?"

She shook her head.

It was only then that I noticed Frelia looked different now. Or at least that's what I *thought* I was seeing. At this point of the evening I could only assume that my eyes and ears had begun to betray me.

Frelia was dressed like a Victorian peasant, with a brown skirt trailing almost all the way down to her ankles and this white thing with strings across her chest. She was carrying a bundle of fabric in her arms, too.

"I need you to get changed into these, if you can," Frelia said, calmly. She dropped the bundle and it landed in a heap by my feet. I then realised they were clothes – similar ones to what she was wearing.

"What's going on?" I asked.

"Just put them on," she said. "Trust me. You need to."

"*Frelia!*" Kev yelled at her. After a long period of time spent simply gawping, it appeared he had regained the ability of speech. "You've bloody done it *again*, haven't you!"

Frelia bit her lip and looked at her feet guiltily.

"Send us back, Frelia!" Kev shouted.

"I can't!" she yelled. She seemed stressed. Which was strange because Frelia rarely lets anything phase her. "I tried! I think it's the mushrooms."

"What's going on?" I asked.

"She's sent us back in time, ain't she," Kev said. "Victorian, or some shit."

"Don't be ridiculous," I said. The last thing I needed right now was people putting ideas like that into my head. My grip on reality was tenuous enough as it was.

"It's even a different time of day!" Kev said. "Look around you. Don't you think it's a bit light for it to be midnight?"

"Mushrooms always make things a little brighter," I said. "Someone like *you* should know that. Get a grip!"

At first he looked offended and he scowled at me, but then his expression transitioned from slighted to smug. "Alright... how about the *moon*, then?" he pointed at the sky. "Explain *that* one."

I looked up and gasped. The moon – which only a few minutes ago had been full – was now just a crescent.

I heard a wail, and turned my eyes to the back of the boat. It was Lenora. She was crying into her hands.

"Will you two quit flirting and just get changed?" Frelia said, tossing some clothes at Kev. "You can fuck each other later..."

Frelia then went to Lenora and started making soothing noises into her ear while she rubbed her back.

It was a bizarre experience, getting changed while under the effect of the mushrooms. It was like I was learning how to do it all over again. Usually, when you get changed, you don't even think about it. Your limbs operate automatically – they are used to the procedure and already know what to do – but I found myself having to navigate and consider my way through every process. Undoing the buttons; they're a little bit peculiar, aren't they, buttons? The way you have to tilt them so that the circle becomes flat and fits through the slit. Sleeves are weird, too. The way your arms vanish inside them – like they have entered an entirely different universe – and then your hand emerges from the other side. And then it has become part of you and you no longer see it as strange.

I heard footsteps and looked up to see that Frelia was approaching me.

"Feeling better?" she asked, curtly.

"I don't know what kind of prank you're pulling here, but it's not bloody funny," I said.

"It's no prank," Frelia said. "Keep your voice down. People might hear us."

"Oh, so you think he's right, do you? That we've been magically whisked away to Victorian times."

"No," Frelia shook her head. "I think this is pre-Victorian, actually. Lenora told me that her father used to be a weaver before they moved to the city and the Cottage Industry didn't fall into decline until the late 18th century, if I remember correctly. The lovely princess Victoria is yet to even kick and screech her way into this world. Let alone become the ever-so-charming Queen we all cherish."

"Whatever, Frelia. I've had enough now. Just take me home."

"I *tried* taking us back home but it's not working! I'm sorry," Frelia shook her head. "We will be pulled back later, I guess. It always–"

"Oh, I see," I slapped my forehead. "*You* travelled us back in time! It all sounded ridiculous before, but now you're explained *that* bit it makes perfect sense!"

"I know it's hard to believe, but it's to do with my father. He–"

"You don't even know who your father is!" I exclaimed, cutting her off.

I know it was a harsh thing to bring up, but I was scared and angry. I regretted it later. I regretted the next thing I said even more.

"I have had enough of you, Frelia! You're nothing but bad news! This is the last time I do *anything* with you."

Her expression changed. I knew then, that I had hurt her – which was quite an achievement, because Frelia is possibly the most thick-skinned person I have ever known.

"Fuck *you*, Pandora!" she said, crossing her arms over her chest. "You know, maybe I am a bit rough around the edges. Maybe I don't know how to smile and put on an act when I am around certain people. Maybe I *do* always speak my mind. Maybe I don't have a fancy job and a lovely little house with all the mod-cons. And, you know what? I probably never will. But at least I'm happy. Look at *you*! You have it all. Or at least you *think* you do, but underneath all of that superficial shit you're fucking miserable!"

That hurt me. It hurt me so much I didn't even have the poise to hide it. It hurt me so much a sharp pain squeezed into my chest and, for a few moments, I found it hard to breathe.

Frelia walked away. I sat down and cried.

It hurt me because it was true. I *was* miserable. I hated my life. I hated what I had become.

But I hated my former self even more. Even if she did have a bit more fun.

I felt my sleeve being tugged upon and I pulled my hands away from my eyes. My vision was still a little blurry from all the tears, but I could see that it was Lenora. She was staring at me.

"Why tune your pipes?" she asked.

I wiped my eyes with the back of my hand. "Sorry, I don't know what you mean."

"There is no use crying over spilt milk," she said. "That's what Daddy always says."

"Oh, the bucket is far from empty yet," I laughed bitterly. "There's plenty more to be spilt, believe me."

"Then put the bucket down until you learn to stop being so clumsy," she said, simply.

I wished it was that simple.

She sat herself down beside me and rested her head on my arm. "Why have you and Frelia gone all surly boots?" she asked. "You both seem plump currant to me."

I still couldn't make head nor tail of much she was saying – and I wasn't sure if it was because of the mushrooms, so I didn't comment. Instead, I put my arm around her. "Thank you, Lenora," I said.

"What for?"

"For just..." I hesitated. "Being here."

I looked over at the boat and saw that Frelia and Kev were sitting together talking. I couldn't tell what either of them were saying because they were out of earshot and Frelia had her back turned to me, but it seemed Kev was consoling her.

I heard a rustling and turned to the source to witness a woman emerge from the scrub. She ran her eyes across the area and then her gaze settled upon me and Lenora.

"That's Mummy!" Lenora smiled.

"And what's Mummy's name?" I asked.

"Jane."

*I'm going to have a word with this **Jane**!* I decided, as I rose to my feet.

Lenora got up to greet her too, but her legs weren't as big as mine so it was me who reached her first.

"What the hell do you think you're doing!?" I said as I approached her. "Leaving her here all alone?"

Jane was clearly startled by me. She drew back and placed her arms across her chest.

"Anything could have happened to her!" I exclaimed, pointing to Lenora. "She could have–"

I cut myself short, because I noticed something peculiar.

There was something wrong with Jane's hands. One of them was deformed. Or damaged, rather. Her wrist was twisted into a terrible angle, and her hand – what was left of it – hung limply. She didn't have any fingers.

"What..." I gasped, putting a hand to my mouth. "What... happened to you?"

She looked down at it and grimaced. "Got caught in the spinner," she said. "My fault. I was careless."

Lenora appeared at her side, and Jane put her good hand on her daughter's head. She didn't take her eyes off me.

"I'm sorry," I said. For the second time that evening feeling guilty over making a hasty outburst. "But... you can't just leave Lenora out at night alone, she–"

"Mr Morgan asked me to stay longer so I could clean the machines," she said. She looked down at the ground briefly and then back up at me and her expression became more assertive. "Look, I don't need no blue stockings telling me what's right and proper for my child. We're in bad bread, but I work hard to bring food to the table..." her voice strained. She sounded like she was close to tears. "I used to make seven shillings a week but now I am lucky if I come home with a crown!"

Shillings! I at first thought. ***Shillings?*** But I was reaching a place by that point where I was beyond questioning it all. I had become desensitised.

I noticed then that Jane was clad in an old fashioned skirt and gown, just like Lenora, Frelia, and myself.

"They're making you work *more* hours for *less* pay?" I asked. "Why?"

She frowned at me. "*This*," she said simply, holding up her deformed arm. "Of course! Why else would he cut my wages?"

I stared at her.

"But... that's just *wrong*..." I whispered.

The most shocking thing was how Jane seemed to think it was completely normal.

"Mr Morgan has more bowels than most," she said. "He kept me. Even though I am not a woman of as many parts."

"Wait here," I said. "I am going to talk to this *Mr Morgan*!"

I turned away and began to walk.

"Don't!" Jane cried. "He will sack me! He–"

"It's okay," I said over my shoulder. "You won't be fired. Trust me."

I marched towards the mill. Or at least in the direction I believed the mill to be; the direction Jane had just come from. I was possessed by a determination and rage more acute than I had ever known.

I became aware that Frelia was walking beside me, and looked at her. I was still angry. I was still hurt from what she said. But none of that seemed to matter as much anymore.

"What's your plan?" she asked me.

Plan? ***Plan?!*** I was too riled to have a plan.

"I don't know..." I admitted.

I was primed to bite back at any snide remark she had mind to make, but nothing came. She just carried on walking.

A group of young women walked past us. I hardly even blinked, or took the time to properly look at the Georgian garments they were clad in. I simply wasn't questioning it anymore. I had stopped wondering how Frelia had managed to pull off such a sophisticated prank and get so many people involved. I was emotionally involved now. Caught in the moment.

We found the mill. It was a large building by the side of the river. It looked quite new. The bricks seemed to have this orange hue about them (but I am willing to admit that *may* have just been the mushrooms at work).

When we entered, a young boy in brown rags paused from scrubbing the floor to stare at us, wide-eyed.

"You can't–" he began to say.

"Where's Mr Morgan?" I interrupted him. There must have been something about how loud and plainly I said it which startled him because he made no further protest. He simply pointed to a door. I opened it and stepped inside.

Mr Morgan was sitting behind a desk and he looked at us.

It was when our eyes met that I remembered I still didn't have a plan.

Nothing.

Mr Morgan was wearing a blue waistcoat and a white frilly shirt which ruffled around his wrists. It was immediately clear to me that he was wealthy. Not just from his attire, but something about his bearing. That self-satisfied and priggish expression he had on his face reminded me of some of the men I work with.

"If you're looking for settlement, come back tomorrow," he uttered dismissively. He turned his attention back to his ledgers and sighed. "And *knock* next time. This is a mill, not a vaulting school."

"I have come to talk to you about one of your employees," I said.

He looked back up at me and his lips parted. "Who sent you here?" he asked, tiredly. "I'll have–"

"None of them," I said, clenching my fists and holding them behind my back. "We came here of our own accord... I heard she had an accident. She lost her hand. She–"

"*Jane* sent you here? Tell her she's sacked," he shook his head. "Impertinent baggage."

This is not going very well... I thought, pressing my knuckles to my mouth. *I've made things even worse! What the hell was I thinking, coming here? I don't know this place, or the situation. I–*

"I don't think you quite understand what she's trying to tell you!" Frelia said, marching across the room and slamming the palm of her hand upon his desk. Mr Morgan jumped at the sound and looked up at her.

"We have not come here to plead with you," she said, ruefully. "We have come here to *warn* you."

She reached inside her bodice, making Mr Morgan's eyes widen.

Oh God, Frelia! I thought. *That's not even appropriate in modern times, let alone* ***now****!*

When she pulled her hand out from her cleavage, she was holding something. In the slightly surreal quality this night had taken, even *I* took a while to recognise what it was. Only God knows what it must have looked like to Mr Morgan.

It was her mobile phone.

"Do you know what this is?" Frelia asked.

He just stared at it.

"This is my Book of Shadows," Frelia said. She pressed a finger to the screen and it began to glow. Mr Morgan's jaw dropped.

Frelia swiped the screen, making the colours and textures fluctuate. It illuminated so brightly it lit up the ceiling. Mr Morgan looked up.

"We are witches, Mr Morgan, and this is how we communicate with our demons," Frelia said. She then pointed the phone at him and pressed a button. It flashed, and he blinked.

"Can you see what this is?" Frelia then asked, turning it around and holding the screen in front of his face.

Mr Morgan stared at it for a few moments as his eyes adjusted. And then he gasped and his hands began to tremble. He looked up at Frelia.

"That's you, isn't it?" she said, smiling. "I have just captured a piece of your soul, and now it is in my Book of Shadows. I could make *very* bad things happen to you now if I wanted to, Mr Morgan. Do you want to know what kind of bad things?"

She leant towards him and put her mouth to his ear. Mr Morgan's eyes widened and then he gasped, turning his eyes down to his lap.

"Now..." Frelia said, as she withdrew from him. "You don't need to worry, Mr Morgan. As long as you meet our *conditions*, none of those things I mentioned will happen to you. *But*, if you break *any* of our terms... well..." she shook her head. "You will regret it…"

"What do you want?" he asked between gritted teeth.

"Are you aware of the term 'compensation'?" Frelia asked.

He squinted at her.

"It means that when something bad happens to somebody whilst they are working for you, *you* are responsible. I want you to give Jane four weeks of extra pay. *And* I want you to put her wages up to twelve shillings."

"I don't know if I can–" he began.

"Don't mess with me," Frelia said flatly. "I am not a very patient person. Am I, Sister Witch?"

She turned to me.

"You don't want to test her, Mr Morgan," I said. "Bigger men have tried to and... well..." I shook my head. "That's all history now. Or they are, rather..."

"You don't understand," he whined. "I am part of a consortium, and me and the other gentlemen have made an agreement. If I put her wages up, *every* worker will want the same, and then the workers in the other factories will hear."

"Well just keep it under your hat then," Frelia shrugged. "I am not planning on telling anyone. Are you going to tell anyone, Sister?" she said, turning to me.

I shook my head. "No. I can keep it quiet. And I am sure you can come to an understanding with Jane, too," I added, turning back to Mr Morgan.

"Money has a way of bringing all sorts of things out of people. I am sure that silence can be one of them," Frelia said. She then pushed a button on her phone and it made a strange whooshing noise. It sounded almost like a gust of wind, but not quite natural.

"That was the demons," Frelia clarified for Mr Morgan, who flinched at the sound. "They will be watching you."

He spat on the floor, a sour but defeated expression on his face.

"I think we are done here now, aren't we?" Frelia said, turning to me and offering her elbow.

"Yes... I believe we are..." I said, linking arms with her.

"Let's hope we don't have reason to meet again, Mr Morgan," Frelia said, smiling at him oh-so-sweetly as we left.

"How did you come up with *that* idea?" I whispered once we were outside. "That was brilliant!"

"I don't know," Frelia shrugged. "I was winging it... I wasn't even sure it was going to work..."

We walked back towards the canal together. Neither of us said anything at first, but eventually I stopped and pulled my arm away from hers.

"Frelia," I said. "The reason why I am not always so nice to you is because I resent you."

It was possibly the hardest thing that I have ever admitted to anyone, but it was out now.

Frelia looked at me ponderously.

"Remember that night? When the police raided that party and you took my drugs for me?" I said.

Frelia nodded and her lips straightened into a grim expression. That was a life-changing moment for both of us. It was when social services stepped in and we were separated. We didn't see each other for years after that. I eventually managed to track Frelia down on the internet.

It was shortly after that night I became Pandora, too.

"I know you meant well, and what you did made complete sense... it was *logical* for you to take the rap, because you already had a criminal record and there was no reason for both of us to go down for all that stash we had... I *know* that, Frelia. And I will be forever thankful for what you did for me. *But...*"

I paused for a few moments as I struggled to find a way to elucidate the next bit. Frelia stared at me.

"But..." I said. "After it was over – after we were separated and they sent you to juvenile detention – I felt so guilty. It was like this constant pain in my chest. And it still comes back sometimes. Even now. Every time I think about it... the truth is a part of me resents you. For not letting me take the responsibility. For making me live with the guilt for all these years. And I know that sounds ridiculous and you don't deserve it, but I can't help the way that I feel."

"It's okay," Frelia said, stroking my shoulder.

"It's not," I said. "I have been such a cow to you..."

"And I have hardly been a saint," Frelia said. "Let's just both try to be nicer to each other from now on, okay?"

I nodded and we embraced.

"Good," Frelia said, once we pulled away from each other. "We can talk about it again another time. Let's go back and find Kev."

We strode towards the bank together. It was odd. I felt lighter now. And that pain that I mentioned – the one which I always felt in my chest whenever I remembered Frelia being arrested – was gone. I looked at her and smiled.

I then – not for the first time that night – noticed something strange. I could see *through* Frelia. She had acquired a translucent quality, almost as if she wasn't fully there.

"What's wrong?" she asked, noticing that I had stopped again.

I stared at her a little longer, wondering if it was just a momentary hallucination which would end, but it didn't. No matter how much I tried to focus my eyes, the effect was there.

Frelia noticed it too. She held her hand up to her face and frowned. "Oh no..." she muttered. "It's happening..."

"What's happening?" I asked.

"We're going back..."

Everything went white.

And then I opened my eyes again, and found myself looking up at an azure blue sky filled with stars.

It was mesmerising. There was something about it which made me feel so small and inconsequential, and yet also, so special, all at the same time.

So many stars. So many galaxies.

It took billions of years of cosmological evolution – a galactic dance of particles and dust coalescing and exploding – for our planet to come into being.

And we are just this one little rock out of trillions. Floating through the blackness of space.

So many astronomical events have led to this moment. Geology shaped our planet. Asteroid collisions filled it with oceans. Species have come and gone. Civilisations have risen and faded away. So many people have lived and died. And all of them had their part in shaping the present.

All of these infinitesimal and infinite events occurred, just for me to be here. *Now*. Tonight. Lying back and looking at the sky.

I stared at it for a long time. The sky turned bluer, and then a hint of yellow joined the aurora. I realised that it was dawn and my mind began to ground itself and return to normality again. Whatever that was.

I watched the sun rise.

"Beautiful, isn't it…" Frelia said.

I looked over and saw that she was sitting behind me rolling a cigarette.

I nodded, only then registering that we were still on the boat. Kev was sleeping.

"Did we really travel back in time?" I asked.

She nodded.

"I am not sure if I believe it," I whispered. "It's crazy..."

"Quite happy to believe in a magical being in the sky who has a creepy fixation with what you're doing with your genitals – just because you read about it in some book – but you won't believe in something you experienced with your own eyes?" she asked, dryly.

I laughed. It did all sound a bit ridiculous when she said it like *that*.

"But we were high," I said.

Frelia shrugged. "High or not, you *know* it actually happened."

I nodded thoughtfully. If reluctantly.

I still believe in God, in my own way, but not like I used to.

I decided to save telling Frelia about that for some other time.

"How do you think Lenora and Jane are now?" I asked.

"*Then*," she corrected me. "It was over two hundred years ago."

"We should have helped *more* people..." I said. "It seems unfair that we only helped two. There were thousands who went through the same as them, weren't there?"

Frelia shook her head. "We can't, Pandora. I know it seems unfair, but it was those people who built what we have today. We shouldn't have helped *any* of them, really. You've heard of the Butterfly Effect, haven't you?"

I nodded sombrely.

"I wonder what happened to them," I said. "I hope we *did* help."

Frelia paused thoughtfully. "We could find out, you know. Well... maybe. Last night was the first time I ever took anyone else *with* me... I didn't even know I could do that..." her voice trailed off, wistfully. "I don't do this all that often because my father doesn't like it..."

"Who is your father?" I asked. "When did you find out about him?"

She shook her head. "The less I say about him the better. For you and me," she drew a deep sigh and then closed her eyes. "Okay, hold on... I will see what I can do."

It all happened so quickly. There was no noise. Our surroundings didn't go blurry. We didn't slip into a tunnel of swirling space-time, or launch into the sky. Nothing like that.

We – Frelia, Kev, I, and the boat – were simply in one place one moment, and then, suddenly, we were in another.

We were still floating in the canal, only it looked a little different.

There was a young lady standing on the towpath and she was staring at us. At first I thought that Frelia had made a mistake but, after a closer look, I realised it was Lenora, only a little older. Probably about Frelia's age by now.

She stared at us and then she smiled.

"Is it really you?" she breathed. "I was just walking to church."

"Yes," Frelia said. "It is us."

Lenora looked healthy enough. A little dirty maybe, but that was to be expected. Her clothes were in better shape and she was fuller in the cheeks. "How is your mother?" I said.

"She's fair," Lenora said. "We have more money now... Dad saved up and opened a bakery..." she tucked a lock of her greasy hair behind her ear. "Me and Mum still talk about you sometimes..."

"I wouldn't tell too many people about us if I were you..." Frelia said dryly.

"Yes, I know that..." Lenora said. She turned her eyes to the ground. "I tried to tell a friend about you once, but she thought I was just making up stories... I never did it again."

She paused and looked at us thoughtfully. "Where are you from?" she then said.

I turned the Frelia, not knowing what to say. It was up to her really.

"We're from the future," Frelia admitted. "To us, this place is the past. Pandora, Kevin and I have not even been born yet, but we will be one day. *You* are actually older than us, believe it or not."

Leona didn't seem as shocked by this as I thought she would be. She nodded thoughtfully. "How far?" she asked.

"About two hundred years," I replied.

Her eyes widened. "Do people still live in cities in the future? I don't like this place... it's getting dirtier every day. And *more* people keep moving here!"

"It'll get a bit cleaner eventually," Frelia said. "They will build things underground which deal with all the shit."

"So things get better then?" Lenora asked.

My initial instinct was to agree with her but, as I opened my mouth to say it, I found myself hesitating.

Are things really all that better?

We have mostly abolished child labour and slavery in the western world, but we endorse it overseas, and there are plenty of countries where people still live in conditions even worse than Lenora's right now. We *have* cleaned up the cities and rivers, but the ocean is pretty screwed and the ice caps are melting. There is still war. There is still poverty.

"Yes and no," I eventually replied. "It's not better or worse, it's just... different."

Lenora nodded. It seemed that I had given her the answer she expected.

I then noticed that Frelia and I – and the boat and Kev with us – had turned translucent again. I looked down and I could see water glimmering beneath the hull.

Lenora frowned. It seemed she could see the change, too.

"I think we are about to return to our own time now," Frelia said to Lenora.

"Farewell," I said. "Be happy, Lenora."

"Bye Pandora," she said.

She reached for me. I reached for her too, and our hands met. Briefly. Then my fingers slipped through hers and everything went white again.

"*Pandora*?" Mr Watts said, unable to hide the surprise in his voice when he saw me.

"Hello," I said.

"Pandora..." he repeated, as he looked me up and down. "Your *hair*... and your... The meeting starts in five minutes!"

I don't think I looked too bad, considering I hadn't slept, showered, or changed.

"Maybe you should go back home and make yourself more presentable..." he suggested. "I can delay the meeting. I'll tell them–"

"It's fine," I said as I breezed past him and made my way towards the boardroom. "I'm ready. Don't worry, Mr Watts. I've got this."

I opened the door before he could make any other protest, and the syndicate – all twelve of them – looked up at me as I made my way to the head of the table. I almost laughed out loud at how symmetrical the sight of them was as I peered down at them. Six of them were sitting on each side. All of them garbed in almost identical suits and with silver watches strapped around their wrists.

"So," Mr Watts began, swiftly recovering his composure as he walked into the room. "This morning Pandora here is going to present us with the research she has compiled. Now – I just thought I would bring this out into the open – she *does* have a few ethical concerns over Equeld, *but* the two of us had a little chat about it and she has agreed to push her personal feelings aside and present us with her findings as impartially as she can."

The members of the board all chuckled to each other like I was a child who just didn't quite understand how the world worked.

And, as I looked at them, I felt a shift in my perspective. A new sense of clarity.

I used to see these people as the cream of the crop. The successful elite. The ones who had really made it in life. I used to crave their approval. I used to feel anxious when I was around them.

I saw them now for what they really were.

Quite pathetic, really. I realised that, hundreds of years from now, if we're still here, it will be these people who will be remembered as being on the wrong side of history. They will be the ones who put profits before people, cherished money more than resources, and prioritised the economy over the environment. They were out of touch. Disconnected. It was *them* who didn't understand the world.

They were vermin.

"Yes," I said, smiling at Mr Watts briefly before I turned my attention back to the rest of them. "I did have a few concerns but, as the honourable Mr Watts often tells me, this is business. And business is blameless."

I plugged my memory stick into the projector and switched it on. "And I am also just a woman, so my opinion is only secondary," I added. "If anything I say makes you feel in doubt, then please feel free to brush it aside and blame it on my menstrual cycle."

Mr Watts laughed, but it sounded forced. I could tell that he was beginning to get anxious. He shifted uncomfortably in his seat.

The machine began to power up and the screen went blue. "I mean, we all know that Fibertine are going to go ahead with the deal anyway, whatever gets said during this meeting," I said as I waited for the menu to load up. "As all this company really cares about is numbers, but it *does* look good on the books if a bunch of us meet up every now and then and talk, doesn't it? And how else are we to validate our jobs without engaging in endless banal procedures such as this one..."

My presentation appeared on the menu and I selected it. "So, without further ado, let us descend into today's exercise in farce together."

"Pandora!" Mr Watts growled, warningly.

The first picture to be projected into the screen was of an orang-utan.

"Why should we care that Equeld are quietly destroying the natural habitat of several dozen endangered species?" I asked. "When, if our profits are high enough, you could get a bonus at the end of the year which could buy you..."

"Ta da!" I exclaimed as I switched to the next picture. "A brand new Bentley! You've had that Porsche for almost a year now, Mr Donald. It's beginning to get a little rusty," I said, winking at him.

Mr Donald blushed. A few people gasped, and a couple of them chuckled nervously, as if they didn't quite know how to respond.

"The next issue I would like to bring up," I said, as I

moved on to a picture of Chinese children working in a rather grey and dismal looking sweatshop.

"*Pandora!*" one of them exclaimed, wincing. "You can't show things like that in *here*. It's most unseemly!"

I frowned at him. "Is there something wrong?" I asked innocently, turning back to the picture. "Surely you already knew that Equeld are one of the great modern pioneers of child labour?"

I shrugged. "Anyway, the reason I brought this up is not because I am trying to talk you out of it. On the contrary! I am actually going to highlight to you a missed opportunity. You see, many of the people who work for Equeld in the developing world suffer accidents and, as there is no social support or compensation scheme available to them, they find it hard to get further employment. I have an idea which would be beneficial for us *and* them. I propose we re-route our office phones and create a call centre for these people to work in. I mean, you hardly need *all* of your limbs to answer a phone, do you? And they will be happy to work for less pay than their more able-bodied peers. To be honest, we're behind the times. Everyone else has call centres abroad now. Why not us? It would take off some of the strain from our rather hefty workloads. And it would also be good for dealing with those awkward moments when Mr Jackson's wife calls and we all have to pretend we don't know he's fucking his PA."

Mr Jackson's face went white.

"So... what's next..." I muttered as I turned back to the screen and prompted the next phase of my presentation. A picture of some of Equeld's product range came up. "Oh yes! I remember now. Equeld have *still* not admitted that one of the additives they add to most of their bestselling beverages is highly carcinogenic, but why should we care?" I shrugged. "We have investments in most of the pharma companies too, so that just means *even more profits* for us! Some of *that* money can go towards funding wonderful events such as this one..."

I flicked to the next picture. A photo of Mr Watts and Mr Davies wearing party hats and with their arms sleazily draped across the shoulders of Germaine and Belinda. "The Fibertine

Investment Bank Christmas Party! That oh-so-enjoyable evening of the year where we pretend to be normal human beings and loosen up those boundaries a little with a few bottles of bubbly. The *real* bonus of that night, is that being drunk is a great excuse to touch female members of staff *even more* inappropriately than usual – or, in your case, Mr Smith," I turned to the grey haired, be-spectacled man at the back. "Thomas, our cute, young, blue-eyed intern. Do not worry, Mr Smith, we do not judge you. We are very modern and progressive here at Fibertine. Everyone is equal. As long as you're not poor or from the third world or something, of course."

The uproar was getting quite loud now, but I carried on regardless. An image of a town which was flooded a few weeks ago came up next. "Now," I said, raising my voice so they could still hear me. "I know that global warming is something we all take very seriously. I mean, all of those *meetings* we have, brainstorming ways to reassure the public, has done a great job of bringing those emissions down. But, I was also thinking, why don't we just screw it? Admit that–"

That was as far as I got before Mr Watts dragged me out of the boardroom.

They sent me home for 'stress related reasons'.

That basically means I'm fired.

Well, not exactly. I have a completely clean record at Fibertine, and they are way too bogged down with bureaucratic formalities to simply sack me.

No. Knowing them, they will give me redundancy. That would be the quickest and sleekest way to get rid of me. And, to do that, they will have to go through a long sequence of procedures. It will take them a couple of weeks at least.

Shortly after I am gone, a new role will be created which will sound remarkably similar to the one I once had.

That's the way Fibertine work.

The severance pay will be fairly handsome. It will keep me afloat for a few months while I figure out what I want to do with myself.

I will think about that another time.

Today I am going to go meet Frelia. At Dinnusos. I am hoping she will introduce me to some of the members of Taxus Baccata.

I know that sounds a little surprising, but I feel a calling.

I mean, they are a little crude – yes. But that is exactly why they need someone with a little sense around.

Someone like me.

I am not worrying about turning into Pandy anymore. But I am no longer Pandora, either. I am both. I am neither. I am regressing. Growing. Unchaining my expectations, and discovering new things about myself.

I am me. And I am still not quite sure what that is. Maybe I will never know.

But does that really matter?

Maybe the secret is to not worry about it. Let yourself be swept away and see where the current takes you.

4
A Distant Melody

The moment I closed the door behind us, I knew that it had been a bad idea.

Ellen hugged herself as she surveyed the room, casting her eyes across the four walls.

It was still strange to see it this way. Until very recently, this room had been the nucleus of our lives. It had been full of instruments, discarded sheets of music, all those tangled black wires which connected us to amplifiers and sound systems, and, most of all, the wonderful sounds we created together.

It was empty now. Apart from Amelia's drum kit – which she had still not removed for some reason – the rest of the band had already packed up their stuff and moved on.

"Why did you bring me here, Patrick?" Ellen whispered.

I wasn't used to Ellen even needing to ask me such things – she had always had an uncanny way of knowing what people's intentions were – but that seemed to have faded now.

As well as many other things.

"I just thought it was a start..." I said.

I *thought* that coming here would help her come to terms with what happened so she could start to move on but, judging from the expression on her face, it seemed I was mistaken.

"Look what I brought with me," I said, feigning a smile as I freed my fiddle from its case. It was my last ditch attempt to pull her out of the dark chasm. "I thought we could–"

She shook her head. "No, Patrick," she said. "*No*."

"Ellen... please, just try," I implored. "I think–"

"No," she said. "It's not happening."

She had not sung a single song since that night.

"What were you hoping to achieve?" she asked, narrowing her eyes at me. She actually seemed *angry*. "By bringing me here?"

"I have been thinking..." I hesitated. I could already tell this wasn't going to go down well but I might as well just come out with it. "I think it is time we try to reform the band."

"Sunset Haze is over," she said. "Don't you understand that?"

"It doesn't have to be," I protested. "We can find a new flautist. It–"

"*No*!" she raised her voice. "Just stop it! Are you *trying* to hurt me?"

"No Ellen!" I said. "Of course not!"

"Then why did you bring me back *here*?" she exclaimed.

And then she pointed to the other side of the room. To the spot on the floor where it happened, all those weeks ago.

The place where we lost Jessica.

I had at least had the sense to clean up a little before I coaxed Ellen here – I came here yesterday and swept the ashes away, and even scraped off all that candle wax which got stuck to the floor during Naomi's ritual – but there were still scorch marks on the panels.

There were still memories.

"Faye was not the only member of the band we lost that night, Patrick," Ellen said, as she walked away. "And *she* can never be replaced."

Jessica.

Sometimes, I try to remember when exactly it was that I first encountered the entity known as Jessica, but I can never quite narrow that one down. Ellen and she were so connected, it's difficult to define where one of them finished and the other began.

I have known *Ellen* since before I could even remember. But childhood is a haze. You don't really think during that period of your life in months and years. Just hours and days. Every day is the present, and the present moves slowly. Every emotion you experience is intense, but brief. You are blissfully ignorant, and yet your imagination is running wild.

When you reach maturity you look back upon it all, and much of it seems like a dream.

And my childhood was a particularly surreal one.

If there is one thing that children like, it's stories. And when there are no adults around to tell them, they make up their own worlds of make-believe.

Ellen and I lived out many stories. Her garden – which had seemed so gigantic when we were children, but became smaller as we grew – was a place we filled with fanciful creatures. They lived in the trees, her pond, and the flowerbeds. In the little woodland on the other side of the fence, too. And the river which snaked through it.

But, of all the marvellous characters we created, there was one who sprang up more often than the others.

And her name was Jessica.

Most of the time, Jessica was like this guardian angel; she seemed to hover around us, but it was only Ellen who could see her or hear her whispers. Sometimes Jessica was an imaginary character – the captured princess Ellen and I had to save from the mischievous pixies, or the tenacious heroine who fought by our side – but, more often than not, Ellen would *be* Jessica herself.

And, whenever that happened, Ellen acted much more boisterous and loud than she usually did.

Once, she hit me. She slapped me across the face.

I can't remember why. It was probably one of those childish disagreements which seemed very important at the time but was actually petty and trivial.

The important thing was that she hit me.

I was shocked. Ellen had always been such a gentle girl. She had only ever been kind to me.

I ran home that day, crying.

That night, I told myself I could never speak to her ever again but, in that childish way, I had already forgiven her by the time I woke up the next morning.

"Jessica is sorry," Ellen said to me the following day when we were sitting in her room.

I looked at her. All those imaginary friends we had and those playful adventures we shared were usually things we lived out in her garden, so it was peculiar for her to bring them into her bedroom. That was a place we were usually a little more grounded.

"Jessica is you," I said. "*You* are sorry."

Ellen shook her head. "Jessica is not me..." she said.

She rolled her eyes up to the ceiling and moved her lips. I didn't hear what it was that she said.

She then turned back to me.

"She wants to know why you lie," she said.

I frowned at her. "I do not lie."

"You do," Ellen nodded. "You and your father tell everyone that your mother is dead. But she isn't."

When she said those words, my stomach turned inside out.

It was that moment I realised that Jessica was much more than just a game.

My father tells everyone my mother is dead. Meningitis, he says.

It is not true, but it might as well be.

My mother is gone, and she is never coming back. She told my father as much, in the very brief note she left him the day she vanished.

I never really knew her. A few dim memories. A blurred recollection of a face. That's about it, really.

I know very little about her. My father refuses to speak of her, unless he's drunk.

One thing I *do* know is that she had a passion for music. She loved to dance and my father loved listening to her sing.

He freaked out when he discovered that I was of similar instinct. It took years of pestering him before he caved in and bought me my first violin.

He told me that I looked like her too, once. But I already knew that.

I sensed it in the bitterness in his eyes when he looked at me sometimes.

It was how Sunset Haze began, really. My father's acrimony. He hated hearing me play because it was yet another reminder of how similar I was to the woman who left him, so it was in Ellen's room I usually practised.

One day she started to sing along, and we discovered she had a beautiful voice. Jessica had a beautiful voice too, but, as we got older, her ability to seize control of Ellen's body seemed to ebb and she 'visited' us less often. Which, in my opinion, was a good thing. It sometimes freaked me out when Jessica possessed Ellen.

Jessica never fully left us though. She often whispered to Ellen from across the ether, and I became all too used to witnessing Ellen's eyes becoming distracted by something which I couldn't see and her muttering to herself as she communicated with her twin. Behaviour like that made people think Ellen very strange but, over time, most came to learn that the mysterious premonitions which came from her lips were things you would not be wise to ignore. Ellen was a girl people regarded with wary respect.

When we got older Ellen and I formed the band. Much of Sunset Haze's original material came from those songs Ellen, Jessica and I had conjured up in that room, it was just a case of adding extra instrumental roles to the songs we had been playing for years.

The original members of Sunset Haze were just Ellen, me, and a few other misfits from our school. They were okay at playing, but I am not quite sure they ever quite got the music. When we hit our late teens they all ended up hiking off to university.

Ellen and I went to the city, and it was there that Sunset Haze matured and reached its golden age.

Jack appeared at our door one day, in that mysterious way of his.

"I hear you need a guitarist," he said. Which was strange as we hadn't even advertised yet and we didn't really know anyone. It kind of freaked me out.

I almost told him to sod off, but Ellen intervened. "Let him in," she called and, within a few moments of him strumming away at that battered old acoustic of his, I knew he was right.

We held auditions a few weeks later, and Amelia was the least charming – and definitely not the most skilled – out of the people who tried out, but Ellen was adamant that it was her we should take on. And it turned out she was right too because, even though she was a little rusty at first, Amelia is a damn good drummer now.

For the first year our flautist was a guy called Sparky. He

was pretty good but he could be unreliable at times and he mysteriously upped and left one day.

It was during that year Jessica joined the band too, in a way. She began to possess Ellen again. But it was a just a sporadic occurrence which happened occasionally during band practice and when we started doing gigs. I didn't mind that so much. For some reason it didn't feel so intrusive when it happened while we were in the middle of a performance.

It was only when we acquired Faye that I felt like Sunset Haze was truly complete. And the later addition of Steve enriched us.

I felt like we were beginning to connect to something special. Something that I could not quite describe.

Something which had been abruptly cut short.

After Ellen left the rehearsal room, I brought the tail of my violin up to my chin.

It ended up being that song Jack dreamed up – that day we came here to practise and ended up doing our last impromptu gig – that I ended up playing. The last song Sunset Haze started to create. The one we never finished.

It wasn't a conscious decision. I simply wanted to fill the silence in a room which used to echo with so many wonderful sounds.

I thought about Ellen.

I had tried everything to pull Ellen out of her despair. I visited her flat almost daily. At first she wouldn't even let me in but I eventually managed to worm my way inside only to discover she had lost weight and grown dangerously thin.

I coaxed her into eating meals again. I tried to talk her into getting some counselling, but she said it would be hard to find a therapist who wouldn't just have her carried away in a straightjacket if she told them the honest truth of the source of her woes. And she had a point, too.

I stayed over. Slept on her couch, most nights, just to keep her company, but she barely acknowledged me.

I drove her to her favourite lake, but she didn't even get out of the car.

I thought that if I could just get her to sing again it would set her back on the right course, but I guess bringing her to Dinnusos was a little too much a little too soon.

I knew that now.

As I played, I became aware of another sound I could hear in the background. A distant melody.

It possessed a unique resonance. It didn't sound like it could have been produced by any instrument I had ever heard before. It was wind based. Its tonality almost reminded me of a flute.

As I listened, a peculiar sensation worked its way up my spine and I became enchanted by a compulsive need to find out where it was coming from so I could hear it louder. Clearer.

I left the room, shutting the door behind me and marching down the corridor, my fiddle and bow in my hands.

I almost felt like I was floating. Like I had become detached from my own body and I was passively observing myself.

It was a weekday afternoon – my brain was so muddled from the music by this point that I could barely remember what exactly a 'weekday' was or how it was different to any other day – but I dimly recalled that, when I walked through the main bar downstairs earlier, it had been empty.

If the bar was empty, just *who* was behind this music? I had never heard anything remotely like it.

I reached the end of the corridor and turned left. Then right. Then left. And then left again. I found a staircase. Strange – it wasn't a staircase I had ever encountered before and, judging from the cloud of dust which sprayed from the cracks when I opened the door, it had not been used for a long time, either.

But the sound was coming from it. It was calling me.

The floorboards creaked a little – and made me briefly consider whether this was such a good idea – but I couldn't resist the pull of the music.

The stairs went down and down and down. When they ended I found myself staring down a long dark tunnel. I couldn't see the end, only blackness.

I carried on walking, only vaguely aware, at first, that my feet were treading through mud and there were tree roots dangling above me.

I pulled my phone out of my pocket and activated the flashlight feature to light my way.

I realised then that I was, in fact, in an underground passage.

And I didn't even care. I just carried on walking.

There was light ahead.

I stepped into a circular chamber. The walls were brown and there were no windows, but candles were burning everywhere, illuminating the scene.

A man was sitting on a little rocking chair, and it was gently swaying back and forth as he played.

The instrument he held to his lips vaguely resembled a recorder, but it was very thin and, most startling of all, there were *two* pipes connected to the mouthpiece. He had one in each hand and he was carefully working his fingers across the holes as he played.

He looked at me, and I found myself unable to turn my eyes away. He had golden skin and amber speckled eyes. His salt-and-pepper beard was the same length and colour as his hair, with no obvious distinction between them. He was handsome.

Eventually he stopped playing and the song's alluring effect came to an abrupt end. It felt like I had been abandoned.

"What was that?" I breathed.

I know it was a peculiar way to open up a conversation with a complete stranger whose home you have just stumbled into, but I was a little bewildered.

"It is called an 'aulos'," he responded.

"I've never heard anything like it before..." I said.

"Not many have, these days," he replied sombrely, as he carefully placed it on a dresser beside his chair.

"Where am I?" I asked, casting my eyes across the room. My mind was starting to clear from its hazy state and I was thinking more rationally.

It truly was a bizarre place. Everything was made from oak and all the furniture looked like it had been individually shaped and crafted. There were colourful tapestries draped all over the walls, and a hearth in the middle of the room. The smoke from it was gently wafting towards a hole in the centre of the domed ceiling. I could smell sage.

"This is my home," he said.

"But how did I get here?" I asked, looking at the doorway behind me. Did that tunnel really lead all the way to the upper floors of Dinnusos, or had I just dreamt it?

"You are here because I summoned you," he said, simply. "The fact that the song I just played drew you here, out of your ordinary life and into this domain of mine, can only mean one thing."

He stroked his chin and stared at me for a few moments before he continued.

"You are my new student."

Our lessons began that very afternoon. Or possibly evening. I wasn't quite sure what time of day it was in that peculiar abode of his. There were no windows.

"No!" he said, when he caught me staring at the aulos. "That doodad is not for you."

"But you said you were going to teach me..."

"Yes! Yes!" he said. "I will *try*. But not all can get it... That fiddle," he nodded at the two halves of the instrument in my hands. "Is for you. *This*," he said, reaching for his aulos and holding it, lovingly. "Is mine."

"But I already know how to play my fiddle."

He frowned. "I want to teach you to play that fiddle the way I play my aulos."

"What do you mean?" I asked. How could one teach another to play a string instrument like one from the wind family? It would be like teaching a bird to swim, or a wasp to make honey.

"Maybe you're not right for this..." he muttered, turning away. "I thought you *felt* something when I played..."

"I did..." I admitted.

"*That* is what I want to teach you!" he said. "How to play that fiddle so that it doesn't just gladden the ears but enflames the soul. I bet you can play a fellow plenty a ditty but, if you listen to me right, you'll be able to *enthral* them. Do you understand?"

I wasn't quite sure I did, but I nodded anyway.

A part of me was relieved. As intrigued as I was by that aulos of his, I feared that it would take me years to play it as beautifully as he did.

"Good... *Good!*" he repeated. He seemed pleased. He smiled and brought the fipple to his lips. "Now, echo my shanty."

He didn't give me much chance to get ready, he simply started playing. I scrambled for my fiddle and tried to mimic each note he played.

I have relative pitch, and I can usually just replicate a simple tune by ear – or at least I *thought* I could – but, after a few moments, I could tell from the expression on his face that he was far from impressed.

"No! No! No! No!" he said, shaking his head. "No! No! No! You are *thinking* too much. *Feel* it. *Know* it."

I tried again. I actually tried *less*, because I was feeling a little disheartened by this point but, oddly, *he* seemed to believe I was going much better.

"Yes!" he exclaimed, after a few minutes. "You *had* it then!"

My hands were still in the exact same position, so I drew my bow across the strings to try and replicate that last sound I made, but he shook his head. "No!" he said. "No... you lost it... Try again!"

After a few minutes of this, I noticed that it was often in the transitory moments that I pleased him most – when I was in the midst of twisting my bow to reach a different chord, or my fingers were sliding into a different note. These moments were elusive and ephemeral. Fickle and fleeting.

It was like he was hearing something I couldn't. An intricacy which completely eluded me.

I tried to humour him for a while, but eventually frustration got the better of me.

"What exactly do you want me to *play*?!" I asked. "It doesn't make any sense!"

"I want you to play that moment when a falling leaf meets the wind," he said.

"You're fucking nuts!" I exclaimed, getting up from my chair. "Screw this!"

He nodded calmly as I walked away, not seeming bothered at all whether I stayed or left.

But, just as I was leaving, he began to play again, and a low note swept across the room and stirred the air around me.

I turned around – I found myself unable *not* to.

His fingers danced across the holes with such an elegant grace that I just stared at the movements for a while, but it wasn't really *that* which was stopping me from stepping out that door.

His melody was pulling me again.

He got up from his chair and walked towards the door – not the door I had been just about to step through, but another one on the opposite side of the room – and kicked it open. I didn't even hesitate. I followed him. Sprinting in my rush to catch him up.

I stepped out of his home to find myself in the midst of a grove. There were trees of all kinds around me. Birch. Oak. Beech. Willow. Gorse. Others which seemed bizarre and I didn't recognise.

He tilted the end of his aulos to the air. That moment, the song changed. It seemed to lose the effect it was having upon *me* and, instead, it stirred the branches of the trees above us.

Birds swooped down. He carried on playing, and they spiralled around him, gently flapping their wings. A pair of them even landed on his shoulders and ran their beaks through his wiry hair.

It was only then that I noticed there was something very dreamlike about the light of this place. It seemed to be neither night or day, and yet everything was illuminated.

Not only that, but the man playing the aulos – my new teacher, it seemed – was no longer a man.

The top half of him still looked the same as it did when I first met him, only now he was naked. His chest and stomach were firm and his skin was smooth.

It was the lower half of his body which shocked me. His legs were now covered in a thick pelt of fur. His knees were bent at a forty-five-degree angle and, where he once had feet, were now hooves.

"*This* is what I wanted to teach you," he said, drawing the aulos away from his lips. The birds circled around him a few more times, and then they gradually dispersed, flying back to the trees.

"Do you still want to learn?"

"What is your name, anyway?" I asked, as he poured us both a murky, musky-smelling drink from a large metal kettle suspended over the fire.

We were back in his home now. His equine limbs had shifted back to human shape the moment we stepped back inside, and it happened just as seamlessly as the transition occurred before.

"Teris," he said.

"I'm Patrick," I introduced myself.

He nodded. As if he already knew or it just didn't matter. I didn't know which one.

"What are you?" I asked.

"You saw what I was back then," he said. His dismissive tone made it clear to me that he had no interest in explaining himself. "I am also what you can see now."

"Where are you from?"

"A land far away from here. Across the seas. One of my forefathers ventured here years ago."

"Why?"

He frowned at me. "Why does anyone travel. Adventure! Work! Life! Experiences! You ask too many questions! I will allow two more."

"How did you do it?" I asked, looking down at his feet. "Change like that?"

He pointed to the door which led to that grove outside. "Out there is a place. People have different names for it. Sidhe, Elysium, Mag Mell, Annwn. Humans feel it or glimpse it sometimes, if they happen to stumble upon the right place at a certain time, but the gates only truly open to those with something a little more supernal flowing through their veins. Now, you have one last question, and then we can get back to work and you will *stop* pestering me!"

I paused for a few moments and considered this final chance very carefully.

"Do you know a song which can make someone happy again?"

He smiled. "Well of course, Patrick! Pick up that fiddle of yours! You can start learning now!"

Progress was slow, but I taught myself to be patient.

Every afternoon I had spare I found myself walking to Dinnusos, down that mysterious passage, and into that strange abode of his. And he was always there, waiting for me.

Within a week I could call the birds. I could never quite get them to circle around me with the elegance that Teris could, though. After that, he taught me to call the rabbits, shrews, and other small mammals – and, for some reason, they were a little trickier to charm than their winged cousins.

I played some of these melodies Teris taught me in Ellen's flat during the evenings, but they didn't make any significant impact upon her. She remained the same.

"You said you would teach me to make her happy!" I yelled at Teris one evening during a moment of frustration.

He had just spent the last two hours getting me to repeat the same string of a mere four notes over and over again. It was starting to drive me crazy.

He frowned at me. "Yes..."

"But all you've taught me so far is how to lure all those sodding animals," I said.

It had been thrilling at first, being able to summon all sorts of creatures – make them rest on my shoulder, run my hands through their fur and tickle their ears – but the novelty was beginning to wear thin now.

And I couldn't stop thinking about Ellen. She wasn't improving. She wasn't really *living*, just going through the motions.

"If you can't summon a mere fox, how do you expect to be able to charm something as complex as a human?" he shook his head. "You're not ready yet..."

He was teaching me to befriend predators now. They were a little more challenging to grace than their prey.

"How do you know that?" I challenged.

"Just trust me..." he said.

"Do you know what I think," I responded. "I think even

you don't know how to."

"You seem to have forgotten how it was you came here..."

"You managed to *lure* me here," I conceded. "Just like we've been doing to those animals. But you didn't *change* my state of mind. You didn't make me *feel* anything. I haven't seen you do that *once*. Not even to a mouse!"

He stared at me. "I could do, if I wanted to..."

"Yeah right," I said.

I consider myself of strong mind. If there was one thing that everyone would agree about me – whether they like me or not – it is that I am very stubborn and not all that impressionable.

And I had also noticed, during my time with Teris, that some animals were harder to charm than others. Even within the same species.

I was willing to bet it was the same with humans, too.

Teris seemed to accept my challenge. He lifted his aulos to his lips.

It was different to anything I had heard him play before, the sound which began to fill my ears, so I listened to it carefully. I memorised the notes and patterns – realising that this was probably the nearest I had got so far to learning the secret to helping Ellen.

I was determined to make the most of the opportunity.

But, as he played, it was *him* I found myself captivated by. I was *trying* to pay attention to the melody, but I found myself instead noticing how finely shaped his eyebrows were. How I could see some of that golden chest of his through the opening of his tunic. The firmness of the muscles in his forearms.

He looked me in the eyes and smiled. By this point my arousal was obvious – my cock was throbbing against my jeans.

Teris brought the song to an end eventually, and then he motioned for me to come to him.

And I didn't hesitate. I strode across the room and, within moments, our lips were joined and we were hungrily peeling each other's clothes away.

The thing about making love with other men is that I have

often found many are possessed by this notion that one of you has to be dominant and the other submissive, but Teris wasn't like that.

He entered me first, but there was nothing forceful or aggressive about it. He seemed more interested in pleasing me than himself. He was sensual.

And then he coaxed me into entering him. I did, and he cried out in ecstasy.

"That wasn't fair..." I muttered into his ear later, when we were lying beneath his blankets.

"Are you going to accuse me of taking advantage of you?" he chuckled as he ran his hand down my back. "You know that is not the case, Patrick. My songs can't *start* a fire, only enflame ones which have already been ignited."

It was true, I guess. There *had* been some unresolved chemistry between Teris and I. Over the last few weeks I had felt it occasionally. During our bickering, and the way we looked at each other.

I had never thought it was something we would act upon though.

We slept for a while, and then, a couple of hours later, he kissed me one more time and I left.

I knew it was just a one-time thing. A moment in time where we connected. An act we would remember fondly, but never repeat.

And that was fine. It was the way of it. It was beautiful in its own way.

Ellen and I had sex once.

It was all a bit cliché. We were fourteen and in the swing of puberty. Ellen's breasts had begun to swell and, in her every movement and posture, they existed as these two extra pieces of weight she wasn't quite used to carrying yet. Which, of course, only made them that much more noticeable.

I had been trying desperately hard not to notice them.

It was in her bedroom, of course. That was where we always were out of school hours, those days.

She suggested it. Flatly. Casually. Like she was mildly

curious, but not really all too bothered either way.

I was eager.

We both undressed, watching each other intensely as we removed our clothes.

When I lay on top of her, it was guilt I felt. Until that moment, the fact that I was male and she was female had never been much of a divide. I was hardly a pillar of masculinity, and she didn't possess many of the traits people typically associate with being 'girly'. I guess that was one of the reasons we had grown so close.

It seemed unfair that now I, by fortune of anatomy, was the one to penetrate her.

"Sorry," I said as I fumbled, trying to find that hot softness between her legs. At first there was resistance and I couldn't figure out why it wouldn't go in.

And then, all of a sudden, I found that right angle and it all slid in at once. Much faster and clumsier than I intended it to. She flinched.

"It's okay," she said.

We both paused for a few moments and stared at each other.

"I think you're supposed to thrust now..." she said.

I began to move my hips up and down. It was clumsy. Graceless. There was no cadence. No rhythm. No harmony. We were just two bodies stiffly rubbing against each other.

I could tell she wasn't really that into it, but she insisted I finish.

We never really talk about it, but it is an incident which lingers between us.

I often think about it. Not the way it was, but the way it should have been.

Ellen. With her eyes closed. Her mouth hanging open a little. And yet she is smiling, too. In ecstasy, and *I* am the one who is making her feel that way.

But I know it will never be.

After a few years of experimenting, with both guys and girls, Ellen came to the realisation that she didn't find physical intimacy with either gender particularly enthralling.

She even discovered it has a name. 'Asexual'. It is not an

orientation people acknowledge often, or even know that much about, but it is apparently quite common.

I, on the other hand, discovered over time that I liked both. I have never been able to sustain a relationship for very long though. The few girlfriends and boyfriends I have had were fleeting. They were all jealous of Ellen. I think they sensed that the two of us shared a bond they would never be able to touch.

"What's with you today?" Ellen said.

It was the morning after my enflamed encounter with Teris, and I had gone for my daily visit to her flat.

"Nothing," I said, as I poured us both tea.

"You got laid, didn't you," she said flatly.

I almost dropped the kettle and spilt boiling water across the counter.

"How did you know?" I asked, looking at her.

She stared at me shrewdly. Knowingly. The way she always used to back when Jessica was whispering people's secrets into her ear.

I wondered if that meant Jessica was back.

"I can always tell when you've got some," Ellen said. One side of her mouth curved upwards. It was *almost* a smile. As much as one could get out of her these days. "You're less... cranky."

No, I realised. Jessica wasn't back. Ellen had just been guessing, and my reaction had given me away.

"So what's her name?" Ellen asked, crossing her arms over her chest. "I thought you'd seemed a little distracted recently."

"There's no girl," I said as I handed her drink.

"*Him* then," she corrected, cradling the mug between her hands and blowing into it before taking a sip. "Go on, Patrick. Just tell me. I am happy for you. *Really*. A least one of us has something to be happy about..."

She managed to whittle it out of me in the end. Everything.

(Well, except for the bit where Teris sometimes grew hooves; the rest of the story was mad enough without throwing mythical planes and creatures into the mix, too.)

I had kept it secret because I thought anyone I told would

just think I was nuts, but Ellen was quite unruffled about it. I should have guessed really, that she – with her own mystic past – would be open to such things.

"Show me," she said.

"Most of the music I have been playing over the last few weeks is stuff I learnt from him," I said. "You've already heard it all. It only works on animals."

"The song he seduced you with," she clarified. "Play it."

I stared at her. "I'm not sure I remember it well enough. I haven't tried to yet."

"Try."

"But what if it *does* work?" I said. "It–"

"Do it, Patrick," she said, insistently. "Please. I *want* you to."

It probably won't work anyway, I said to myself as I reached for my fiddle.

I lowered my bow to the fingerboard and tried to recall the details of that song he played me. I could vividly remember the main sequence, but the melody was filled with so many nuances I wasn't sure I would be able to do it any justice on my first attempt.

I played it anyway. I tried to. I wasn't sure if the sound I filled the walls of her living room with was anywhere near as beautiful as the piece Teris played for me, but it was definitely uplifting.

Eventually I stopped trying so hard to recreate what Teris had played for me, and I just let the sound shape itself. It felt strange. Like I was channelling something rather than repeating or rehearsing. I closed my eyes and lost myself in the euphony.

When I finished playing, a heavy silence hung across the room.

Ellen was staring at me.

And there was something in her eyes which I had never seen before.

She leapt upon me.

I dropped my violin. It clattered clumsily upon the floor. I didn't care.

It was how I imagined it all those times, and much more.

Ellen was hungry. She took control. She was on my lap, ripping my shirt open. Caressing my chest. Kissing my neck. My shoulder.

She freed my penis and guided it between her legs. It entered her warm folds and we both gasped.

We kissed again. She lowered herself, drawing me deeper into her, and she moaned while our mouths were joined and I felt it as breath. She then pulled away a little, and began to gyrate, and I felt the whole length of my cock slide in and out of her. Over and over again.

We climaxed together. As one. Our bodies twitching as we both came. I grabbed hold of her and held her tight. She rested her forehead on my shoulder.

We slumped against each other for a while, both breathing deeply at first, but gradually returning to normal exhalations.

And then she climbed off me, rolling onto the other side of the couch.

"Oh..." she said, running a hand across her forehead. "I didn't realise..."

"You enjoyed that?" I asked, still in disbelief over the whole thing.

"I did..." she admitted.

I grinned. "Teris said that that song can only enflame something which is already there, not ignite it. So that must mean–"

"I am not a robot, Patrick," she said. She finally brought herself to *look* at me then, drawing her palm away from her face. "I have *thoughts,* sometimes. Feelings. About you, and other men. I feel... drawn to certain people. I have just never been able to enjoy the actual act before."

I put my hand upon hers. "Are you happy that you can now?"

"It was distracting..." she said. She turned her eyes to the window. "I forgot about everything for a while... but now it is over I..."

She shrugged.

"Teris will teach me that song soon," I said. "The one which can make people happy."

"I don't know if I want to be happy."

"What do you mean?" I said, looking at her.

"Not without Jessica," Ellen shook her head. "I don't *want* to be happy if she's not here. I don't deserve it."

She pulled her hand away from mine and crossed her arms over her chest. After a few moments, she drew her knees up to her chest too, and curled up into a ball.

"What do you mean you don't deserve it?" I asked. "Of course you do!"

She shook her head. "Have I ever told you *how* Jessica died..." she said, softly.

I shook my head.

"We were joined."

I wasn't too surprised. I think I had always suspected. It just wasn't something I ever felt I could ask though.

There was also that scar on Ellen's back. The one she never talks about. I had wondered about that a few times...

"We couldn't both live," Ellen said. "So they had to make a choice... and I think they picked the wrong one."

"*Ellen!*" I gasped. "How can you say that?"

"You've met Jessica plenty of times," Ellen said. "She is the bright one. She is confident. She is sexual. She could have made someone happy. Even though she is dead, she is more alive than I will ever be. It should have been *her* who lived. Not me."

"No, Ellen!" I said. "Don't you realise how special you are?"

"That was why I did it," she looked at me. "That is why I asked you to play that song. I wanted to be like Jessica. I wanted to figure out why everyone is so obsessed with something I can never understand. Do you think that I have never felt jealous about those girls and guys you introduce me to? They all give you something that I never can. And I really wish I could sometimes."

I gasped. "Really?"

She nodded.

"But sex isn't everything in a relationship," I said. "We could have–"

She shook her head. "No!" she said. "Don't! Just don't. Please. I am broken, Patrick. I am not complete. You deserve to be happy. I *want* you to be happy. All I could do is bring you down with me."

I got up and fastened my trousers. "You deserve to be happy too!" I said. "And I am going to help you."

Ellen didn't say anything. She just stared at the ceiling.

I went to her and kissed her on her cheek. "Wait for me, Ellen. Please! I will be back."

For the first time I could remember, Teris was not in his home when I got there. I waited for him for a while and eventually decided to go for a stroll around the glade outside his home.

I took my fiddle with me and began to play.

First I called the starlings. They flocked and circled around me as I drew my bow back and forth along the strings. I called the rabbits next. They bounded, sat in a circle, and stared up at me with their little noses twitching.

I called up every creature I knew how to. One by one. In the very same order Teris taught me to draw them.

I then tried to call the foxes – the one which Teris started to teach me yesterday, but never finished – somehow, I knew how to now.

I noticed a rustling in one of the gorse bushes nearby, and a little creature crested with red fur peeked its head. And then more began to reveal themselves. They slowly stalked towards me.

I then became aware of a large figure – a tall human – striding towards me, too. At first I believed it to be Teris, but I swiftly realised it wasn't him.

It was a man, clad in a large brown coat. He looked at me and our eyes met. I gasped.

It was Jack.

But not as I had ever seen him before. His face was hairy – it was not just that shabby beard he sometimes grew when he couldn't be bothered to shave, it was all over his cheeks too – and there was ivy tangled in his hair.

I stopped playing and all the foxes which had been slowly making their way towards me halted. They looked around themselves, as if unsure of where they were, and then padded over to Jack and gathered around his feet.

"Jack?" I whispered in disbelief.

"Hello," he said. "I felt something calling them so I..."

"What *are* you?" I asked. He looked different and yet he looked the same. It was like when Teris stepped into this peculiar place. Jack had morphed into something else, but it was a different kind of being to Teris.

He hesitated. "I'm not the only one with a secret here..."

"What do you mean?"

He looked me up and down and raised one of his eyebrows. "You don't *know*?"

"Know what?"

"Never mind," he shook his head. "How is Ellen?"

"Not great..." I said.

He nodded sombrely.

"How are *you*?" I asked. I had not crossed paths with Jack for a while – the last time I saw him he was taking part in one of those protests which had been going on in town recently. I had been tempted to approach him and say hello, but he seemed busy and he was with all of these people I didn't know. I'm not very good with strangers.

"I'm okay..." he said. He scratched his head. For a moment I thought I glimpsed a squirrel underneath all of that hair of his but just as quickly it was gone. Probably just a trick of the light, knowing this place. "I miss the band."

"Me too..." I agreed. "The good old days..."

"I should go now," Jack said. He put his hands back into his pockets and then turned and walked away. "Be careful what you eat here, Patrick. And remember, *always* remember how you entered. When you venture to places like this, it can be hard to find your way back."

A few moments after Jack had gone, Teris appeared.

"How long have you been watching me?" I asked.

"A while," he admitted. "Was that man a friend of yours?"

I nodded. "We used to be in a band together... he said something to me. He said that he was not the only one with a secret and he looked at me funny. What am I? Am I not human? Am I like you or him?"

"I think the question is more what was your *mother*," Teris replied.

I could tell from his eyes he knew more.

"Don't look at me like that," he said, putting a hand on my shoulder. "I will tell you, one day. But we have something else to deal with first. Come, let's go inside. I'm going to teach you that song you've been wanting to learn."

"*Really*?"

He nodded. "You're ready now."

It only took him a few minutes. It was surprising, really. After all that time spent feeling like I was getting nowhere, it seemed I finally *got* it.

The trick was not in trying to imitate; that was where I kept getting it wrong. It was in letting go. Losing myself. Letting the song shape itself.

It was like guiding a boat along a river: I had to let the current take me. All that Teris could do was push me out from the jetty.

When I finished playing I opened my eyes again and Teris was smiling at me.

"You've done it," he said.

"I know..." I replied. "Thank you."

"It was a pleasure," he said, dipping his head at me. "Now, you should go to her, Patrick. Play her what you just played for me, and I promise you, you will see her smile again."

I packed away my fiddle with giddy hands. I couldn't wait to see Ellen happy.

Just before I left, I shook Teris's hand and he patted me on the back. I could feel something different in the way he regarded me now. More like I was an old friend than his student.

I turned and made my way out of the door. Along that dark old tunnel again. I had walked it so many times now that I no longer needed to pull out my phone to light the way. I could almost do it with my eyes closed.

As I was walking, a sound began to gently echo down the passage.

It was Teris playing his aulos.

It was different to anything I had heard him play before. High-pitched, and it quickly built momentum.

I couldn't explain why, but I felt a sudden compulsion to

run. To get to the other side of that tunnel as fast as I could.

And I did. I sprinted.

I heard rumbling. My legs picked up speed, and the ground beneath my feet quivered. A cloud of dust formed around me so I covered my head and closed my eyes.

When it had cleared, I looked behind me to see that the tunnel had collapsed and it was completely blocked up now by rocks and chunks of earth. There was no light at the end.

"Goodbye Teris," I whispered.

I knew that I would meet him again, one day. It would be a day of his choosing, but we would meet again.

When I arrived at Ellen's flat, the door was locked. Which was unusual – she typically just leaves it on the latch, unless she is out. A rare event these days.

I have my own key though, so I let myself in.

She wasn't there, but there was a letter waiting for me on the coffee table.

Patrick,

I had to go. I'm sorry. I needed to get away for a while.

I am not sure when I will be back... or even if I ever will, but please don't bother trying to find me. You won't.

I will be okay. I promise.

Forget about me. I am not capable of being in a romantic relationship with anyone. You know that.

If I was, it would have been you. It has always been you.

You need to find someone who will make you happy. I am broken. I am not complete. You deserve better.

Please forgive me.

Ellen.

I read it several times. The words never changed.

Eventually I stopped reading and I just stared at it. My eyes went out of focus. The letters blurred. They faded. Just like her.

When I left her flat, I don't know why, but I was really careful when I closed the door behind me to do it gently. Which was ridiculous. There was nobody inside there to be disturbed.

Maybe it was just my way of convincing myself that a part of her was still there.

I walked down the street with my violin in my hand.

I began to play the song. Ellen's song. The one which would have made her happy.

I noticed the effect it had on the people around me immediately. They all halted from what they were doing and stared.

I wandered, causing a trail of elation in my wake. Some of them followed me. Big gleeful smiles on their faces. Some of them even tried to give me money.

I ignored them. I felt nothing. It seemed I was immune to the effect of my own song. It didn't do anything to fill *my* emptiness.

I carried on playing. I carried on walking.

I will play it every day that I live, until I find her. Until I see that smile. That face again.

Ellen.

5

The Picture Changes

So somehow I had wound up at the afterparty.

Well… actually this was the party *after* the afterparty… come to think of it…

And I wasn't even sure how I ended up there. Everyone around me was totally wired. They were the dregs. The stragglers who were still clinging on to the bitter end and not ready to admit that the night had already burnt out. Snorting up lines which they didn't even seem to be getting much out of anymore, as they chased the high.

And, to make it all better, some of them had just begun attempting to delve into discussions of philosophical and political natures – they had reached *that* point of the night – and, trust me, they were conversations their addled brains were beyond channelling elegantly.

I wasn't high, but I was beginning to wish I was. I was simply there because I was tired, my hangover was starting to kick in, and I had not quite worked up the energy to drag myself out of my chair yet.

"I don't care what you say, there is something dodgy about it," Kev said, as he inhaled a cloud of marijuana from his vaporiser.

"Is this going to be another one of your conspiracy theories?" Pikel groaned. He was chief-cynic among our group of friends, and it was usually his duty to be the first to supply Kev with the voice of reason.

"No! *Listen*!" Kev shook his head. "Just hear me out! Don't you think it is a bit dodgy that the two guys who *apparently* died in that explosion just happened to both be single men with no families?"

"What are you getting at?" Pikel asked.

"They had no commitments. Nothing tying them down!" Kev exclaimed. "They're just the sort of men who could be easily convinced – if you offered them enough money, and the means – to do a disappearing act."

"That's a little far-fetched…" a young man on the other side of the room said. I didn't know his name; there were so many members of Taxus Baccata these days that I had given up trying to remember them all.

"I found these records online, and do you know how many employees they had at that place?" Kev asked, casting his voice across the room. The few who were listening shook their heads. "Sixty-seven!" Kev answered. "And sixty-five of them had children, or a husband or wife. Someone they cared for or were responsible to. Don't you think it's a bit strange that the only two people who had no connections just happened to be the only ones who died?" he shook his head. "I don't buy it. The whole way the media has been about that story has been dodgy from the very beginning. When they first reported it, they were calling it a 'family-run farmstead' or some shit, but it was actually a massive industrial cruelty factory."

"Oh, we all know that," a girl said. I didn't know her either. There seemed to be a lot of new faces in Kev's house that evening. "But what difference does it make? It still got blown up. People died."

"But did they *really* die?" Kev challenged. "I'm not so sure. The whole thing has the stink of false flag to me. It's been like, what? Two months now? And they are *still* talking about it every day. Talking about how they suspect Taxus Baccata were behind it. They've mentioned Taxus Baccata so many times now most of the public think we *did* do it, even though there is no evidence. It's been ingrained into their minds."

"But *we* all know we weren't behind it," a girl said. This one I *did* know; her name was Halann. "So who cares? I don't give a shit about '*the public*'."

"You probably will do if that new law comes in at the end of the week!" Kev said loudly. "Have you *seen* that piece of legislation they've drafted up. It's some scary shit!"

"What law?" someone asked.

"They're basically trying to ban political demonstrations and movements like Taxus Baccata," Pikel smirked. "I wouldn't worry too much, Kev. The whole of Westminster is going to be voting on that. It'll never get through."

"Banning political demonstrations wasn't the half of it, mate," Kev said. "If the National Conciliation Act *does* go through they'll have the power to shut down any business, charity or organisation which is perceived as having a 'subversive agenda' – whatever that means – like *that*," he clicked his fingers. "They'll bring tighter restrictions on the internet, *again*. They want to make it illegal for employees to speak badly about the companies they work for, and turn civil disobedience into a criminal – rather than civil – offence. I mean, I know all the parties will vote against it, but still, the fact that they are even *attempting* something like that scares the shit out of me. I was talking to Pandora the other day and she–"

Pikel laughed and rolled his eyes. "Ah, here we go again…"

"What do you mean?" Kev frowned at him.

"You do realise that is like the twentieth time you've mentioned her tonight?" Pikel said.

"I have not!" Kev crossed his arms over his chest. "I mentioned her earlier, but that was just because–"

"If you like her so much why don't you just ask her out or something?" Halann suggested.

"*Pandora*?" Kev gasped. "No… she would never… I mean, she's–"

"So you *do* fancy her then!" someone laughed.

"Shall I just ask her out *for* you?" Halann offered. "Get it over and done with so we don't have to listen to you talk about her all the bloody time?"

"Don't you *dare!*" Kev yelled, pointing his vaporiser at her and causing a rupture of giggles.

"Has anyone seen the acid?" someone sitting on the floor piped in.

They looked like they already had more than enough acid.

"Don't look at me!" Kev said. "I don't do acid anymore! It's not natural."

"Didn't Parmella take the acid?" a wide-eyed young man sitting beside them responded, dreamily.

"When?"

"You know. When she came in and did that dance and fed us gooseberries…"

"Oh my God. You're right!"

"The gooseberries are still here though…"

"But where is the acid?"

"Parmella took the acid and left us with *gooseberries*!"

"Where is Parmella?"

"I think she went outside."

"We *can't* go outside!"

"Quiet down!" Kev interrupted their dialogue. "My neighbours have already complained twice."

"Kev can you go outside and find the acid, please?" one of them asked.

Kev groaned.

"*Please*?"

"Fine!" he said, getting up from his chair. "I'll find her. Just *keep. It. Down*!"

Kev walked away and everyone began to talk in small groups again.

"You've been quiet," a voice beside me said.

It was my friend Namda. She was lounging beside me with a patchwork blanket draped over her knees.

"So have you," I replied.

"I'm tired," she admitted, running a hand through her wavy locks of mulberry hair. "You, on the other hand, have been *distant*. And not just now, either. You've been acting strange all night. What's up, Tristan?"

It is always hard to hide things from Namda. I don't think she's psychic or anything. Just perceptive.

"It's a bit difficult at home at the moment," I said. "Neal is stressed."

"I thought Dinnusos was going well now?" she narrowed her eyes.

"Oh yeah, it's doing great," I said. "Financially, anyway. It's just the authorities came to visit the other day and asked Neal all these questions. Apparently they heard rumours that drugs were being dealt under the counter and he's been serving underage kids. It's really spooked him. He's worried about his licence."

"Janus is *full* of underage kids, and we were taking drugs in there for years," Namda muttered. "Half the bars in town are full of people who're high, but nothing has ever happened to those places. Why have they got it in for Dinnusos?"

"Well, what Kev just said then got me thinking… maybe it's because they know that a lot of people who come to Dinnusos are connected to Taxus Baccata. Do you think that might be why?"

"I wouldn't put it past them…" Namda muttered.

Our conversation was interrupted. We both heard raised voices – not only that, but you know that feeling you sometimes experience when the atmosphere of a party takes a sudden turn and a bad energy sweeps into the room like a cold wind? We felt that too.

Kev raced in. "Shit!" he said, leaning on the doorframe. "Someone attacked Parmella!"

"Is she okay?" Pikel asked.

Kev nodded. "Elaine and Amelia are looking after her. I found her in the garden! She's bleeding from her head!"

Pikel and a few of the others got up and raced towards the back of the house. I initially felt an urge to follow them, but realised that Parmella was probably going to already have more than enough people crowding around her.

A few minutes later, Pikel and Amelia guided Parmella into the room, each of them supporting one of her shoulders. She was holding a cloth to the back of her head and looked a little dazed. The room went silent again and two of the guests swiftly vacated one of the chairs to allow her to sit.

"Are you okay?" someone asked.

Parmella grimaced, but nodded. "Don't worry," she said, lifting the cloth from her scalp and looking at the patch of blood which had formed. "I don't think I need stitches or anything. I'm just a bit shaken…"

"Who was it?" Halann asked.

"I don't know," she shook her head. "I have never even seen him before… I went outside to get some air and he followed me. He hit me with a bottle and then ran away."

"Did he mug you?"

"No," she said. "Not that I know of… he wouldn't have found anything valuable on me even if he did."

"That makes no sense…"

"Don't worry guys, I've called the police," Kev announced as he sat himself back in his armchair.

The room went silent and everyone stared at him.

Kev casually inhaled from his vaporiser and turned his eyes up to the ceiling.

"You did *what*?" Pikel asked.

"I called the police," he repeated.

"You're kidding me, right?" a girl sitting on the floor asked. She had a rolled up note in her hand and there was a tray on the coffee table in front of her which had several lines of white powder ready to be inhaled.

"No," Kev shook his head. "I called them as soon as I found out. Don't worry. They should be here really soon."

"Oh fuck."

"Shit."

"Shit shit shit shit shit shit!"

What followed was a mad scramble. Several people got up from where they were sitting – chairs or floor – and began rummaging around the room, collecting illegal substances and paraphernalia, sweeping their hands over all the surfaces to clear any remaining piles of dust, and emptying ashtrays.

"Wha…" a guy lying on his side on the floor mumbled. "What's going on?"

"The fuzz are coming!"

"Shit man!"

"Where shall we put all the drugs?"

"Just hide them!"

"But what if they bring sniffer dogs?"

"Why would they bring sniffer dogs?"

By the time the police arrived, they had not done all that great a job of covering up what had been going on in that house. Sure, all the *evidence* had been removed. But the air was thick with smoke, the place was a mess, and the officers, when they entered the house, were greeted by several pairs of very wide eyes.

"What do you have going on here, then?" one of them asked, casting his gaze across the room.

"Nothing much, Sir," Kev responded. "Just some good ol' clean fun."

I repressed a strong urge to thump him.

"We received a report about an assault?" the other officer said. His gaze then settled upon Parmella, who raised her hand.

It was only then that I realised I recognised the second officer.

Oh shit, I thought, as I made to turn away and hide my face, but it was too late. Eye contact had been made.

"Would you like to come speak with us?" the first officer asked, while his colleague and I stared at each other.

"Yeah, sure," Parmella said, raising herself from the couch.

"Are you coming, Thomas?" the policeman I didn't know was eventually forced to ask, nudging his partner.

He finally stopped staring at me.

"Sure…" he said.

"What was that all about?" Namda whispered in my ear a few moments later when they were both safely out of earshot.

"I know that policeman," I murmured back.

"How?"

"We kind of…" I hesitated. "Well–"

"Oh… I see," Namda smirked. "You *know* him."

"It's not like that!" I hissed. "We dated. It was a few years ago. He wasn't even a copper then."

"Teenage romance, huh?" she chuckled. "And let me guess. Now you're all embarrassed because he's a respectable officer while you're attending benders which go on till the early hours of the morning?"

"No," I mumbled. "It's not like that."

"So why did you both go all weird when you recognised each other?"

"We didn't exactly part on good terms."

"Just go say hello," she suggested. "You said it was years ago."

"He was in the closet and wanted us to sneak around. It kinda pissed me off so we had a massive row one day and never spoke again…" I shrugged. "Who knows? He's probably still in the closet now. It's probably best I leave him be."

"You're worried you'll blow his cover, so to speak," she chuckled.

"Maybe it is time I went home," I said, rising from my chair. My departure was well overdue.

"Okay, sleep well," she said.

The two of us briefly embraced and then I left the room.

When I reached the hallway he was waiting for me.

"Tristan?" he said.

I held back a sigh. *Here we go.*

"Hello, Tommy," I replied.

He chuckled softly. "Not many people call me that these days. Just boring old 'Thomas' now." He looked me up and down. "How are you doing?"

"Fine," I said.

"Still doing the painting?" he asked. The way he said 'the painting' vexed me. He made it sound like a whimsical hobby. When we were in college together he was studying 'sensible' subjects, like Psychology and Politics, and I kind of felt like he looked down upon the arts.

"Yes," I said, putting a hand on my hip. "I'm making a living off it now, too."

His eyes widened a little, and I have to admit I did get a bit of satisfaction in that. I guess he had assumed I was just a deadbeat now, finding me in a place like this.

"That's really impressive," he smiled and reached into his pocket. "It would be great to catch up sometime. I'll tell you what, I'll give you my number if you–"

"I have a boyfriend," I found myself saying.

He did look a little disappointed. "That's cool… I didn't mean anything like *that*… I just thought it would be nice to catch up. Just friendly like. Here, just take this," he said, handing me a card. "It's up to you."

I didn't make any promises, but I did place it in my pocket.

"You seem to be one of the only ones here who isn't totally wired," he then said conversationally. Like he was just trying to fill the silence.

"I don't know what you're talking about," I said. I felt defensive. I *did* know this guy but he was still a copper. I didn't know whether I could trust him.

He grinned knowingly. "Don't worry, Tristan. The way I see it, if we're called out to deal with an assault, we'll deal with the assault. I don't want people to feel like they can't rely on us if there is something serious going on just because of their habits."

"Do you think they'll find him?" I asked, nodding my head

in the direction of the kitchen, where Parmella and the officer were sitting at the table together.

"I doubt it, to be honest," Tommy replied. "My partner will take some statements from any witnesses, and then Parmella will have to come to the station so we can photograph her wounds and note his description. Weird thing is, this isn't the first time this has happened this week. Some colleagues of ours were called out to a different house party last night, and it sounds like it might be the same guy too."

"We should warn everyone," I said. "If it's a serial crime…"

"Don't worry, PC Rolfe and I will talk to the people here after we have taken some statements. You can go home if you like. As long as you weren't a witness to the event?" he checked.

I shook my head. "No, I was in the living room the whole time."

"You can leave then," he said, and shuffled aside to let me get to the door. "No offence, but you look really tired."

"Thanks," I said as I pulled it open.

"Just so you know," he then said. "I am sorry for the way I was back then. I've changed now. I came out to my family a couple of years ago. Just in case you were wondering."

"Good," I said, smiling at him. Maybe he wasn't so bad after all. "I'm glad for you… I'll call you, if you like. We can have a coffee or something.

He nodded. "I would like that… oh and one more thing. Be careful, Tristan. What I said to you earlier about me not making a fuss over what's been going on in this house tonight… not all officers see it the same way I do."

I nodded. "Okay. Thanks for the heads up."

We shook hands and I left.

It is a bittersweet feeling when you're on your way home from a night out and begin to hear the dawn chorus. It is beautiful, but you are also struck by the dawning reality that the day ahead of you is likely going to be a write off.

When I reached my flat I stumbled up into the bedroom and collapsed into bed.

"You stink of booze and fags," Neal groaned as he shuffled

aside to make room for me. "What time is it, anyway?"

"About five," I replied. It was a slight softening of the truth. The exact time was 5:43.

"It's only a few more hours till I need to get *up*."

"Try not to wake me when you do," I said, rubbing his shoulder.

"What, like you've just done to me?" he grumbled. "Did you have a good night then?"

"It was okay," I said. "Someone hit Parmella over the head with a bottle though."

"Really?" he muttered, turning his head a little and looking at me. "What happened?"

I told him the story.

"Eventful night then," he muttered. "I got into a bit of a ruckus with some of the punters in the bar, too."

"Why?" I asked. It was rare anyone caused trouble in Dinnusos. It just didn't seem to draw that sort of people.

"I kicked a pair of lads out because they were being all rowdy and it was bloody obvious they were high as kites… thing is, a load of their friends got shitty about it and left too…"

"I guess they were surprised," I said. "The reason people come to Dinnusos is there're fewer rules."

"Yeah, well I've got to do something to clamp down on all the drug-taking which has been going on recently or there won't even be a Dinnusos…" he sighed. "I don't like acting like a bloody matron either, Tristan, but I have to… it feels like I am caught between a rock and a hard place."

I rested my forehead on his collar.

"Should I be jealous then?" he asked.

"About what?"

"About you going to meet up with one of your exes."

"Of course not," I said. "We're just going for a coffee."

"Yeah, and we all know what 'coffee' usually means."

"*Actual* coffee. It's not like that, Neal. I don't even find him attractive anymore."

"Meeting up with a nice young man your own age…" he murmured. "At least it'll get you away from the old fart for an afternoon."

"Stop it," I said. "You know I wouldn't."

He grinned and then planted his lips on my forehead. "I know. I was just teasing."

He then rolled over and put his back to me.

"Oh yeah, I forgot to tell you, your paintings have changed again," he then said. Like it was an afterthought.

"Oh…" I replied. It was still a bit surreal for me to hear someone else speak about that little secret of mine in such a frank manner. Until recently the only other person in whom I had confided about it was Namda – and I got a strong impression she was very sceptical when I told her.

But Neal knew it was true – he had witnessed it too many times now. It was actually a bit of a relief in a way. At least I knew I wasn't crazy anymore.

"Which one?" I asked.

"Loads of them," he said.

"More than one?!" I exclaimed. Usually when my paintings changed it just occurred to one of them at a time. I had never had it happen to multiples before. "Are you sure?"

He nodded. "Yeah. These weird shadows have appeared all over the murals you did on the walls of Dinnusos. You'll have to have a look."

I woke up at around lunchtime, and by then Neal had already left.

I didn't actually feel as bad as I was expecting to. A little groggy, but it was nothing a cup of tea and some breakfast couldn't cure.

I couldn't quite summon the energy to make the walk to Dinnusos though, so decided to head towards my studio on the other side of the flat and work on my paintings.

I checked the piece I was currently working on to see if anything had changed since the last time I had laid my eyes upon it but, as far as I could remember, it was the same.

It is a bizarre phenomenon, the things which occur to my paintings. I often return to them after time away to find that they have been mysteriously altered. Most of the time it is just something subtle – like a slight variation of a certain colour or texture – but occasionally it can be more dramatic. Sometimes key details can change to a degree where the piece is almost unrecognisable.

At one point I thought I was going nuts. I tried to confide in Namda about it, but she didn't help much to be honest – she just came up with this theory that I have a habit of getting up in the middle of the night and painting in my sleep. Don't you find sometimes that the 'rational explanations' people try to make for mysterious events, can be even more farfetched than just accepting that the world is a bit weird?

Neal believes me though. Since he opened Dinnusos he has basically moved into my flat – we hardly ever get the chance to visit his rural home outside the city anymore – and he has witnessed it with his own eyes. The changes in my paintings have often occurred during nights I have slept in his arms, so he knows it isn't me who is doing it.

There is also the case of the murals I painted upon the walls of Dinnusos: the customers often make comments about how nice it is that I go to the trouble to change them a little every now and then. Neal nods and smiles when they say that, but the truth is, I have never done such a thing.

I am not sure if the same thing ever happens to the paintings I have sold and are now mounted upon the walls of my clients, or if it is just a phenomenon exclusive to the ones I haven't parted with yet. My pieces, once they are finished, are usually sent to a lady down the road who owns a gallery and sells them for commission, so I have had very little contact with the people who have bought my work. The few I have met have never reported anything unusual.

One thing I *do* know, is that the shifts in my paintings have often, in hindsight, proven to be prophetic, so over the last few months I have begun to pay more attention.

The piece I am currently working on was inspired by the political movement which stirred within the city recently.

It was of a crowd of people, dancing in hedonistic revelry.

My compositions are usually grounded in realism, but this was one of the exceptions. The dimensions were completely warped. The background scenery was of buildings and streets – urban – but these motifs were dismally grey and visibly dwarfed by the primary focus of the piece; the dancers. They shone out brightly, in vibrant colours. I guess it was symbolic of them rising up from the establishment and becoming liberated.

Without even thinking about it too much, I found myself adding green textures to the edge of the painting. I do that sometimes; begin to paint a colour without even consciously knowing what it is for or where it is leading, at first, but it always comes clear to me what I am doing eventually.

Trees. That was what I was painting. They were encircling the city. No – not just that – it seemed almost like they were *enveloping* it. Encroaching. Strangling. Laying it under siege.

I then heard the door open and was pulled back into reality.

It was Neal.

"You're back early," I said.

I turned my eyes to the clock on the wall. It was actually 8:45pm. Not quite as early as I had first assumed – where did all that time go? – but Neal didn't usually return until gone midnight.

"It was quiet so I decided to take an evening off. Elaine is locking up tonight."

I nodded and placed my brush into a jar of water. It was good Dinnusos was busy enough for Neal to hire some extra staff now. When it first opened he couldn't afford any and he didn't get a single day off for months. He was really stressed and it worried me.

"I guess everyone is preparing themselves for tomorrow," I said. "It's a big day."

He nodded. "I watched the news earlier. They're predicting hundreds are going to turn up in this town alone."

"Yeah," I said. "And for a good reason. The National Conciliation Act sounds frightfully Orwellian. Like something from a dystopian novel. Are you coming to the protest?"

He shook his head. "No, I've got to keep an eye on the bar."

"Why don't you just close for the day?" I suggested. "I think pretty much everyone who hangs out at Dinnusos is going to be at the demonstration anyway."

"Yeah, I know. And that is why I am going to be there. If anyone dares walk into that bar I'll give them a piece of my mind and ask them why the hell they're not out there protesting with the others," he said, winking at me. "Don't worry, I'll be doing my part."

I smiled. "Fair enough. Shame you're going to miss out though. I think it's going to be fun."

I don't think any of us realised how big the turn out for the protest was going to be. When I reached the meeting point I was truly astounded by the size of the crowd I found there. I recognised a few of the faces, but most of them were strangers. There were more 'respectable' looking people than usual. I had recently become accustomed to taking political action as part of Taxus Baccata – whose members were mostly young and schismatic – but on this day the turnout seemed to span all ages and walks of life. There were even families there; mother and fathers guiding children with their own little placards.

The police were there too, but they were not there to intimidate us that day. This rally had been organised conventionally through all the correct channels. It wasn't even officially a Taxus Baccata event, but most of its organisers were members of the movement.

That was probably a wise decision. The media had not deviated from their obsessive agenda to demonise us. I had a feeling most of the people who were here that day wouldn't have turned up if it had been under the banner of Taxus Baccata.

I eventually caught sight of Pikel and Kev and squeezed my way through the crowd to reach them.

"Morning," Pikel said.

"Quite the turn out!" Kev said. He had a huge grin on his face.

I nodded. "Where's everyone else?"

"Not sure," Pikel shrugged. "Frelia couldn't make it. Something came up."

"I wonder where Pandora is," Kev said, casting his eyes around. "She said she'd be here…"

Pikel and I both rolled our eyes.

Someone surprised me by wrapping their arms around me from behind. It was Namda. "Found you!" she exclaimed.

Jack and Parmella were the next to appear. Parmella seemed to have made a remarkably swift recovery from her injury – she wasn't even wearing a bandage.

"How are you, hun?" Namda asked as she embraced her.

"I'm fine," Parmella said. "They still haven't found the bastard though. Apparently the same thing happened to another girl last night."

"*Really*?" both Namda and I said in unison.

Jack nodded. "I was at a party in Yesterville, and it was almost the exact same thing. A girl left the house to walk home and was hit over the head just after she stepped out of the door. She never even saw him, but a couple of others did through the window."

Namda shuddered. "And he just ran off? He didn't mug her or anything?"

Jack shook his head. "And the police who turned up weren't as kind as yours. They ended up searching everyone and three were arrested for possession. And the house was a squat, so the two dudes who were living there have been kicked out."

"What's the motive?" I asked. "It just doesn't make any sense…"

"Well, actually, when they got arrested, it got me thinking. Maybe *that* was the motive," Jack shrugged. "Stir trouble. Get some of us in the click. Make us scared."

"You mean it's an attack on Taxus Baccata?" Kev exclaimed. He slapped his forehead. "Oh my god! Yeah! It makes sense! Of course they would–"

"Who do you think it is *this* time," Pikel asked sardonically. "The Illuminati, or those lizard people? The world isn't quite the conspiracy you think it is, Kev. We shouldn't jump to any conclusions."

"We should be careful, in any case," Jack said, measuredly. "I told my father about it and he said he'll look into it."

That did actually somewhat reassure me. Jardair did seem to have a mysterious way of getting things… well, 'done', I guess.

Shortly after that conversation, the march began. There were so many people I couldn't even see who was leading, we just simply followed the people in front of us, making our way past the City Hall and then on to the library, towards the high street.

It was all very civilised and controlled at first.

I am not quite sure how the trouble started. We heard shouting, and I looked over to see a commotion going on a few dozen yards away between a group of teenagers and the vendor of a market stall. I thought that a fight must have broken out, but I couldn't quite make out what was going on. Everything was happening so fast. It was chaos.

And then, between all the mayhem, I spotted something in the background – a group of youngsters running out of one of the high street shops with stolen goods clutched in their arms. They were laughing.

They were looting.

"Shit man!" Kev exclaimed.

The people around us began to get agitated – nobody seemed to know what to do or where to go. The march had come to a halt because the police had formed a blockade.

I saw a flash in the corner of my eye and looked over to see a glass bottle spinning through the air. It had been thrown by someone in the crowd – I never saw who – and it was bearing down towards the policemen. They scattered. I heard it smash.

And then all hell broke loose.

"We need to get out of here!" Pikel said. I cast my eyes around us – looking for somewhere to go – but there was too much confusion. The crowd were starting to panic. People were pushing and shoving at each other. In the distance I could see a group of policemen charging towards a group of young men and hitting them with their batons.

"Is that *Tilly*?" Namda said.

I looked over to where Namda was pointing and saw her face. It *was* Tilly. She was crying. A man was dragging her away and she was trying to fight back – kicking and screaming – but it was useless. He lifted her over his shoulder.

"It's *him*!" Parmella gasped. Her mouth was hanging open.

"Who?" Jack and I said in unison.

"That man!" she screamed. "He's the one who hit me! He's got Tilly! That's *him*!"

Without even a word being said, we all – me, Jack, Parmella, Pikel, Kev and Namda – began trying to fight our way through the crowd to reach Tilly. It was useless. Futile. Everyone was panicking and they wouldn't let us through. I caught a flash of Tilly's face again as she was carried away.

She was crying.

"Move!" Pikel shouted at a group of men blocking our way. "Get out of the fucking way!"

We were too late. The man hauled Tilly all the way to the blockade. Which I thought was strange – why would he try to kidnap her right before the very eyes of the police? – but he reached into his pocket and showed something to the officers.

And then, to my utter disbelief, they let him through.

Pikel, Kev and I finally reached the blockade a few minutes later. Somehow in all the confusion we had lost the others.

"That man!" I exclaimed when the three of us reached them. I was so out of breath my speech was stalled. "Who was he?"

"Stay back!" one of the officers warned.

"No," I said. "You don't understand. We–"

"He took Tilly!" Kev exclaimed. "And you let him through!"

"I told you to *stay back*!" the officer shouted.

"I think everyone just needs to *calm down*!" Pikel said, trying to play the mediator. He positioned himself between us and the policeman. "There was a man," he tried to explain. "With a girl. She–"

The officer swung his baton at Pikel, striking his shoulder.

"What the fuck?" Pikel asked, staggering away. "Take it easy! I'm just trying to–"

"Stay back!" the officer yelled.

"You *bastard*!" Kev screamed, launching himself at him.

What occurred next happened so fast I can't even recall all the details. Kev came at the officer but he was met by a wall of swinging batons. As they clobbered him, some instinct within me I didn't even know I had was triggered and – against my better sensibilities – I found myself charging into the fray. I think I remember Pikel being beside me too.

Everything after that was a blur.

And then I found myself facedown, staring at the ground, my whole body ringing with pain as they held me down and cuffed my hands behind my back.

The three of us were loaded into the back of a van.

"Nice one, Kev…" Pikel uttered.

"Hey! They started it!" he exclaimed.

"But you didn't have to bloody take it further, did you!"

"It's okay," Kev said, his eyes lighting up as an idea came to his mind. "Frelia can sort this out, can't she!"

"No," Pikel shook his head. "I don't think she can this time, Kev…"

I stared at the two of them during this exchange. I had kind of guessed Frelia had a secret – a bit like the one I had concerning my paintings – but I had never quite worked up the guile to ask her about it. She started acting all mysterious last year, and told us all that something bad was going to happen in a nightclub we used to go to called Janus. It turned out she was right in the end and, thanks to her intervention, we were all there to stop it.

"But–"

"No Kev!" Pikel hushed him. "You need to *stop* talking about that, or you'll get not just Frelia, but everyone who knows her into some serious fucking shit. Do you understand?"

Kev turned his eyes down to his feet guiltily and nodded his head.

We were there for a long time. Or maybe it just felt like that – I had no way of checking my watch with my hands cuffed so tightly behind my back. More people were loaded onto the van. Most of them were teenagers and clad in gothy black clothes. They seemed oddly pleased with themselves.

"Your Mum is going to kill you!" one of them said to her friend. The two of them chuckled nervously.

"And yours!"

Pikel and Kev carried on bickering. I tried to be the peacemaker but I eventually gave up.

It was a relief when the engine started.

When we reached the station we were dragged out of the van and into a crowded room. Eventually I was called up to a desk. The woman sitting on the other side informed me I had been arrested for 'violent disorder', and began to ask me a series of questions.

I kept trying to talk to her about my real concern – Tilly – but she just pulled an irritated expression and carried on filling out my details on a form.

I was asked if I wanted a lawyer, but I declined. There didn't seem to be any point. I did ask if I could make a phone call though, and rang Neal. He was really pissed with me at first, but when I explained to him about Tilly, his anger shifted to concern. He said he would send word out.

The three of us were then thrown into a cell together and, almost instantaneously, Kev and Pikel began to bicker again.

I claimed one of the bunks and lay down.

They questioned us the next morning. I was called in first.

"I need to talk to you about a friend," I said, as soon as I sat down. There were two officers on the other side of the table. One of them was portly and bald – his pudgy arms were resting over his pot-belly stomach, and he had a rather sour expression on his face. The other was skinny, and his skin was all wrinkly and shrivelled like a prune. "This is all a misunderstanding. We were just trying to find out what happened to our friend. She was taken away by this–"

"We will be asking the questions," the portly one said. He leant over – nudging the table with his belly as he did so – and turned a recording device on. Which I thought was strange. I was (supposedly) here for assaulting an officer, which seemed fairly straightforward to me. I didn't understand why there was a need for all of this.

The other officer then presented a photo to me, holding it up to my face.

It was of Jack.

"Do you know this man?" he asked.

"What, Jack?" I replied. "Yeah, of course I do. He–"

"So this man is a friend of yours?" the bald one asked me. His eyes lit up.

"I guess so… Why?"

"I need to ask you some questions," he said, leaning forward and placing his large red elbows on the table (and nudging it with his belly, once again). "And I would like to remind you that this conversation is being recorded, so it is important you answer truthfully."

I nodded. There was a peculiar tension in the room. It confused me.

"Did you have anything to do with the bombing?" he then asked.

"The bombing?" I repeated.

He nodded.

"What, you mean the farm?" I clarified.

He nodded again.

"No, of course not! I mean, not even Jack… it wasn't anything to do with–"

"Do you know where Jack is?" he interrupted me. "When did you last see him?"

"At the protest…" I said. "But we lost him. Why do you keep asking me about Jack?"

"Do you know where we might be able to find him?"

I paused for a long time before I responded to that one. I *used* to know where to find Jack, but that squat he used to live in was now the headquarters for Taxus Baccata. He had moved. I had no idea where.

I shook my head.

"What about this man?" the other officer said, presenting me with a second photo. This one was of Jardair. It wasn't a very good picture – a little blurry, like it had been taken from afar – but it was definitely him. "Do you know who he is?"

I saw no reason to lie – everyone who was affiliated with Taxus Baccata knew who Jardair was – so I nodded.

"Do you know where we could find him?"

They interrogated me for over an hour, and almost all of it was about Jack, Jardair, and Taxus Baccata. It seemed they wanted to know about every interaction I had ever had with them to the tiniest detail, and they had a particular interest in my activities a couple of months ago – around the time of the bombing. I felt very much like they thought I was hiding something and they were trying to whittle it out of me.

When it was over, I was escorted out of the room and I passed Tommy in the hallway.

"Tommy!" I exclaimed.

He stopped midstride and stared at me.

"*Tristan*?" he said, his eyes widening. He turned to the

officer who was guiding me. "Wait, James."

We drew to a halt.

"Can I speak to him, please?" Tommy asked, walking up to us and looking at the other officer. "I can take him back to his cell."

He left and the two of us were alone.

"What's happened?" I asked him. "They kept asking me all these questions about Jack."

"Is Jack a friend of yours?"

"Kind of…" I said, cautiously.

"Tristan," he said, leaning towards me and lowering his voice. "You need to be careful. That explosion which happened a few months ago… the forensic team just uncovered new evidence which connects it to him. And they think his father is implicated too. All key members of Taxus Baccata are being treated as suspects and accomplices."

I stared at him for a long time because it took a while for all of that to sink in.

"That can't be true…" I whispered. "Jack would never…"

"It is, I'm afraid. How well do you actually know this Jack?"

"We're not close or anything… but still, he's not the sort… I mean, he would never…"

Tommy shrugged. "I know *you* would never be involved in anything like that, Tristan. All I can tell you is that your friend has been implicated and you need to be careful. Especially now the National Conciliation Act has been passed."

"It was *passed*?" I exclaimed.

He nodded wistfully. "Yep. I don't think what happened during the protest yesterday helped... It made national news. They announced that they had proof connecting Taxus Baccata to the bombing just an hour before the final vote. It was close in the end, but it got through…"

"This is like a bad dream…" I muttered.

"Between you and me," he said. "Even most of the police force aren't happy about that piece of legislation… it's not going to be very good for us either."

"I need your help," I said. "I've been trying to talk to the other officers about something which happened yesterday but none of them will listen."

"What is it?"

I told Tommy about what happened to Tilly. He narrowed his eyes.

"Now that is very strange…" he pondered out loud. "I will talk to some of my colleagues and see what I can find out, okay?"

"Thanks," I said.

"I'm sorry, but I am going to have to escort you back to your cell now," Tommy said with a grimace. He seemed rather embarrassed about it.

"That's fine."

After I was returned to the cell they came for Pikel. His interrogation didn't seem to take as long as mine.

Kev's, on the other hand, took over two hours.

"You didn't tell them anything you shouldn't have, did you?" Pikel asked when he returned.

"No!" Kev said, incredulously. "Of course not!"

"Why did you take so long then?"

"We got talking about crop circles."

"Crop circles?" Pikel repeated.

"Yeah," Kev smiled. "You know. Those–"

"I know what crop circles are," Pikel interrupted him. "My question is, *why* were you talking about them?"

"They didn't seem convinced at first but I think I brought them round," Kev scratched his head.

Tommy came to visit us a few minutes later.

"Did you find out anything?" I asked as soon as he entered the cell.

He sighed and I immediately knew he had come bearing bad news.

"I spoke to some of the officers and they said they only let one man through," Tommy said. "He had a badge."

"A badge?" I repeated.

He nodded. "A police badge. It wasn't from our county though… I guess they must have assumed he was undercover or something. I'm not so sure though… I think it was likely a fake."

"A fake?" Pikel repeated. "How is that possible?"

"It's actually much easier than you would think," Tommy said, turning to him. "They are all different, you see. The badges we have in this city look completely different to those officers in other districts have, so figuring out which ones are real can be difficult. Especially when you are busy trying to manage an unruly crowd."

"So we don't know who he is, or how to find him?" I clarified. "Do you know if Tilly is okay? Has anyone seen her?"

He grimaced. "Tilly's grandmother reported her missing yesterday…"

"Fuck!" Pikel exclaimed. He kicked the wall.

"You bastards!" Kev yelled.

"Stop it!" I said to them. "He's trying to help us."

"We have officers searching for her as we speak," Tommy said. "And I am going to need to take statements from the three of you… I promise I will do everything I can to help get to the bottom of this. And find Tilly."

I was finally released – on bail and pending charges – the following morning.

"Now you're a sorry sight," Neal said when he saw me.

"You're not looking so great either," I said. He looked more tired than I had ever seen him and had these huge dark bags beneath his eyes.

"Well, the last couple of days haven't exactly been great for me…" he said as we stepped out of the station. "Are you okay?"

"I think so…" I nodded. "Could do with a drink though… can we go to Dinnusos?"

"We can if you like," he said. "But I'm not sure you'll like what you see."

"What do you mean?" I asked. We stopped in the middle of the street. "What's happened?"

Neal looked at me. He had tears in his eyes.

"Dinnusos has been shut down," he said.

"You're kidding?"

He shook his head. "The National Conciliation Act," he spat out those words like they were bile. "They didn't waste any time… Dinnusos is being investigated for its alleged connection to dissident groups. Taxus Baccata is now classified as an illegal organisation."

I went there. Just to see it. Neal didn't come, I think he still wasn't quite ready to face it.

When I inserted the key into the lock it was a little stiff and rusted at first, but I eventually managed to get the knack of it and it clicked open.

It was eerie to see the bar so empty. It had not been this dim and gloomy since the days Neal and I spent furbishing it before it opened. Back then it was just an old derelict building in need of patching up. Now it was a domicile we had nurtured, cherished, and filled with wonderful memories.

I began to tidy up a little. I guess when the authorities came to shut the place down it was very sudden and there was some resistance, because some of the chairs had been knocked over and there were still glasses on the tables. Some of them were still half full. I righted some of the chairs and cleared the glasses, stacking them by the washer.

It was just as I was passing through the lounge that I glimpsed one of my murals and stared at it.

During all the things which had occurred over the last few days, I had completely forgotten what Neal had said to me about them changing…

A few hours later, someone knocked upon the door and I answered it.

"Hi," Faye said, greeting me with a grimace. "I brought Naomi with me. I hope you don't mind…"

"No, it's fine," I said, opening the door wider to let them both in. "Come inside."

"Are we *allowed* to?" Faye asked, cautiously. "I heard–"

"Yeah, just come in," I said. "As long as we're technically not open, it's fine. I won't turn the light on or anything."

I closed the door behind us. It was approaching evening now and the bar had become even dimmer.

"What's going on, Tristan?" Faye asked. She played with her hands. "We were just helping with the search for Tilly…"

"I'm sorry about that," I said. "We tried to get to her in time but we couldn't."

"You were there?" she asked.

I nodded and told them how she was dragged away during the protest.

"Do you have any idea who that man could be?" I asked her. "Has she mentioned anything to you which might give us a clue?"

"No," Faye shook her head. "Tilly and I… well, we haven't been getting on very well recently… she's been acting strange. I should have–"

"Stop blaming yourself," Naomi said, placing a hand on Faye's shoulder. She then turned to me. "Tilly's been going through a bit of a destructive episode. Faye tried to reach out to her but she pushed her away."

"Where are the others?" I asked, turning back to Faye. "I tried to ring Ellen and Patrick, but I couldn't get hold of them. And Jack's gone missing."

"Well, that's not surprising, considering his face has been broadcast all over the news and the police are after him," Naomi said, dryly.

"I still don't think he did that…" Faye shook her head. "It doesn't make any sense…"

"They say they have evidence," Naomi said. Not unkindly, but in a matter-of-fact way.

"I know…" Faye whispered. "But I *know* him, Naomi. He wouldn't do that."

"I don't think he did it either," I said.

"What is this about, then?" Faye asked. "You said you tried to contact Ellen and Patrick too, but what would you want the three of us and Jack for? You must have heard the band split up. It happened months ago."

"I need to tell you something," I said. "I have this secret… and it's a bit weird. You're going to think I am crazy, but please can you just try to hear me out?"

"Naomi is a witch," Faye said. "And, trust me, we have had our fair share of weird recently… Try us."

"You know my paintings?" I began.

They both nodded. Anyone who came to Dinnusos knew I was an artist. The murals I had painted over its walls are quite the talking point among the customers, so my name comes up a lot in this place. Naomi and I were introduced to each other a few weeks ago, and we ended up getting into a lengthy discussion about the finer aspects of painting. She was an artist too, and we had talked about me visiting her studio to see her work sometime. I hadn't quite got around to it yet.

"Well sometimes they mysteriously change… It just happens. Like that," I clicked my fingers. "When I'm sleeping, or out of my studio, or–"

"What kind of changes?" Naomi asked, raising an eyebrow.

"Lots of things," I said. "Colours, textures–"

"Are you sure it's not just a trick of the light?" she interrupted me. "Sometimes things can just *seem* different because it's a different time of day. Or the paint dries and–"

"No," I shook my head. I was beginning to feel a bit under the spotlight because they were both staring at me now with rather perplexed expressions. "Sometimes it can be dramatic. An entire scene changes. Almost to the point where it is not even the same painting anymore. Just hear me out please? The thing is… I realised a while ago that often the things that change in my paintings have meaning."

"I have never heard of a form of divination like that before…" Naomi said.

"What do you mean?" Faye turned to her. "It isn't all that different to Tarot cards, is it? The pictures have meanings."

"No," Naomi shook her head. "Tarot cards don't change *themselves*. You just shuffle them and different pictures appear by chance…" she sat herself down on one of the chairs. "All the tools of prophecy – whether they be Tarot, tea leaves, I Ching, or whatever – all work on the same principle, really. You randomise them – if it is cards, you shuffle them; if they are sticks, you drop them and see what order they fall; if it is tea leaves, you drink the tea and see what patterns appear on the bottom of your cup – and then people interpret meanings from the order which arises from the chaos. How it actually *works* is subjective," she shrugged. "Some people think the cards, leaves, or whatever you're using are influenced by a mysterious force of nature which arranges them a certain way. Personally I think it is more likely that all of these forms of divination are just aids to draw intuition out from your subconscious."

She then narrowed her eyes at me. There was still acute scepticism there, but also an element of intrigue now too. "What you are claiming you do is something different."

"I want to show you something," I said. "Follow me."

I turned my torch on and led them deeper into the bar towards one of my murals. I then shone a beam of light upon it.

It was one of those I painted before the place even opened. A historic depiction of how I imagined this building looked when it was first built back in Georgian times. The walls were spotlessly clean and all the windows were still intact. The canal was there too, and there was a small boat being towed along it by a pair of horses.

"See this?" I said, pointing to the shadowy figure which was standing outside the front of the building. "It wasn't there before, but it is now. It just appeared. It looks like a girl, doesn't it?"

"One of the punters here could have just done that," Naomi said.

"There is more. Come, I'll show you," I said, leading them further into the bar.

I showed them more paintings. A landscape of a riverside village which now had the same shadowy figure walking along the bank. Some of my cityscapes which had her too. I then took them up the stairs and along the corridor to where there was a large, life-sized version of her on the wall.

"But this isn't even a painting," Naomi said.

"Well technically it is, in a way," I said. "It was *me* who painted the walls of this corridor white just before it opened. I mean, I know it isn't art or anything," I conceded, touching it. "But it is still something I *painted*. It surprised me too… I didn't realise it worked like that…"

I took them to the next example further along. It was also life-sized, but the girl was in a slightly different pose and you could see the outline of her face more clearly.

"It was when I saw this one that I realised I recognised this girl," I said, shining my torch upon it. "It looks a bit like Ellen, doesn't it… but there is something about her posture…. You know how sometimes when you were gigging Ellen became, well… different… more confident, I guess. Almost like she was another person. *That* side of Ellen. Do you know what I mean?"

The two of them turned to each other and a look passed between them. I felt a peculiar tension at that moment.

"I think *that* is the Ellen we are seeing in these paintings," I said. "Come back downstairs. There are two more examples I want to show you."

I guided them back to the lounge, where one of my canvas paintings was leant against the wall.

"After I saw all the changes to the murals in this place I went home to see if anything had happened to any of my pieces there. Two of them had. And I think they are the most important," I said. "Take a look at this."

They both took a few steps closer and examined it. It was the painting I had been working on the day before I got arrested. Of the crowd of people dancing in a hedonistic, rebellious revelry.

"Look," I said, indicating to the very centre of the painting, where, in the pinnacle of the crowd there were now two new figures. One of them was the girl. Her hands were outwardly drawn and her mouth was wide open, almost like she was singing.

And beside her a young man was playing a fiddle.

"Do you think that is Patrick?" Faye asked.

"Possibly," I said, turning to her. "It's hard to tell. That was why I tried to contact him. Are you sure you don't know where he and Ellen are?"

Faye shook her head. "We didn't part on good terms… I haven't heard from either of them for months. It's… complicated.

"Some other things have changed about this painting," I said, circling my finger around the edge of the canvas. To the trees and flora which surrounded the urban setting. There were now peculiar faces and figures camouflaged between the green and earthy-brown textures. "These were just trees the last time I saw this piece, but now there are all these weird things…. I didn't paint it like that."

"That is *very* strange," Naomi said, peering closer. She then turned to me and she seemed almost angry. "This is the kind of art *I* do – I paint seemingly normal landscapes and add mythical elements into the background – and it takes me *hours* to add details as fine as that… it's a very subtle technique and it took me years to perfect it."

"These is one more thing I need to show you," I then said, reaching for one of my scrapbooks on the table.

"This is a sketch of Tilly I did once," I said, showing them one of the pages. "She was on the bar one night and she seemed a little sad. I told her she was pretty, and she laughed at me and said I was just being kind, so I secretly drew her from behind the bar and showed it to her later. It made her smile."

There was now a shadowy figure in the sketch too. It was the same girl. Ellen. She was standing in front of Tilly with her hands on her hips. Defiant and protective.

"I think this is important," I said. "I have never had a mere sketch alter itself before, only paintings. Tilly looks a little different now to how I remember drawing her… she seems more vulnerable – like she's in trouble. And can you see how Ellen is standing in front of her? It looks like she is trying to protect her."

I placed the scrapbook back on the table, but I didn't close the page. I let them stare at it a bit longer.

"I think," I then said. "That this is a message. Tilly is in trouble, and if we want to save her we are going to have to find Ellen."

6
Dreaming Her Back

After Tristan escorted Faye and me out of Dinnusos, he shut the door and the two of us walked away.

A prominent silence hung in the air as we made our way down the dimly-lit streets towards my flat, dwelling upon his revelations and their implications.

I couldn't stop picturing that shadowy image which had appeared all over the walls of Dinnusos. Each time I tried to purge it from my mind it would appear again and make the hairs on the back of my neck stand on end.

It was Jessica. It had to be. I knew it, and Faye knew it too. That was why neither of us could look at each other.

I thought we had rid ourselves of her forever, but it appeared I was mistaken.

As soon as we entered my flat, Faye kissed me.

I took her in my arms and we stumbled towards my room, slipping each other's clothes away and leaving a trail of discarded garments on the floor, our lips never parting.

She pulled me to the bed and we made love. There was an urgency to it. A need.

It was almost like we were preparing to say goodbye.

When the moment was over, Faye lifted her head up from beneath the covers and kissed me one last time before she rolled onto the side of the bed and draped one of her arms across me.

"We're going to have to find a way to bring Jessica back..." she eventually said.

"I know..." I whispered.

"Do you..." she began and then hesitated. "Do you know how to?"

"No..." I said. "My mother taught me to banish only... I guess she never thought I would have a reason..."

I am not sure I would do it even if I ***did*** *know how*, I thought, repressing a shudder. Banishing Jessica was one of the hardest works of magic I had ever done. She fought me the entire way.

"I understand if you don't want to help me…" Faye said, stroking my shoulder. "I know that you… I mean–"

"No," I shook my head. "We are in this together, Faye… but I am not doing it for *her*. You need to understand that. I *hate* the idea of bringing her back… I'm going to do it for Tilly."

Faye's face fell a little. "I thought you were going to say you were doing it for me…"

Neither of us said anything for a while. The last few months we had spent together had been wonderful – I don't think I have ever had a partner who has brought me as much joy as Faye does – but we never talked about Jessica. We swept it under the carpet. We ignored it, but it lingered like a bad smell and I often sensed that Faye felt a lot of guilt over what banishing Jessica did to Ellen and the band.

"What do you think it's going to do to us?" Faye asked, her hand tightened around my arm. "I don't want to lose you…"

"I don't know, Faye," I admitted. "I'm not going to give you any false promises… let's just focus on finding Tilly for now. That's the most important thing."

She nodded sombrely and then rested her chin upon the back of my neck. "Maybe we should try to find Ellen," she suggested. "She might know how to bring Jessica back."

"No," I said. "I think if Ellen knew how to bring Jessica back she would have done it already … I know what we must do, Faye. Go to sleep. We have a journey ahead tomorrow."

"Where are we going?"

"To meet my mother."

"You have a car?" Faye exclaimed.

She stared at it wide-eyed. Like it was a spaceship.

"Yes…"

"Why didn't you tell me you had a *car*?" she asked, turning to me and frowning.

"Did you ever *ask* if I had a car?"

"No," she shook her head and turned her eyes back to it.

"But… you could have mentioned…"

"Hello, my name is Naomi and I have a car. Pleased to meet you," I said flatly. "Would that have been a better introduction?"

"We've been together for what, three months? You *never* thought to mention you have a car?" Faye asked.

"I hardly use it…" I shrugged. "College is a ten-minute walk away. Your place takes about fifteen. And the roads in this city are awful."

"Oh my God! You're *middle class*, aren't you!" Faye pulled a face. "I can't believe I never realised before…"

"Not really," I said. "My mother is a holistic therapist."

"Yep," Faye nodded. "Definitely middle class."

I was finding it difficult to discern whether she was genuinely miffed or being playful.

She turned her gaze back to the car. "Look at it! It's all shiny and red!"

"It's my ex's old car," I said, trying my best to veil my irritation. I wasn't quite sure how successful I was. "He gave me a good deal."

"*He*?!" Faye's eyes went wide. "You had a *boy*friend?"

"Are you getting in the car or not?"

"Talk to me," I said, once I had steered the car out of the city and reached the motorway.

"Sorry," Faye mumbled, stretching her arms behind her head. "I keep thinking about Tilly…"

"Tristan said if we bring back Jessica we will find her," I tried to reassure her.

"I knew there was something wrong…" Faye said, as if she didn't even hear me. "I should have done something…"

"You *tried* to help her," I reminded her. For a period of time there was not a day which went by that Faye didn't come to see me after she finished school upset because she had tried to reach out to Tilly and only been given the cold shoulder.

"I gave her those pills…"

"Now *that* was stupid," I admitted. I could have slapped her when she told me how she had lied to her doctor to get contraceptives for Tilly. It was one of those moments which made me very aware she was a bit younger than me. "But still, it was *she* who asked you for them in the first place, and you stopped once you found out it was risky. You can only help your friends if they *want* to be helped, Faye. Don't blame yourself for their foolish decisions."

"How long will it take to get to your Mum's?" Faye asked, turning her eyes to the window.

"A couple of hours, I guess," I said. "As long as this old banger holds up."

"Can't believe this was your boyfriend's," Faye uttered, looking around the interior. "What was his name, anyway?"

"Are you *still* on that?"

"So when did you figure out you were a lesbian?" she carried on.

"Oh great. And now you are gay-washing me…"

"What does that even *mean*?"

"Every girlfriend I have ever had has referred to the times I had a boyfriend as 'before you turned gay', and all my boyfriends have referred to the times I have had a girlfriend as a 'phase'. I thought *you* would be a bit more open minded than that."

"So you're bi?" Faye said.

"Music is wasted on that great mind of yours," I said dryly.

"I don't even know who you are anymore…" Faye muttered. "Boyfriends! Flashy car! What next? Is your real name even Naomi?"

"If this car bothers you so much you *can* get out of it, you know."

That shut her up for a while.

"I'm sorry," she eventually said.

"What's with us?" I asked, turning to her. "Why are we being like this with each other?"

"Maybe we are realising we made a mistake…" Faye said wistfully.

"No," I shook my head. "If I could go back I would do the same. Jessica was out of control. It wasn't fair on you. Or Ellen. Even if *she* doesn't recognise it."

"Are you sure, though?" Faye asked.

"Well, it's what I think," I shrugged. "I guess I am subject to my own biases."

"But you're a witch," Faye said. "I thought you were all supposed to be wise."

I chuckled. "Why do people always see witches as these all-knowing, enlightened goddesses. Go visit any old witchy gathering and, trust me, you'll soon learn otherwise. We can be just as clueless, flawed, and dysfunctional as the rest of you."

"Really?"

I chuckled. "Yep. Just wait until you meet my mother."

When we reached my house my mother stepped out of the front door and waved as I pulled up into the driveway.

"Is that your Mum?" Faye asked.

It was hardly rocket science. My mother does have a rather clichéd witchy look about her; dark and billowy garments, curly red hair, and all that jewellery dangling from her neck.

"It's like she *knew* we were coming."

"She will probably claim she did," I muttered. "But it's more likely she just heard the engine."

"She seems nice."

After I finished parking Faye got out of the car and ran straight to her. "Hi!" she said, giving my mother one of her sweetest smiles. "I'm Faye. Nice to meet you."

The way she had been grouchy with me all morning and was now being all light and sunshine with my mother irritated me.

"Merry meet. I am Cynthia," she responded, opening up her arms and embracing her. "I have been expecting you."

And then my mother looked at me. "Hello, Naomi. It's been a while since I last heard from you…"

I grimaced, feeling a twinge of guilt. When I first moved away I wrote to my mother almost every week, but I had stalled a little over the last couple of months. I had been busy. Distracted.

"It has," I admitted, walking up to her and kissing her on the cheek.

She looked me up and down and then turned to Faye and stared at her a while with a sage look in her eyes.

My mother is intuitive – why else would I have come to her in this time of need? – but she does irritate me sometimes.

When she meets new people she often goes into this weird mode where she postures. Every word she says, every motion, and expression she pulls, are all wilfully executed to create a certain air about herself.

"Yes…" she eventually said. "I sense you need guidance…"

I resisted the compulsion to roll my eyes.

"Come inside," she said, ushering us into the house.

She guided us into the living room. Not the living room at the front of the house which is pretty mundane and has a television, but the second one at the back which smells of incense and has gaudy tapestries dangling from every wall and ceiling. The one my mother receives people in when she wants to make an impression.

Faye ogled all the decorations. The giant dreamcatcher dangling from the ceiling, the shelves of crystals, effigies of various deities, and the reindeer skull above the fireplace.

And then, a few minutes later, my mother returned bearing a tray with three cups and a pot of some kind of fancy herbal tea which *I* didn't even recognise. And I know my herbs quite well.

"It's nice to meet you, Faye," my mother said. "Naomi has mentioned you in her letters. How long are you staying?"

"Not very long, I'm afraid," I said, deciding to cut to the chase. "We need your help."

"As you will," she said, placing the pot down and crossing her arms over her chest. "So tell me. What's your trouble?"

We told her the story. Faye was a bit cagey about the exact nature of the relationship she had with Jessica, but I sensed from the look in my mother's eyes she guessed that bit herself. She listened mostly, nodding her head every now and then and asking the occasional question.

When we had finished, my mother took a deep breath and turned her eyes to the window.

"This is quite an unusual situation…" she said. "I, nor anyone else I know has ever had reason to bring a spirit *back* once it's been banished… it's something most wouldn't even contemplate."

"But Tilly," Faye squeaked. "She–"

"I didn't say I wouldn't help you," my mother cut her off sharply. "But neither is this something I am going to do lightly… what you are asking me to do for you is extremely dangerous… you need to understand that," she looked at both of us. "But yet I also suspect that if *I* don't help you, the two of you will do it anyway, and it will just increase the chance of you causing harm to yourselves. And others."

She pursed her lips before she continued.

"I think I need to consult the cards…" she said, raising herself and gracefully making her way over to the dresser on the other side of the room.

She returned a few moments later, freeing her Tarot cards from their silk pouch.

"Shuffle them," she said, placing them on the table before Faye.

"How long for?" Faye asked.

"Until you feel a desire to stop," my mother replied.

Faye mixed them for a while and then placed them back on the table. My mother gave them one last shuffle before she began to flip some of them over.

I do not know all that much about Tarot – my mother tried to teach me the art but I never had much success so we accepted that my talents lay elsewhere – but I recognised the formation she was using. It was a slight variation on the Celtic Cross spread.

My mother stared at the cards. I followed her eyes. She seemed to look at each one individually and then at the spread as a whole.

She traced her finger across one of them.

"You have a gift," she said, looking at Faye. "You must use it to get you through this time of need."

"Dreamwalking," I murmured.

My mother nodded. "Yes."

She then turned her eyes back to the cards. The Fool and The Moon were crossed over each other in the very centre of the spread. "Yes…" she repeated. "I see it now… dreams are a gateway to the unconscious. The divine. It is a mysterious gift you have, Faye – quite rare, and difficult to control – but it can open doors which are closed to most people."

"You will go with her," my mother then said, turning to

me. “The cards are telling me it will take the two of you to bring her back.”

“How?” I asked. “I can’t–”

“Faye can take you there,” she replied. “She will be your guide.”

I heard Faye swallow a lump in her throat beside me.

“I don’t know how to…” Faye said. “I–”

“I will help you,” my mother said, looking at both of us. “There are certain things I can do – things I know – to set you upon the right path… but I cannot go with you. Do you understand?”

I nodded. My mother then stared at Faye, and she nodded too.

“I will begin making preparations,” my mother said. “It will happen tonight.”

My mother told us we would have to fast for the ritual, so we weren’t allowed to eat. I didn’t mind. I was so nervous I didn’t have much of an appetite anyway.

I took Faye for a walk in the woods around my home. It wasn’t until we were in the trees again that I realised how much I missed this place. I love living in the city – I had never had such a rich diversity of cultures and people right outside my doorstep before – but now that I was back here I was remembering how much clearer the air was and how pleasant it was to hear the sounds of birds instead of the drone of car engines in the background.

“Your mother seems nice,” Faye said. “Why are you always groaning about her?”

“She *is* nice,” I said. “It’s just… I don’t know… she annoys me. She’s always being all showy and acting ‘the witch’.”

“But she is the real deal, isn’t she?” Faye said. “She said she was going to help us bring back Jessica.”

“Yes, she is the real deal,” I conceded. “But I don’t see why she has to be so sensational about it. I *know* her Faye. As soon as you stepped out of that house she probably poured herself a cheap cup of coffee and lit up a cigarette.”

“So she *is* the real deal, but you get annoyed because she *looks* and *acts* like the real deal,” Faye said.

"Exactly!"

"That's a strange reason to get irritated by someone."

"I guess when you say it like that…" I muttered.

"You're nervous, aren't you," Faye said, looking at me thoughtfully.

"Of course I am!"

"Good," Faye whispered. "Because I'm nervous too…"

Faye and I returned to the house just before sunset when my mother was making the final preparations. The entire room had been rearranged. The table had been removed and the rest of the furniture had been pushed to the corners to free a large empty space in the middle. A ritual mat with a large white circle filled with occult symbols had been spread across the floor, and there were candles glowing everywhere.

"The circle has been cast," my mother said, extending her palm. "I invite you to enter."

I took her hand and she pulled me into the circle. I felt a change in the atmosphere as soon as I stepped across the threshold. The air felt heavy and I could feel energy as heat prickling my skin.

My mother then invited Faye into the circle too, and then she gestured for the two of us to sit upon a pair of pillows in the centre.

"I call upon the Gods and Goddesses," my mother began. She raised her head to the ceiling and extended her hands. "To ask them to aid these two loved ones on their journey. To watch over them."

Her opening speech went on for a while, and I have to admit that I zoned out a little. My mother and I have a slightly different approach when it comes to ceremony. Hers tend to be more elaborate and long-winded than mine, but I respect that we all have our own methods. Hers *do* certainly seem to work for her; I could feel the energy in the room raising as she called upon the deities and elements.

Eventually she finished and then handed us each a goblet full of a warm concoction she had brewed.

"What is it?" Faye asked.

I held it to my nose and breathed in the aroma. I recognised a few of the scents. Star anise. Damiana leaves. I suspected there was mugwort in there, too.

"Drink it," my mother said.

It tasted vile, as expected, but I am well practised in imbibing my mother's potions. I also happen to know how potent they can be.

Faye flinched and pulled a face after she took her first gulp, but then she looked at my mother – who stared at her tenaciously, waiting – and she necked the rest of it down.

My mother then brought out a small vial filled with oil, poured it over her fingers, and traced a symbol upon my forehead and then massaged more of the oil into my temples. It made my skin tingle. She muttered an incantation. I caught the odd word, but she was speaking too fast for me to catch it all. That potion I had just drunk must have been strong, because my mind was already beginning to go a little blurry.

She then moved on to Faye and applied the oil to her. By then my eye-lids were feeling heavy. It was a struggle just to keep them open.

"Lie down," my mother said. Her voice sounded oddly distant…

I did so in a rather ungraceful manner. My body slumped to the floor and I was only vaguely aware, a few moments later, of my mother placing a cushion beneath my head, and that Faye was lying beside me.

I took her hand into my own and held on tightly.

Darkness. A Ferris wheel spinning. The carriages were full of limp bodies. Their limbs swung each time it moved. Lightning flashed, and I saw their faces. They were laughing.

I ran. I didn't like that place. It scared me.

Everything went dark again. At one point I thought I heard a familiar voice call my name and a hand grab my shoulder, but when I turned around no one was there.

I carried on running, eventually reaching an old house in the middle of a forest. The walls were decayed and the windows were boarded up.

The door creaked open as I approached and I stepped inside. There was a woman there.

"Do you know the Way?" she asked, opening her mouth in a toothless smile.

"No…" I said.

"A sacrifice must be made," she said.

I checked my pockets but all I had was seashells. My pockets were full of them. I emptied them out and they clattered in a pile at my feet.

The old hag cackled.

"Stop it!" I yelled, but she carried on laughing, lifting her head up to the ceiling. The walls of the house trembled and I then became aware that my feet were wet.

I looked down and a wave of frothy seawater swept across the floor. The old woman was up to her waist in it.

"Let the tide take her," she said. "Drown in her. Her body is the vessel."

"But–" I began to say, but then something grabbed hold of me and I was pulled out of the room.

My initial urge was to kick and scream, but then I realised that I didn't like in there anyway so I let myself be carried.

When I eventually turned around I found myself face to face with Faye.

"I found you!" she exclaimed.

"Run!" I cried. "The sea is coming for us!"

"No," Faye shook her head. "That was not real."

"What do you mean it's not real?" I challenged.

"This is a dream," Faye said. She grabbed my shoulders and shook me. "Your mum gave us that potion. We need to find Jessica!"

And then I remembered and my mind was abruptly pulled back into a cognisant state. I gasped.

"Are you okay?" Faye asked.

"Yes… I think so," I said, running my hand over my forehead and through my hair. I then brought my palm up to my face and stared at it for a while. "Hold on… just give me a few moments. This is very weird…"

"You'll get used to it," Faye said. "Don't worry."

It took me a few moments to gather my thoughts. It felt like I had been born again. I was remembering. Reminding myself of the situation we were in and why we were there.

I took a glance around us. It was a truly bizarre place. There was no source of light, but yet somehow my eyes could make out most of the details. We were in a glade. Most of the trees were oddly shaped, with twisted branches, gnarled roots, and irregularly shaped leaves. They seemed to undulate but yet there was no wind.

"Are you okay now?" Faye asked.

I nodded. "Where are we?"

"I don't know…" Faye replied. "Usually when I dream like this I can change the scenery and control everything… but it seems we're stuck with this," she said, casting her arm around us. "Sorry if it's a little gloomy…"

A burning torch suddenly manifested in Faye's hand. She smiled and swept it through the air. "I can still do *some* things though."

I attempted to do the same – I looked at my palm and tried to envision a torch appearing there – but nothing happened.

"You can't do it?" Faye asked, an expression one could almost term 'smug' on her face.

"We have enough light anyway," I replied curtly. I couldn't help but feel a little incensed. *I* was the witch. It was supposed to be me who had the knowledge and skills when it came to the world of the arcane, but now we were in a realm where Faye was the savvy one and I was powerless.

"What do we do now?" I asked.

"I don't know…" Faye replied. "I don't even know where we are, let alone how to find Jessica…" she began to walk. "Come," she said. "We'll take a look around."

I followed her through the grove. Every now and then I caught a movement in the corner of my eye – a fleeting sight of a creature jumping between the branches of the trees or stirring in the undergrowth – but I never saw any of them for long enough to discern what they were. I hugged myself, not because I felt cold, but for comfort.

Faye led the way, veering her torch from side to side as she examined our surroundings. I didn't know why. Our surroundings never changed. The trees never seemed to end.

Eventually we heard something and we both stopped and stared at each other.

"What is that?" I asked, as it became louder. It sounded like footsteps but there were dozens of them and it gradually merged into one ominous cacophony.

Faye's eyes widened and she grabbed my hand. "Come!"

she whispered.

She dragged me away and the two of us crouched behind a bush. Shadows began to emerge from the trees. We both watched silently as a horde of creatures made their way along the path in front of us.

They were led by a man. He was tall, with glowing eyes and pearly antlers protruding from the sides of his head. Several white dogs prowled around his feet – their ears were red, and for a brief moment one of them looked in our direction. Faye placed a hand over her mouth and bit upon her fingers. She seemed terrified.

It was what came next which made the hairs on the back of *my* neck stand on end. Behind the pack of dogs, the cavalcade was followed by an entourage of ghoulish, pale beings with gaunt faces and blackened eyes. Their heads clumsily rocked back and forth and side to side as they walked and their gait seemed to lack any animation or purpose.

Once the last stragglers had passed us, Faye put a hand to her chest.

"What's wrong?" I asked.

"They were *real*!" Faye said.

"What do you mean?"

"Usually when I dream like this everything else isn't real, so I can control it. I can even make things vanish if I want to because they are just fictional – a mere figment of my imagination. I just tried to do the same with them – I tried to make them disappear – but they didn't. They were *real*, Naomi! They were actually *here*."

She cast her eyes around us and hugged herself. "This is not just a dream. This is something more."

I had already assumed as much. My mother *did* say that she would help us reach the place where we would find Jessica – and she warned us it would be dangerous too – so I had been quite prepared for the idea we were going to travel to a place where we would encounter other beings and not all of them would necessarily be benevolent.

But I then realised that, to Faye, this place must be terrifying. To her, it *felt* like a dream – a place where she'd become accustomed to having near-omnipotent mastery over the environment and the events which unfolded – but now she was at the mercy of a realm in which she had little control and bound by a set of rules she did not understand.

"Come," I said, offering her my hand to help her up. "Let's find Jessica so we can get the hell out of this place."

She nodded and we began to walk again.

"How about another one of those torches," I asked.

She summoned one. We didn't even really need the light that much, but I thought a reminder that there were *some* things she could still do might boost her morale. It seemed to work; she began to stride with more confidence again.

"Where are we going?" I asked.

"I don't know," Faye replied. "I just…"

"Ok, well let's just stop for a while and *think*," I suggested. "The scenery hasn't changed since we got here, so I don't think walking around aimlessly is getting us anywhere."

"This place is familiar, though," Faye said. "I have been here once before…"

"When?"

"The last time Jessica visited me while I was sleeping."

"There's got to be a reason for that," I said. "What happened that time?"

"Well… we argued…" Faye recalled, scratching her head. "And she kept coming for me, so I made the roots of this tree grow and grab hold of her."

"Is that tree here?" I asked.

"I don't know…" Faye said, looking around us. "I don't remember."

"Was there anything else?" I asked.

"There were these cats," Faye said. "At the beginning of the dream. They led me to her…"

"Well maybe that's it!" I said. "How did you find the cats?"

"They just appeared," Faye shrugged.

"Call upon them," I said.

"How?"

"You're the dreamwalker!" I reminded her. "Just try."

She stared into space and blinked a few times. "No," she then said, turning back to me. "Nothing."

"Try harder."

She shook her head. "Usually if I want something to

appear, I just think of it and it does," she said.

"But this isn't a normal dream, is it," I reminded her. "Do you think when I banished Jessica it was easy? No, it was bloody hard, and took a lot of energy and concentration. Try again."

"Okay, hold on…" she said, drawing a sigh.

She closed her eyes and let her hands fall to her sides. The features of her face relaxed and became completely still.

I felt something then. An energy within her. It was strange because in the waking world I can often sense it when another person is weaving magic – or if they are gifted in some way – from their aura, but I had never detected anything like that within Faye before. Dreamwalking seemed to be a more mysterious and elusive ability.

I looked around. We were suddenly surrounded by several pairs of glowing eyes. I yelped and almost backed away, but then my vision focussed and I realised that each of them belonged to a cat. Black, shadowy ones. They were creeping towards us. Cautious, and yet intrigued at the same time.

Faye smiled.

"Come here," she cooed, dropping to her knees and coaxing them towards her. One of them sniffed her fingers and then the rest followed, slinking up to her and rubbing the backs of their heads against her hands. She petted them.

"Tell them to take us to Jessica," I said.

The cats flinched at the sound of my voice and pointed their luminous eyes at me suspiciously.

Faye gave me a look which said, *let me handle this*, and then began making her soothing noises again. They all turned their attention back to her and their postures relaxed. Faye whispered to them softly as she tickled the backs of their heads and ran her hands down their backs.

One of them – the leader, it seemed – rose to its paws and began to saunter off, its tail swaying, and the rest followed. Faye followed them. I did too, but I maintained a careful amount of distance to not startle them again. I was humbled enough by this point to know that they seemed to have an affinity with Faye which they didn't share with me, so I thought it best to not get too close.

Our surroundings changed. Trees began to be replaced by

small rocky outcrops and then, later, towering silvery karsts which jutted out from the ground and towered into the purple welkin above. The light still remained the same – a little dusky – but the slightly green haze was replaced with blue, almost as if we were lit by moonlight.

"Can you hear that?" Faye asked.

"What?" I whispered back. I pricked my ears but I couldn't pick up anything.

"I don't know…" Faye replied. "I just… I thought I heard something then. It reminded me of that feeling I used to get when I was in the band and Jessica was singing. It's gone now…"

The cats carried on stalking their way across the rocky terrain. I soon grew frustrated. It *felt* like we were getting somewhere when those creatures showed up, but now it seemed we had merely transitioned from one repetitive never-ending landscape to another.

I heard a squawk and looked up to see a several pairs of dark wings flapping through the sky above. At first I thought them to be birds, but they were far too large and their wings were webbed and leathery.

They were circling above us.

"What are they?" I asked.

Faye and the cats, as one, turned their heads up. Faye's mouth gaped open and the cats all hissed. They scarpered away, leaping off in different directions to hide between the rocks and crevices.

"No!" Faye cried, trying to coax them to stay, but within moments they had all vanished and we were alone.

One of the winged creatures swooped, drawing its wings into its body as it dived towards us. I saw its face, gaunt and white, with eye sockets which were empty and yet still seemed to be looking at me. I grabbed Faye and pulled her beneath one of the karsts for cover.

The creature raked its claws across the opening with a shriek, and then it swerved away, taking to the sky again. Its wings stirring a cyclone as it ascended.

"I thought I heard something then…" Faye said, dully.

"If you could open your bloody eyes too, that would be great!" I snapped. "Pay attention, Faye! That thing would have had you in its claws if it wasn't for me!"

"No," Faye shook her head. "I'm not talking about that thing… I heard Jessica. I think she's close."

I peered up. The creatures were still circling above us and they were getting closer. "What are we going to do?"

"I can hear her…" Faye said. She rose to her feet.

"Faye!" I exclaimed. I tried to stop her but I was too late. She stepped out from beneath the rock and boldly walked into the open. I cried out her name again but she didn't even seem to hear me.

I then noticed the space around Faye darken and looked up. A shadow was descending upon her.

"Faye!" I cried. "Come back!" But it wasn't until the creature was a mere few feet away that she seemed to pay it any heed. She tilted her head up to the sky, almost serenely, and clenched her fists.

I got up and ran to her, but what happened next stunned me so much I skidded to a halt and my entire body froze.

A sphere of purple light manifested around Faye, almost like a lightbulb within her had been ignited. The creature flew into its contour and was repelled in a flash of bright radiance. It howled, its mercurial form writhing through the air as it spiralled away and collided into one of the crags.

Faye then turned back to me and offered her hand. "Come, Naomi."

I gulped down my fear and walked towards her.

"What was that?" I whispered once I reached her.

"I don't know…" she said. "It's weird… I don't know when, but I feel like I have been to this place before and I just suddenly *knew* how to do that…"

"Are they going to come for us again?" I asked, turning my eyes upwards. The winged creatures were still circling the sky but they seemed a little warier now.

"Don't worry about them," she sneered. "They're not as scary as they look. There are much more terrifying things in this place than *those* things."

She walked up to one of the rockfaces nearby and placed her hand upon it.

"What's going on?" I asked.

"I can hear her…" Faye said, pressing her forehead against

the stone and closing her eyes. "Can't you?"

I shook my head and looked up at the sky again. I was a bit more worried about those winged beings than some bloody rock. They seemed to be gaining confidence again, drawing nearer.

"Faye–" I said.

"Shhhh," she whispered, drawing a finger to her lips. She was pretty much hugging the rockface by now, with both her hands and the side of her face pressed against it.

I drew a sigh and kept an eye on the creatures looming over us. They seemed to be getting closer with each loop they made.

"Faye!" I yelled, as I noticed one of them preparing to dive. "Whatever you're doing you need to hurry up. They're coming!"

She ignored me.

I scanned the area around us for somewhere to take cover, but the nearest shelter I could see was the one we hid beneath last time and it was too far.

"Don't worry, Naomi!" she said. "I've done it. Look!"

I turned to where she was gesturing and saw there was now an opening.

There was something about its darkness which sent shivers down my spine, but it was either that or face the winged being swooping down towards us.

"Come!" Faye said, grabbing my hand and pulling me in.

We walked silently down the long dark tunnel. The hairs on the back of my neck were standing on end.

Faye led me into a chamber which seemed to glow, and Jessica was there. I knew it was her as soon as I glimpsed her silhouette, even though her back was turned. She was kneeling upon the ground with her face turned to the wall. She lacked any colour and seemed to only exist in a monochrome of black, white, and shades of grey.

"Jessica?" Faye said.

She turned her head and, for the first time, I saw her face. She looked like Ellen, only the way she held those almost identical features was different. Her expression was more imperious. Her hair was longer and a little messy.

She rose to her feet. It might have just been my imagination but she seemed a little taller, too. Or maybe she just stood in a bolder posture than her twin. It was hard to tell.

"So you have come back for me," she said. "You took your time..."

"Jessica," Faye began. "Tilly and Ellen. They are–"

She put a finger to her lips. "I know. Don't worry." She looked at me and then turned her gaze back to Faye. "The three of us will resolve our differences later... we have more important things to deal with. We all did wrong. We all have things to atone for."

Fat chance of that! I thought – as far as I was concerned I had *nothing* to apologise for – but for the sake of simplicity I kept my mouth shut. Jessica was right about one thing. We had more important things to deal with.

Jessica looked at me with a discerning expression. Almost as if she heard my thoughts.

"We do not have much time..." Jessica said. "One of you is going to have to carry me back. And I am going to need to borrow your body for a while when we wake."

"I don't think that will be necessary–" I began.

"I just said we don't have much time!" she cut me off sharply. "Do you want me to help your friends or not?"

I scowled at her. "Fine!" I hissed. "Just do it."

I offered her my hand. I hated the thought of her possessing me, but Tilly's life was at stake and I didn't want that on my conscience. "But I swear! If you do *anything*–"

Jessica shook her head. "You can't be the vessel. You will put up too much of a fight. Even if you don't mean to, you will. And you know it too." She turned to Faye. "It is *you* who has the strength to pull me back into the mortal world."

"No!" I exclaimed. "You are not doing that to Faye!"

"She will," Faye said, turning to me. "It's my choice. Not yours."

I then remembered the hag's words. *The one you love is the vessel.*

I thought that was just a meaningless dream, but perhaps it wasn't...

It was also that moment I realised that I was in love with Faye.

Jessica crossed the cavern. She didn't walk. Her opaline feet left the ground and she seemed to hover. She spread out her arms, like a bird stretching its claws as it prepares to snatch its prey.

And then everything went dark.

I opened my eyes and stared at my mother's ceiling, blinking as my sight gradually cleared.

We were back. It was daylight. Morning.

My mother's face peered down at me and she smiled. "You're awake!" she said. "How was it? Did you–"

She then stopped mid-sentence and her eyes widened as they were drawn to the figure next to me.

I turned, following her gaze.

Faye sat herself up and rolled her neck from side to side to stretch the muscles. There was something peculiar about the way she moved.

She looked at me and I saw her eyes. I remembered.

"You're not Faye, are you?" my mother whispered.

Jessica bared Faye's teeth in a grin. One which made both my mother and I shudder.

"I think it is best you both leave…" my mother then said.

I have never, in my all years, seen my mother scared before.

I kept trying not to look at her, but I couldn't help it. Every time I finished navigating my way through a turning or junction and reached a straight section of road, I found my eyes being drawn to her and chills went down my spine.

She stared out of the car. Her forehead resting upon the window and her eyes flitting as we passed the scenery. As if she was fascinated by every event which went by and trying to register all the details.

"Will you stop that?" I eventually said, hating the fact that it was me who caved in first and broke the silence. We had not uttered a single word to each other yet. "It's starting to freak me out."

She turned her head – Faye's head – to me. She had Faye's face but I *knew* it wasn't her. Everything about her expression and that crazed look in her eyes was wrong.

"Sorry," she said, dully. Her eyes then circled the space around me dreamily. "These eyes see things differently to the way Ellen's do. I'm getting accustomed to it."

She turned back to the window.

"I need a burger," she then said.

"I thought you said we didn't have much time?" I muttered. "And anyway, it's 8 o'clock. People don't eat burgers in the morning."

"Faye is running low on calories. She will not have enough energy for what she needs to do today if I don't give her sustenance."

I flinched at the way she spoke with Faye's voice in the third person.

"You know, I could expel you out of that body like *that*," I said to her, clicking my fingers. I had done it once before when she was in Ellen's body, shortly before I banished her from this world completely. All it took was placing my hand on her forehead and channelling a bit of my will.

"Yes…" she said. "But you won't. Because you know I am the only one who can save Tilly and sort out everything else."

"Everything else?" I repeated. "I thought you were just here to help us save Tilly."

"Tilly is just part of it," she replied. "Taxus Baccata. The National Conciliation Act. Jack. Ellen. The closing of Dinnusos, even. It is all connected."

"How are you expecting to sort *all* of that out?" I asked.

"You will see… and I am going to need your help," she said. "But first I need a burger."

I pulled into a service station and Jessica marched into the nearest fast food restaurant like she owned the place, placed her hands on her hips, and turned her eyes – *Faye's* eyes – up to the large, illuminated menu above the service counter. She muttered and mumbled incoherently to herself for a while as she scanned it, almost like she was figuring out some complicated equation.

She then strolled up to the counter and flatly delivered her order. The server could barely keep up. She frantically tapped away at the screen, almost as if she could sense Jessica's urgency.

"This is for you," Jessica then said, handing me one of the paper bags once the money had changed hands.

We sat down at one of the tables.

"Faye isn't very fond of beef," I said as she unwrapped her burger and took the first bite.

She shrugged. "Beef has more calories," she said, after swallowing.

I grudgingly began to eat. I was surprised how hungry I was – and how much I enjoyed it – but I was determined not to let it show because it would have felt like I was giving Jessica a small victory. She seemed to have gained far too many of those that morning already.

I guess it shouldn't have been too much of a surprise how hungry I was. Faye and I had eaten almost nothing the previous day.

"So Tilly is still alive then?" I eventually asked.

She nodded. "For now."

"Where is she?"

"Not now," she shook her head and gestured to my unfinished food. "Eat. We will have plenty of time to talk in the car."

"So what do you mean by it all being connected?" I asked.

"Everything is connected…" she whispered. She was back in her former pose again, with her forehead pressed against the window. Like she was registering every feature and occurrence which passed us by in minute detail.

"Don't give me all that mumbo jumbo," I groaned. "My mother is the queen of that shit. I grew up on it. Just speak plainly. What does saving Tilly have to do with The National Conciliation Act and Taxus Baccata?"

"It's too hard to explain," she said.

"Try me."

"You humans are limited to only four dimensions," she said. "It's beyond your comprehension."

"*Try*," I repeated through gritted teeth.

"There is a shift about to happen," she said. "And we are all part of it."

"What kind of 'shift'?"

"There is this… force… I guess you could call it that…"

she said. "That is the only word you have which comes close to describing it… It guides things. Everything is connected to it. It pulls upon all creatures and beings. The planet. The Universe."

"Like a god?" I said.

She chuckled. "You people and your gods… You all have these different ones and you argue over which ones are real. Has it ever occurred to you that maybe you are all right, and you are, also, *all* wrong? That the divine is something which is so complex it is beyond the comprehension of your limited human brains? You really need to stop thinking you can quantify everything. You can't."

I paused. I guess what she was saying kind of made sense. Even my mother and I have slightly different opinions when it comes to the gods. She actually sees them as literal beings, whereas I have always thought of them more as archetypal forces of nature.

"So anyway, back to this *force*…" I said.

"A shift is about to happen," she repeated.

"You sound like *Star Wars* now," I said, dryly.

"What's that?"

"Never mind," I said. "Carry on."

"Me, you, Tilly, Jack, Ellen, Patrick, Taxus Baccata. We are all ripples in that shift."

"Why us?"

"Various reasons…" she uttered. "I mean, you must have noticed something a bit peculiar about Sunset Haze, right?"

"I guess…" I replied. I thought back to when I saw them do their gig the night I met Faye. It wasn't only sensing Jessica's ghost hovering around them – and then later, her actually possessing Ellen – which was odd about the whole experience. When they played, I felt something tugging upon me. Almost as if they were taking me and everyone else in that bar to a different place. "There is something about the music they play… and the members too," I added. "I mean, Jack and Patrick both have really strange auras."

Jessica nodded. "Do you think it is a coincidence that a clairvoyant, a dreamwalker, and people like Jack and Patrick all happen to be in the same band?" she asked. "Of course not. They are in it because I picked them."

"Why?"

"That is another thing which is hard to explain."

"You didn't do too badly with the last thing which was 'impossible' to explain, so try me," I replied.

"Remember how I said earlier that you humans are limited to only four dimensions," she said.

I nodded.

"The band," she said. "Sunset Haze. The music they play resonates with some of the other dimensions. Ones which you don't consciously perceive, but affect you all the same. That is why you experienced that strange feeling when they played… it's like… I don't know… imagine a group of people who are colour blind, but can actually paint in a way which seems like they are somehow aware of colour. That is what the members of Sunset Haze do. I mean, don't get me wrong. It is very crude… rudimentary… like a child… the only one out of the lot who has reached a degree of sophistication in it is Patrick, but that is because of his bloodline. But the point is they *can* do it. Which is remarkable."

"We are getting closer to the city," she then said. Her eyes suddenly changed. Like she was becoming more focussed. She sat up. "I am going to need your help."

"What do you want me to do?"

"Drive me to Yesterville."

"That's simple enough."

"When we get there we will part ways," she said. "I have errands to do. I want *you* to find Jack."

"Jack is missing," I said. "The police are–"

"I know where he is," she said. "I will give you the address. He is the one who is going to save Tilly."

"How?" I asked.

"Tell him to head to the eastern side of the city. And to take his nose with him."

"What does that mean?" I asked.

"He will know."

"That's it?" I asked. It all seemed too easy. Deliver a message. Tell Jack to rescue Tilly.

Some 'ripple' I was.

She shook her head. "No," she said. "I have bigger things

planned for you. After you have spoken to Jack, I need you to go back to your car and ring this number," she reached into my dashboard for a pen and my pad of sticky-notes. She began to write. "His name is Laurence. He's a journalist. One of the good ones. Tell him you know where those two men are hiding."

"What men?" I asked.

"The two who were supposedly killed in that factory when it was bombed. They're still alive."

"*Really*?"

She nodded.

"How's that possible?"

She shook her head. "Why do you think? It's obvious. By convincing everyone that Taxus Baccata were a terrorist organisation they managed to pass the Conciliation Act. It was all cunningly schemed."

My fingers tightened around the steering wheel.

"What's the address," I asked.

"I have written that down too," she said, peeling off the note and sticking it to my stereo. "It's a village a couple of hours away."

"You're different," I said, looking at her. "You've changed…"

She nodded. "Yes. Before I was just a ghost clinging to my former mortal life. Now I have been beyond and come back. One does not go where I have been and stay the same."

That was followed by an awkward silence.

"Don't worry," she said, looking at me. "Like I said earlier. We all did wrong. I forgive you."

"There is *nothing* to forgive," I muttered.

She looked at me flatly. "Really?" she said. "So you *had* to banish me? You had no other, less permanent, options which would have given me time to cool my heels? It had *nothing* to do with the fact you wanted Faye to yourself?"

"*You* were the one in the wrong!" I said. "You were harassing Faye and using Ellen's body like it was some kind of fairground ride."

She nodded. "That *was* wrong of me. But you could have done something a little less dramatic. The real victim of this whole thing has been Ellen… anyway, it is all water under the bridge now. It was actually a good thing you did what you did in some ways. Thanks to you, I am different now. I am more capable of helping you."

"We're almost there," I said, as I steered the car out of the motorway and into the city.

She nodded.

"Where in Yesterville do you want me to drop you off?" I asked.

"Carry on and take the third right," she replied. Her eyes were now staring straight ahead of us but they seemed oddly out of focus.

I complied and, for the next few minutes which followed, we only communicated when she gave me further directions. A nervous feeling crawled into the pit of my stomach. I could feel the tension rising. Almost like that feeling you experience when a storm is brewing.

When she finally told me to stop, I pulled the car up on the side of the road and we both climbed out.

"This is where you will find Jack," she said, handing me another piece of paper with a little map drawn upon it.

I scanned it. It seemed easy enough to figure out.

Jessica then stepped up close to me and did something I truly did not expect.

She kissed me.

Not directly. It was on the side of my mouth.

It wasn't sexual, but it wasn't purely platonic either. It was something in between.

And the most shocking thing about it, was that it *didn't* feel inappropriate.

"Good luck," she then said into my ear. "I will contact you in an hour or so to find out how you are getting on."

"How?" I said. "I don't have a phone."

She looked me in the eyes.

I have learnt a few new tricks while I was away.

I heard her then. Not with my ears. A voice – one which I didn't immediately recognise but instantly knew belonged to Jessica – resounded in my mind.

She turns and walks away. Smiling. Confident.
It is time to change things.
It is time to put things right.

7
Bakkheia

I am of form, but not one you can fathom. I have no outline. I am neither wind nor matter. I exist in the spaces in between. Dimensional ambits which are beyond your senses. Occasionally you may catch a flash of my existence – a flicker in the corner of your eye, or the feeling you sometimes get that someone is watching you – but the moment you try to look at me directly, I am gone. I am empyreal. Ether. I am here. I am everywhere.

I am neither male nor female. The visage I don when mortals glimpse my entity is but a vestige. I wear it for simplicity. Also, perhaps, because a part of me still clings to an epoch which was cut short and I am bound to a soul I was once joined to.

I am riding a corporeal body. Her feet are compelled by gravity, and at the moment I am constrained by the rules of space and time. They carry me across a breadth of concrete composite. I feel like I am floating.

I read the sign dangling above the door of the building ahead of me. My destination. 'Dinnusos', it says, its angle askew. I enter and step into the foyer. Upon wooden floorboards. Up the stairs, her feet carry me, and then through another door.

I hear sounds. It is him. The one whom I seek. He is playing an instrument. It is a crude thing, but I guess it has a certain beauty when heard through these human ears.

I step into the room. He doesn't even notice me at first. He just keeps on playing.

Then he looks at me.

"Faye" he gasps at the sight of me.

"Not Faye," I say, walking towards him. I smile.

His eyes dance and then widen. He recognises something. Perhaps it is my gait. My expression. Who knows? The next thing he says is, *"Jessica?"*

I nod.

"How did you?" he whispers. Looking at the being who is Faye and yet also me, up and down. "Is Ellen coming back too?"

"Yes," I say. "Yes, she will."

"When?" he asks. "I–"

"No time," I cut him off. "I need you to do something for me, Patrick. I need you to play a song. A special kind of song."

His shoulders slump a little. "I had a teacher, but he left me… I come here sometimes, hoping he will come back, but…"

"Don't worry," I say. "This is a new song. I can be your teacher…"

I place my hands on the sides of his face and look him in the eyes. I begin to sing. Faye is not as blessed as Ellen with her vocal ability, but I at least manage to get the pitch right. The rest is not important. I am not just merely humming a tune. I deliver its essence – its pith – to him in a manner which is difficult to explain. The nearest term you have for it in your vocabulary is 'telepathy', but even that doesn't quite explain it.

"Do you understand?" I then ask.

He positions the fiddle beneath his chin and begins to play. A sonance fills the room and a heavy feeling swirls around us like a burst of wind. The very air seems to stir.

I smile. He *does* understand.

This sound was exactly what is needed for what I intend. It is insurgent. Inciting. Defiant. Liberating. Invigorating.

It is *rebellion.*

We step out into the streets of Yesterville. Patrick walks beside me, playing his new tune. Faces appear. At first they merely peek out from the doorways and windows. They are intrigued. They can feel something – a calling within them – but they are also wary. Very aware of the edict which has been placed upon them. They fear the consequences of breaking it.

The melody begins to take effect and they dare to venture outside. A crowd starts to gather. At first there are dozens.

We march through Yesterville, and then on to other neighbourhoods. And we become hundreds.

A young woman makes her way up to the front of the crowd. Maybe she knows it is the calling of Patrick's violin which is sparking this revolution – or perhaps she is just acting out of some strange compulsion she doesn't quite understand – but she approaches Patrick and attaches a small device to the bout of his violin. She is carrying a large speaker on her shoulder, and she switches it on and Patrick's tune is amplified from a secondary source.

She begins to mingle around the outer reaches of the crowd, holding the device in the air so more can hear it and be charmed by its call.

By the time we reach the centre of the city there are thousands. The police are called. They march towards us, grim-faced and imperious, but, as they approach, their stern expressions and their austere manner falter. They stop. They stare. Their eyes widen.

They remove their hats and rip off their badges. They wander into the crowd. Immerse themselves. Join in the revelry.

We march on, deeper into the city. The crowd grows at a mounting scale. New members are swarming in hundreds by now. Workers and consumers alike are rushing out of the high street stops, discarding their merchandise, badges and uniforms.

My work here is done.

The shift has been set into motion. I have cast the stone. The ripples are forming. Spreading.

I let myself be carried by the wave.

I relinquish my hold over Faye's body, rise into the space above her, and look down as I float away…

Faye casts her eyes up at me, smiling faintly as I drift. She is not one of those people who has the ability to sense me, but she knows I am there, somewhere.

And I know that smile is meant for me.

I will see you soon, my love, I whisper into her consciousness.

For a moment I see Jack. I feel myself pulled towards him. He is one of the ripples. He is in the outskirts of town, marching purposefully with that squirrel of his buried beneath his hair. He is looking for Tilly. He is close. That squirrel will soon pick up her scent.

I hope he finds her before it is too late.

The next place the torrent sweeps me is to a girl. I have never met her before, but her name is Pandora. She has her own part to play soon.

But for now she is preoccupied with other things. She is amidst the crowd. Part of the swarm of anarchy which is arising around Patrick. She is elated. She feels like she is *part* of something, and yet for the first time in her life she doesn't feel like she has compromised herself in any way. She has never felt more free.

As chaos ensues around her she suddenly, in a moment of compulsion, grabs hold of a young man and pulls him into an alleyway. His name is Kevin. She kisses him. His eyes widen as their mouths meet and his whole body tenses up.

"Are you sure?" he says, as she begins to unbutton his shirt.

She kisses him again.

"I am very sure."

I am pulled towards Patrick. It is hard not to be drawn towards him. He is not just an undulation in this shift I am observing. He is an instigator. A whirlpool of energy. It is swirling around him. Spreading.

He is also, for the first time in weeks, happy.

Ellen is returning soon, and his life will be complete again.

I am then drawn to Tristan. He has already played his part. It seems small, but it is thanks to him I am here now. That I am able to incite this moment. When I was stuck in the darkest reaches beyond the mortal world, it was he – with his mysterious gift – and he alone, that I could reach out to. He didn't understand my message but he passed it on all the same.

He and Neal have just noticed something is occurring. They're staring out of the window of their flat, watching all the throngs of people making their way towards the centre of the city.

Neal marches over to the TV and switches it on.

"What the bloody hell!" he exclaims when he sees Patrick and Faye on the news. They are standing in the centre of a large crowd and he is still playing his violin.

And then, through the speakers of the television, Tristan and Neal hear the song too.

They grab their coats and leave.

Naomi. She has just parked her car outside a cottage in a small rural village. The one I gave her the address for. There are two men with her, and one of them has a camera.

They march towards the front door and she knocks upon it. A few moments later, it opens. A man on the other side sees the camera pointed at him and gasps. His face betrays a dismayed and guilty expression. He tries to slam the door on them but Naomi blocks it with her foot. He backs away. The reporter asks his first question.

Well done, I whisper to her. *Well done. Now the world will see.*

There is one person left. One more who has a role to play.

If she is still alive, that is.

I pull myself back towards the city.

Hold on, Tilly. Hold on. Just a bit longer...

8
Scars

The morning that Jack carried me to Faye's house, all those weeks ago, was the most shameful moment of my life.

I can't even remember it very well. When I think of it now, I can only recall a hazy sequence of sensations. The feelings of my legs dangled over of the crook of his arm. My forehead rocking against his shoulder as he took each step. The way my heart beat numbly against my chest. The light of dawn stinging my eyes whenever I tried to open them. The intermittent hot flushes, and those moments in between, when my body went so cold I trembled.

But it was the aftermath which was the worst. Waking up in Faye's bed and knowing it had happened.

"Tilly!" her voice rattled my consciousness and I stirred, awakening to an entire ensemble of pain and discomforts.

I groaned and pulled the duvet over my face in an attempt to escape the world that little bit longer.

"Are you okay?" Faye appeared at the side of the bed. "There's water here. Drink it. I'll get you a cup of tea as well, okay? Just wait there."

I don't know if it was because I dozed off or she already had one prepared, but she seemed to return within moments.

"Here," she said. "Drink this."

"Leave me alone…" I mumbled, turning away.

"What happened to you last night?" she asked. "Jack brought you here… has he been giving you drugs?"

"No!" I said, flinching at the sound of his name. I was already wondering how I was ever going to bring myself to face him again.

"Then *who*?" Faye asked. "Don't lie to me, Tilly. I know you did something last night… when you first got here you were shaking. I couldn't get any sense out of you. I almost called an ambulance!"

"I just went to a party with some friends…" I said. "Don't worry, I am not going to do anything like that *ever* again. Trust me."

"Some friends," she huffed. "You're lucky my mother wasn't here… even *she* would have freaked out."

I didn't respond to that. I drank some of the tea though. It seemed to lack any taste.

"Your grandmother rang…" Faye said as she sat herself down on the chair by her desk.

"Oh…" I said. Usually the thought of being in trouble with my grandmother terrified me, but I was strangely numb. "What did you say?"

"I told her you were sleeping," Faye carried on. "Technically it wasn't a lie. Although 'dead to the world' might have been more accurate."

"Thanks…"

"She said that your boss called because you didn't turn up to your paper-round this morning."

"Oh…" I said.

I forgot I even *had* a paper-round.

Faye stared at me. "You told me you were fired from your paper-round months ago, Tilly…"

Shit…

I forgot I told her that little fib, too.

"I'm sorry…" I said.

"Why did you lie to me?" Faye asked. She seemed hurt. "When you asked me to get you those pills from the doctor you said it was because you couldn't afford them anymore. Are you spending your money on drugs?"

"No!"

"Then why do you want me to get you those pills?" she asked.

"I…" heat rose into my cheeks. "I can't tell you…"

"You *can* tell me," Faye said. "I'm your friend."

"I can't…" I whispered. "I'm sorry."

I was saving up for my sexual reassignment surgery. That was why I asked Faye to supply me with birth control pills. I used to purchase a more conventional form of hormone therapy online, but it's expensive.

Every penny that came my way was going towards surgery now. I was even skipping meals sometimes so I could save that little bit more.

But do you know what was really depressing?

It was hopeless. The surgery I need to correct my body would cost me thousands. The pittance I earn – and have been storing away over the last few months – hasn't even touched the total sum.

I *could* wait to see if I could get it done for free, but there are many hoops you have jump through to get in on the health service. Not only is the whole process bogged down by endless procedures, but there's a distinct lack of funding and resources too.

Even if I *do* eventually get them to refer me, I would likely face a rather lengthy waiting list.

And who knows? The way this country is heading it really wouldn't surprise me if sometime during the whole process the national funding gets cut even further. Maybe I'm just paranoid, but I don't trust the people who are currently pulling the strings in this country. They haven't exactly proven themselves friendly to vulnerable minorities.

"I'm not getting you those pills anymore…" Faye said.

"*Faye!*" I cried. "Please! I–"

"No," she shook her head. "While you were sleeping I did some research. You told me it was safe but all these people on a forum I found are saying it's dangerous. You need proper medication."

"They're just exaggerating…" I said. "It's not that bad…"

"Some of the side effects they mention here…" she said, swivelling her chair over to her computer and opening up a window on her browser. "Say that they can cause nausea, vomiting, heart problems, blood clots, damage to your liver and kidneys. Depression and inclinations towards destructive behaviour…" she then looked at me with a shrewd expression. "I'm sorry, but I'm your friend and I am not going to help you harm yourself."

I turned away, with a sinking feeling in my chest.

There was another lifeline gone…

I knew she meant well, but I felt betrayed.

I'm never going to be able to afford that surgery... I thought, wretchedly. *I might as well just give up.*

I felt like crying, but I fought back the tears which were pressing into the back of my eyes. I had already shamed myself enough during the last twenty-four hours without showing any more weakness.

"Are you okay, Tilly?" Faye asked, her voice softening. "You've been distant recently… I'm worried about you."

"I'm fine," I lied.

"Are you sure? You don't sound fine…" she frowned. "I tell you what, Naomi is supposed to be coming over later but I'll cancel. We can spend the evening together. Just you and me. We can watch a film or something."

She was just doing the 'good friend' thing. I could tell.

I could see it in her eyes she really wanted to spend the night with Naomi.

"No. It's okay," I said. "I'll go soon."

"It's no trouble," she said. "Naomi will understand. She said the other day I should see more of my friends anyway…"

"No," I repeated. "Don't. I'll be fine. My grandmother will want me home tonight."

Faye carried on staring at me. "Are you *sure* you're okay, Tilly?"

There was a brief moment then when I almost told her.

I am having suicidal thoughts again.

But I didn't. I said nothing.

"I'm fine," I lied, just before I downed the last dregs of my tea. "I'll go home soon. Don't worry about me."

It surprised me how calmly I was contemplating ending my life.

I am no stranger to suicidal thoughts. They have occurred frequently throughout my childhood and my teens.

It is not exactly surprising. Transgendered people have one of the highest suicide rates in the world. And it also just happens to be the same way my mother left this existence – though hers was for different reasons.

So here I am. Back here again. For a while I became known as the girl who overcame her issues. People kept telling me how much better I was doing and how nice it was to see me blossom and come out of my shell. I fooled them very well.

Hell. I even fooled myself.

I thought I was cured, but I wasn't. I was simply in remission. It came back.

Maybe suicidal ideation is like your shadow. You never truly escape it. You just don't see it when the sun is in its zenith and everything is shiny and bright but, as soon as the sun creeps towards the horizon again, it grows, everything turns dark. And then you remember.

This time felt different to all the other times I have experienced it though.

I have spent many sleepless nights, during my short lifespan, in states of emotional misery which are so unbearable I can only stuff my face into my pillow, grind my teeth, and whisper to myself over and over, "I can't go on… I can't go on…"

This time I was oddly composed.

When I got home that evening I began researching. If I was going to end my life, how did I want to go? It was not the thought of dying which scared me. It was the pain involved in getting there.

My grandmother didn't have many prescription drugs in the house, so my overdose options were limited. Paracetamol would do the trick, but I didn't want to spend my final moments with my head halfway down a toilet basin.

Opening my veins was an option. And I guess there is something poetic about lying in a warm bathtub as your life slowly ebbs away, but slitting your wrists is actually much harder than you would think. I have tried it before.

I, very briefly, considered hanging myself, but then a memory of that day I found my mother entered my mind and I shuddered.

No… definitely not *that* way.

As I began to read through all the alternatives, I actually found myself becoming *excited*. It was strange…

I wondered what would be waiting for me on the other side. The idea of oblivion was attractive, but I knew it was unlikely. I have never been religious, but I have witnessed too many mysterious things to believe that we are simply just matter and there is nothing more.

Would my soul, when it left my body, be female? Or is the afterlife without gender? Would I breathe? Would I feel pain?

Would I see my mother again?

There was just one thing though… one thing I wanted to do before I ended my life.

I didn't want to die a virgin.

But how is someone like me ever going to do that?

You do hear stories about transgendered people finding love – finding someone who cares enough to see past the fact they were born with the wrong set of genitals – but that is something which requires two things I am seriously lacking; time and luck. Luck doesn't follow me and, in the state I was in, there was only so much time I was willing to stay alive for.

So that left me with no other option but do something I had always promised myself I would never even contemplate.

Fetish websites.

I had heard rumours that there were men out there who had kinks for people like me, and a quick search online confirmed that. I even found a website which facilitated 'trannies' and their 'chasers' to connect with each other and set up a profile for myself.

It didn't take long for my inbox to start filling with messages. They were all a lot older than me, but I chatted with some of them. I was shocked to discover that many found the fact I still possessed male genitalia desirable.

But most of them were hundreds of miles away – not to mention creepy – so I eventually signed out.

I kept the profile active though, just in case someone more local surfaced.

That night I went to bed and thought about Jack.

About his face. His eyes. The way those baggy clothes of his dangle from his lean body. That messy tangled hair. His voice. His smile.

It was a peculiar thing, love.

I think Faye is in love. I have never seen her so happy. Naomi is the nucleus of her life now. They are completely absorbed in each other.

I was in love and it was killing me.

I felt so ashamed about the incident on Friday night I told myself I would avoid him from now on – I just didn't think I could face him again, and I was thinking about him so much it was driving me crazy – so I thought it best I stayed well away.

But, being the pathetic, hopeless, besotted fool that I am, I found myself walking to his place the very next morning.

Ever since Jardair had come to town Jack's home had turned into a hub of activity, and that day was no exception. I passed several groups of hippies and vagrants loitering in the street leading up to his house and there appeared to be some kind of bizarre New Age picnic going on in the garden. Dozens of people were lounging upon blankets which had been spread across his lawn, drinking wine from shiny goblets and dropping grapes into each other's mouths. A young woman was carving up a roasted deer with a hunting knife and a piper mingled, playing a tune.

I recognised a few of the faces. Norma, Sandra, Jimmy and Leo were among the crowd who had taken me out partying on Friday night, and they were sitting in a circle by the fence. I walked over to them.

"Hi," I said. "How are…"

Norma looked up at me for a fleeting moment, but then she turned away and drew the hose of the hookah pipe back to her mouth.

I let my voice die. It wasn't just Norma; they were *all* ignoring me. It was like they were making a point of out of it, too. They suddenly all went quiet and turned their eyes to the grass, each other, the sky – anywhere but me.

"Never mind," I whispered as I walked away. I began to wonder if I had done something that night to offend them and forgotten about it.

Some friends, Faye's voice echoed in my mind.

I guess she was right.

I opened the door to Jack's house and made my way up the stairs.

"Tilly!" Jardair said, getting up from his armchair and

grinning at me as I entered. “How are you?”

“I’m okay,” I lied.

A look crossed Jardair’s eyes which made me suspect he knew I was lying too. Jardair’s eyes were a bit mysterious like that.

“Is Jack here?” I asked.

He shook his head. “Jack doesn’t live here anymore.”

“Oh…” I said, and that bleak feeling in my chest, that I had recently become all too used to, twitched.

I looked across the room and noticed that Jack’s collection of books had gone and some of the furniture had been changed. It made me a little sad.

“This is the headquarters for Taxus Baccata now,” he said.

“Where is Jack?” I asked.

“Somewhere…” he shrugged. “He’s keeping the location of his new home a secret. I think all the crowds got to him a little. He does like his solitude, my son.”

After all that time I had spent fighting an inner battle trying to convince myself that I should try to avoid him, and now it seemed destiny had made that decision for me.

And it felt like I had been stabbed.

“Do you want to leave him a message for next time he pops by?” Jardair asked. “I can find you a pen and some paper.”

I hesitated. What exactly could I write to him?

I need you.

I am thinking about you all the time.

No, I couldn’t write any of those things. I had already made myself look pathetic enough recently without adding something like that to the list. And anyway, the last exchange we had didn’t exactly go well.

Perhaps it was best I distanced myself a little…

If I kept him close, it will only make it more painful for him when I do what I intend.

“No, it’s okay,” I said, scratching my head. I feigned a smile. “What’s coming up this week then? Is Taxus Baccata up to anything I can help with?” It was time for a distraction. Something to focus on.

“Yeah, of course,” Jardair said, smiling. “I have some flyers I need spreading around… I’ll go and get them.”

“Flyers?” I repeated. “You want me to distribute *flyers*?”

He grimaced. "Jack made me promise to keep you–"

I groaned. This was a tired old argument. Jack was always getting worried about me being too involved in the movement because he thinks I am too young. I usually end up worming my way back into the grittier activities eventually though.

"Fuck Jack! He's not even here!" I exclaimed. After that outburst I came to a sudden realisation. "Wait… is that why Norma and the others are ignoring me? Did you or Jack say something to them?"

He didn't deny it. He simply said; "He only does these things because he cares for you, you know…"

*If he cares for me so much, then **where** is he?*

"What are the flyers for, anyway?" I muttered, crossing my arms over my chest.

"Have you heard about The National Conciliation Act?" he asked.

I nodded. It was all over the news.

"We're organising a protest against it," Jardair replied. "It's a couple of months away, so you've got plenty of time to recruit. This one is going to be a more button-down affair. We're doing it by the book and we are not officially connecting it to Taxus Baccata either. Kids. Families. All ages can be invited. It's an important one, Tilly," he added.

"Fine," I said, through gritted teeth. "Give me those bloody flyers."

It was bizarre. Even though I was contemplating ending my life I was still determined to get my hands on more oestrogen. I was hell-bent on saving up every penny I could for sexual reassignment surgery I would probably never have.

I guess I wanted to die as close to being a woman as I possibly could.

I was going to have to find someone else to supply me with birth control pills soon or I would start to run out.

Faye was only one of my sources of Microgynon. I am taking two a day to speed up the feminising process. My other supplier is Harriet; a girl I sit next to during French classes.

Who else could I ask? I am not really that familiar with many of the other students here. At my last school I was bullied horrifically, so I have learnt to be wary and keep my head down. Faye, Steve, myself, and a few other misfits in our year group have formed our own little social bubble and we mostly keep to ourselves. There weren't really any girls outside of it whom I am friendly enough with to feel comfortable asking to do such a thing for me.

The fact I am transgendered isn't exactly a secret in this school. I transferred here last summer – shortly after I met Faye – and I was already passably female by then. They don't remember Charlie here, like my former classmates did. I think most of them have heard the rumour, and I am pretty sure lots of things are said behind my back, but nothing is ever said to my face. I wouldn't say that this school was accepting. 'Apathetic' is more accurate.

I spent most of Monday morning considering my options. Wondering whom I could trust. I avoided Faye. We usually meet in a corner of the hall during the first break, but I didn't turn up that day.

It was when I walked out of my second class that the plot thickened and my situation became even more dire.

I heard someone call my name and turned around.

It was Harriet. She was walking towards me and her friend Amy was with her.

There was history between Faye and these two girls, but I have never quite got to the bottom of it. I *do* know the three of them used to be a clique. Faye drifted apart from them shortly before I met her.

Harriet is nice enough – she's just not very bright – but whatever you do, ***don't*** *trust Amy*, Faye warned me once, when she noticed I had become friendly with her.

"I need to talk to you…" Harriet said.

Something squirmed in my gut. I already had an idea what this was going to be about.

"I can't–" she began to say.

"Can we speak alone?" I asked, glancing warily at Amy.

"Of course! How thoughtless of me…" Harriet said, slapping her forehead. She turned to her friend. "Amy… sorry, but is it okay if we…"

"Of course," she said, walking away and leaning against the wall – at a distance which, I suspected, was still well within earshot. She pretended to play with her phone, but I could tell she was eavesdropping.

I let that one slide. I had a strong feeling that Harriet had already told her what we were about to discuss anyway.

"I can't give you those pills anymore," Harriet said. Once we were 'alone'.

"What did Faye say to you?" I asked tiredly.

"She told me it was dangerous!" she squeaked. A little too loudly. "So I looked it up too, and she's right! Tilly, you need to be careful…"

"Whatever," I said. I turned away. "Mind your own business."

"Tilly! Wait!" Harriet called. She tried to follow me but I quickened my pace. I wasn't interested in hearing anything she had to say.

I found Faye on the green.

"Oh, so you've stopped avoiding me now?" she said as I approached her.

"Is there a girl in this school you *haven't* told about my…" I was so angry I stumbled over my words. "My *condition*?"

"Calm down," she hushed. "I only spoke to a couple of girls. And I was tactful, too. I just dropped a couple of hints about you needing medication, that's all. I read online that it usually takes two pills a day to get the effect you desire, so I knew there must be someone else getting them for you."

"Are you *trying* to fuck up my life?" I asked.

"No," she shook her head. "I am trying to *help* you."

"You don't have a fucking clue how to help me!"

"Sit down," Faye patted the spot next to her. "Let's just talk about this. We can find a solution together."

I stared at her.

I knew she cared, but I felt betrayed.

Maybe it's best I distance her too, I realised.

"No…" I said. "I think I have had enough…"

"*What*?" Faye's eyes widened.

"You heard," I said. "I've had enough of you. Let's face it, you are far too busy canoodling with Naomi these days to give a shit anyway."

I have started cutting myself now.

I actually quite like the pain. It's distracting. I like the way the blood trickles warmly down my arm. That feeling of release.

I'm still not quite sure *why* I'm doing it. I don't cut deep enough to class it as a suicide attempt, but if it is merely an act of self-harm, why am I choosing to do it on my wrist?

It is certainly not a cry for help. I know that much. It is my secret. I don't want anyone to know. I don't want anyone to help me.

I let people help me before. They convinced me, for a while, that my life was worth living.

But I know now that it was a lie.

I am flirting with suicide. Building a relationship with it. Testing how far I will go.

Throughout the next few weeks my relationship with Faye continued to deteriorate.

She tried to reach out to me – every time we passed each other in the corridor or were sitting in the same class she tried to talk to me and make amends – but I retained an icy veneer. I wasn't unpleasant. I was aloof. I didn't burn the bridge. I razed it.

I never saw Jack. I didn't even go back to his old house to see Jardair.

I carried on cutting myself, but I managed to keep it secret. I took to wearing long sleeves and I even wrapped a bandage around my arm just in case anyone ever had reason to see underneath. This was one of the few occasions where being transgendered was a blessing; I didn't have to worry about people seeing my scars during PE lessons – I had been permanently excused from them anyway.

Something in me had changed. I could feel it.

I was on the precipice. I had lifted my foot. I was stepping out into the chasm.

I don't think there was any going back now.

I didn't want to.

I finally found someone on that dating website who was willing to meet me.

He was in town on business. Or so he said, at least. He wouldn't tell me exactly what kind of 'business' he had here, or anything much else about himself really.

My theory was that he was most likely married.

We met in a hotel room.

I was nervous as hell when I entered the lobby, but the receptionist hardly even looked at me.

"Upstairs," she droned after briefly calling him on the phone. "Third floor."

When he opened the door he looked a lot older than the pictures on his profile had made me believe, but I wasn't all that surprised. Apparently that sort of thing is common practice when you meet people online – or so I had heard, at least. I would have guessed him to be somewhere in his mid-forties. He wasn't ugly. Maybe there was even once a time he could have been considered somewhat handsome, but it certainly wasn't now.

I wasn't attracted to him. But did that really matter?

It wasn't like I had come here looking for love.

"Hello," he said, after closing the door behind us. "Do you want to sit down?"

I looked around. It was a small room but it was reasonably clean. I guess he picked a hotel like this because they were less likely to ask questions.

The only place to sit was on the bed, so I perched myself on the end of it and tucked my hands underneath my thighs to stop them from shaking.

"So you're Tilly?" he said.

I nodded.

He smiled. "What was your name before you became Tilly?"

I flinched. It wasn't a question I particularly liked being asked. Especially during a moment like this.

"Charlie…" I whispered.

He began to unbutton my blouse.

When it was open, he removed my bra too, and then took a step back and looked at me.

"Can I see it?" he asked, his eyes voyaging from my breasts down to that place between my legs.

No! a voice in my head screamed.

But another said:

Who cares? You'll be dead soon. You might as well do what he says...

I found myself nodding.

He put his hand inside my underwear and cupped my genitals. I cringed and closed my eyes.

After caressing them for a while, he finally pulled his hand away.

I opened my eyes again. He was undressing himself. His body was hairy and a little saggy. His stomach wobbled as he moved.

And, as I watched him, all I could think was.

I wish you were Jack...

This was nothing like how I had imagined it would be.

"What is this?" he asked, as his hand went to the bandage around my wrist.

"I just… sprained it," I stammered. "I–"

He ignored me and unravelled it.

And then my arm – in its current condition; red, welted skin and scars – was, for the first time, seen by eyes other than my own.

I was expecting him to be horrified. To throw me out of the room. Or, even worse, attempt an intervention.

But instead, he grinned.

"You really are the full package, aren't you…" he said.

Something twitched in front of my face. It was his cock stiffening.

He pinned me to the bed.

This is as good as it is ever going to get for you… I thought, as I let him run his hands all over me.

Nobody ***you*** *love is ever going to want you.*

I thought it would make me feel more like an adult.

But, as I made my way home, I felt more like a child than I had for years.

I hugged myself as I walked down the street. I felt paranoid. Like everyone I passed somehow knew what I had just done and how disgusting I was.

When I got home I got into the shower and I lacked the will

to even soap myself down. I sat in the bottom of the bathtub and pulled my legs up into myself, pressing my forehead into my knees and feeling the hot water stream down my back and through my hair.

When I towelled myself dry and returned to my bedroom, there was a text message waiting for me.

It was from him. He had somehow talked me into giving him my phone number just before I left. I guess considering what we had just done it seemed like such a small thing to concede at the time, but, as soon as I saw his name come up on the screen, I knew it had been a mistake.

This is Ian, it read. I doubt that was even his real name. *You were fun. Let me know if you wish to meet again. I'm in town for another week.*

There is an old aqueduct on the outskirts of the city. It used to connect one of the canals to the coast but it dried out years ago, and it is now part of a popular countryside walk.

That's how I wanted to go. The drop is over two hundred feet. It was more than enough to do the job.

I finally gave in and raided my savings to buy a bottle of whiskey and several tablets of Valium. They would help give me courage if I began to hesitate.

I was ready now.

Saturday. That was going to be the last day of my life.

I know it sounds strange that I didn't just go through with it straight away, but I was oddly excited about it and the anticipation was the nicest thing I had felt for quite some time.

And anyway, if my absence from school was noticed it would have only caused suspicion and people might have come looking for me. I didn't want anyone to interfere.

I just needed to get through five more days, and then it would all be over.

When I returned home from school on Monday, I found Jardair waiting for me in my room.

"What the fuck!?" I exclaimed when I saw him. He was standing by the window.

"Hello, Tilly," he said, smiling.

"You scared the fucking life out of me," I said. "How did you get in here? My grandmother–"

"You haven't popped by to see me for a while…" he commented as he opened the curtain a little to let some light in. "I was worried."

"I've been busy," I said.

"So busy you couldn't distribute those leaflets I gave you…" he said, turning his eyes to the stack which was piled on top of my desk.

I looked down at the carpet guiltily.

"Are you okay, Tilly?" he then asked me. His tone was concerned. Almost fatherly.

I nodded.

"I know you wanted to have more to do with the movement… and you feel that spreading flyers is beneath you, but the march is *this* Saturday and it is very important. Do you want to live in a world where the National Conciliation Act has been passed?" he asked.

I am not even going to be alive to see it… I thought.

"And I am sure Jack would like to see you there," he added.

I had not heard that name spoken out loud for weeks and it kindled a familiar feeling in my chest. One which I think I hated, but I wasn't quite sure.

"Fine! I will do it!" I found myself saying.

"Good…" he said. He then walked up to me and ruffled my hair. It was something he used to do quite often – I would always complain that he ruined it, and he would laugh, but secretly I enjoyed the affection.

But not anymore. After Ian, the experience of another man touching me – even if it was just playful – made my whole body tense up and the hair on the back of my neck stand on end.

Jardair then opened the door. "See you on Saturday, Tilly. And remember, recruit as many people as you can."

I sighed as he left.

It looked like I was going to have to go to the march now. If I didn't show up, Jardair might suspect something and come looking for me.

And there was something spooky about that man; I had a

feeling he wouldn't find it too difficult.

And I have to admit, a part of me wanted to see Jack one last time.

A few minutes later, I finally dared to venture downstairs. I was not looking forward to explaining to my grandmother why an eccentric middle-aged man with long hair had come to visit me in my room.

"Hi…" I said cautiously, when I reached the living area.

"Evening, Tilly. Supper is almost ready," she said, and then turned her eyes back to her newspaper.

She didn't even see him, I realised.

My grandmother is starting to go deaf – so it is not surprising she didn't hear him – but the fact she had not even *seen* him beggared belief.

Just what ***are*** *you, Jardair?* I wondered. Not for the first time.

The following day I began spreading some of those leaflets around. I began with my school, pinning them to the noticeboards, lockers and walls. I even scattered some across the floors of the corridors, but only when no one was looking. I was careful not to be seen (I had already been sternly reprimanded by my head of year a few months ago for 'spreading political propaganda').

I was just tacking one of them to the wall in the toilets when I heard the door open.

"Hi Tilly," someone said.

I turned around and saw it was Amy. She stared at the leaflet I had just attached to the wall and her eyes lit up.

I had been caught red handed.

"So it *is* you who's been spreading those leaflets around!" she exclaimed.

I grimaced. She had only ever been nice to me, but I was still wary of this girl. It wasn't just Faye's warning which made me cautious… there was something about her I didn't trust. Her eyes never seemed to express the same things as her words and she seemed a little calculated and false.

"Is it true, then?" she asked. "Are you part of Taxus Baccata?"

"Not really," I mumbled. "I just… know some of them."

"You *know* them?" she squealed. That seemed enough to excite her. "Have you ever met their leader? I heard his name is Jadar, and he is–"

"*Jardair*," I corrected her.

"So you *do* know him!" she said, her eyes widening.

I nodded.

She stared at the leaflet for a few moments. "How many of these have you got? I can help spread them around if you like?"

I couldn't think of any reason to say no. In fact, I was quite happy to offload some of them so I handed her a stack.

"Cool!" she exclaimed, with a big smile on her face. "Thanks, Tilly! I'm going to Janus tonight… I bet loads of people there would love to come to this!"

I almost flinched when she said that word.

Janus.

I went there once, but it wasn't a pleasant memory. It was not a place I would ever return to.

After four more days of school, Saturday finally came.

I packed that Valium and the bottle of whiskey into my bag and left the house. My grandmother was at some WI event that day, so I didn't get a chance to say goodbye. Which was a little sad, but possibly a blessing; if I had been too emotional about it when I left that morning it might have aroused suspicion.

I felt wistful when I stepped out of that house and shut the door behind me that last time. When I was dropped off there by social services all those years ago, traumatised and newly bereaved, my grandmother had no other choice than to take me in. She was the only relative I had left. I felt like a guest. Not even a particularly welcome once. We were two very different people. We never really understood each other, but we learnt to respect each other, over time.

It was surprising, realising that I had come to finally think of that place as home.

I made my way towards town. The plan was to turn up to the protest, show my face – maybe even see some of my friends one last time – and then, while everyone was distracted by the post-rally-high, I was going to make my way to that aqueduct.

When I reached the meeting point I was truly astounded by the number of people I found there. I had not been to any Taxus Baccata events for a while. It was surprising seeing how much the movement had grown during my absence.

I spotted Jack. He was standing several dozen feet away, with Parmella, Kev, Namda, Pikel, and Tristan. A part of me was tempted to attempt to squeeze through the crowd to greet them, but I thought better of it. I had not seen them for such a long time it might have been awkward. Or, even worse, they might be so warm to me I would start to have second thoughts. I didn't want that. I had worked a lot of courage to build up to this day. I didn't want to falter.

"Hey Tilly!" a voice called.

I turned my eyes away from Jack and saw it was Amy. She was with Harriet and several other girls.

I had never seen Amy and Harriet outside of school before. They looked almost identical in their matching black corsets and purple tights. The only real difference was that Amy had spiked bracelets around her wrists, whereas Harriet was wearing a necklace with some kind of faux-tribal symbol.

"Tilly's the one I was telling you about," Amy said, turning to the gang of girls behind her. They were also dressed very similarly to her and Harriet, but I didn't recognise any of them so I guessed they must be from different schools. "She's part of Taxus Baccata!"

I heard a few 'ooooos' and 'ahhhs', and then Amy wrapped her arms around me. In a fashion which made it seem we were old friends and far more familiar with each other than we actually were, and she did it with a grace which gave me the impression *she* felt I should be honoured by that gesture.

"Come!" she said, grabbing my hand. "The march starts soon!"

She began to pull me towards the crowd. I wasn't sure I liked the vibe I was getting from Amy and her friends, but I didn't really have any particular reason to object. I guess it was good to get some distance from Jack.

Amy eventually let go of my hand a few minutes later when she spotted a group of teenage boys she knew. She ran over, squealing as she embraced every single of one of them like they were her favourite person in the world. It was during one of these – slightly empty – interactions that I caught a familiar face in the corner of my eye, and my heart lurched inside my chest.

It was Ian.

He was amongst the crowd, and there was something about that which I found acutely suspicious. I am not completely sure why – maybe it was the way he was casting his eyes around, almost as if he was sizing up the people around him, as he mingled among them – or, possibly, it was because I just *knew,* from the brief time I had spent with him, that he was not a man of conscience, and definitely not the sort to concern himself with societal issues.

So just what was he *doing* here?

His eyes wandered in my direction, so I quickly turned my back to him and walked away, praying he didn't see me. Amy and Harriet certainly didn't notice my departure. They were too busy chatting to those boys. I was far from their minds.

I found myself amidst a different crowd of people. Strangers.

And it was that moment the rally started. I had no other choice but to march amongst them. Blend in.

I eventually dared to turn my eyes back to look for Ian and, to my horror, I found him talking to Amy and Harriet.

Get away from him, I thought. *He's bad news.*

I was now faced with a moral dilemma. Neither of those girls were people I thought of as close friends or anything, but I was still concerned for them. I felt like I should warn them – tell them to stay well clear of him – but the idea of exposing myself in the process, and encountering that man again, terrified me.

As I was battling with my conscience, more of Amy and Harriet's friends began to gather around Ian. He was making a speech, and it seemed to be drawing attention from the people around him. I didn't catch any of the words. Loads of the people around me were shouting political chants, so it was all lost in the clamour of noise.

When Ian had finished making his speech, he then turned and walked towards a stall on the side of the street – it was one of those little huts which sold newspapers and snacks to people on the go – and some of the youngsters who had just spent the last few minutes listening to him followed. They marched up to the stall and began helping themselves to large handfuls of the merchandise. The seller got up from his seat and yelled an objection but they ran away, laughing. Ian grabbed the man by his collar and threw him to the ground.

By this point, people around me began to notice something was amiss. They stopped and stared at the commotion as the youngsters – Ian's minions – began looting the high street. They ran into the shops in packs and emerged a few moments later holding stolen goods to their chests. I saw Amy and Harriet among them; Amy was carrying a shiny new guitar, and Harriet a large black speaker. They laughed to each other as they fled.

I turned my eyes back to Ian and caught him in the action of throwing a bottle at the wall of police which had formed a blockade in the road ahead of us. I didn't get a clear enough view to see if anyone got hurt, but I heard it smash and a woman screamed.

People were panicking now. The havoc was rapidly escalating and many were trying to escape, but in every direction they tried to run they came across blockades. Some of them became angry and tried to fight their way through but they were bludgeoned by batons. No one knew where to go or what to do.

And, among all the mayhem, was Ian. Standing there with a triumphant smile on his face.

That was the moment I realised what had just occurred here.

He had been sent here by someone. To rile the crowd. To incite a riot. To cause chaos.

I had heard rumours that such things happened sometimes during demonstrations, but I had never, until that moment, thought it more than a conspiracy. The sort of ideas people like Kev came out with when they were waffling during the early hours of the morning. I had never thought I would actually see it with my own eyes.

I stared at Ian as the gravity of that revelation struck me. I couldn't help but feel like I was partly responsible. Because I knew him. Because many of the youngsters he managed to beguile had been invited by Amy.

He then turned his head and his eyes met mine. I was too stupefied by the shock of it all to realise he was staring at me at first but, when I did, a cold, terrible feeling crept down my spine.

He came for me. I tried to run but I wasn't fast enough. He grabbed me by the back of my neck and lifted me from the ground.

I fought him, but it was no use. I was a girl and he was a full-grown man. He was so much bigger and stronger than me. I screamed for help but there was so much chaos nobody seemed to hear. I even found myself calling Jack's name, for some reason. Which was stupid. He was too far away to hear me.

Ian dragged me towards the barricade. Strange – why was he attempting a kidnapping before the very eyes of the police? – but then something even weirder happened. He flashed them some kind of ID and they let him through.

I guess it wasn't all that surprising. It wasn't the first time in my life authority had catastrophically failed me.

"Get in!" he growled, pushing me through the doorway of his car so roughly I bashed my shin on the way in. I yelped but he warned me to be quiet and cast his eyes around us to make sure no one had heard.

There was no one there. I could hear an uproarious clamour from the protest going on but it was quite distant now. Everyone was distracted.

He then slammed the door and made his way around to the other side of the car to get into the driver's seat.

As soon as he had sat himself down next to me, I heard the central-locking system engage and it was followed by a heavy silence.

I began to cry.

"Shut the fuck up!" he yelled but I couldn't stop. Hot tears poured from my eyes uncontrollably.

A few moments later I felt something cold pressed against the side of my temple and I opened my wet, blurry eyes, and saw it was a gun. A shiny black one. I had never seen one in real life before, and my entire body froze. He had his finger on the trigger.

"Now this is what's going to happen," he said. "I am going to drive, and you are going to stay quiet and not move a single fucking muscle. If I catch you doing *anything* funny, I will shoot you. Do you hear me? And stop crying too, it looks suspicious."

I found myself laughing. Hysterically. He frowned, and I felt a peculiar sense of power in that because it was clearly not the reaction he was expecting, and it seemed to put him on edge.

"What the fuck is wrong with you?" he asked.

"Do it!" I exclaimed, turning to him and pressing the barrel to the centre of my forehead. "Go on! You'll be doing me a favour anyway. Do you have any idea what I was planning to do today?"

He stared at me for a long time.

And then he drew the gun away from my head and directed the barrel to my belly.

"Do you know how long it would take you to die if I pumped three bullets into your bowels?" he asked. "I have heard it is a very slow way to go. And painful. Especially if I dump you somewhere afterwards where no one will hear you scream."

The blood drained from my face, and a few moments later I found myself nodding. Agreeing to do anything he said. I don't know what the hell I was thinking that moment. Maybe I was in such a state of shock I had become compliant.

Or possibly it was because, even though I wanted to die, there was something else I wanted even more now.

I wanted it to be on *my* terms. Not his.

I wanted it to be by anyone other than him.

He drove and I just sat there. The city passed in a blur. I wasn't even watching. My eyes were open but I wasn't seeing. I wasn't even *thinking*. I just stared into space. He kept muttering to himself. I didn't catch many of the words apart from the odd curse.

Eventually I realised that our surroundings had turned green and the car drew to an abrupt halt.

We were in a field.

"Fuck!" he then exclaimed, kicking the inside of the car

and slamming his fists upon the steering wheel. Like he had been holding all that rage within and was finally letting go.

"Did you tell anyone about me?" he then asked.

"No," I shook my head. "Of course not!"

He stared at me suspiciously.

"Just let me go," I found myself saying. Against my will my voice came out all croaky. "I won't tell anyone. I promise!"

"No!" he shook his head. "You will! I know you will!"

I said nothing. Probably because it was true. At this moment in time I was so terrified I would say pretty much anything to get myself out of this situation but, once free, I would tell someone eventually.

"I can't let you go. You know too much. Shit!" he kicked the inside of the car again. "Shit, shit, shit!" he then looked at me and his eyes widened. "Wait… where is your phone?"

"In my pocket…" I whispered.

"Give it to me."

I handed it over.

He took it and then got out of the car. "Wait here!" he said. "And don't fucking *do* anything. If you move I'll know about it because I am going to turn the alarm on and you'll set it off."

He then slammed the door shut and engaged the central locking system again. I sat back and watched as he walked away, pulling out a mobile phone from his pocket and placing it to his ear.

"Hello?" he said a few moments later. "Mike! I need your help! It's all gone fucking wrong… No… yeah, everything went to plan, I did exactly what you wanted… but there's this girl… she's in my car…" a longer pause. "No, of course I didn't tell her my real name, but she's got my fucking phone number and she knows where I have been staying, that's enough! She could blow the whole fucking thing."

He began pacing up and down. "No!" he then yelled. "Listen. You need to fucking help me… No, I am not going to do *that*… if you want to do that, you can do it your-fucking-self…"

He then glanced at me and our eyes met. His expression went angry. He had just realised I could hear everything he was saying. "Fuck sake! The bitch is listening even now! Hold on a moment…"

He walked away, out of earshot, and then began to talk again.

They carried on arguing for a few more minutes, and then he hung up and let out a series of curses.

I ended up being sat in that car for what seemed like hours, but I had no real way of knowing the time.

Ian smoked a few cigarettes and made a few more phone calls. A lot of the time he just scowled at me.

Later on, another car drove into the field. It was black and the windows were tinted, so I never saw who was inside – which I guess was the whole point.

Ian walked over and spoke to the driver for a while. After a few minutes he then made his way to the boot, opened it, and lifted out a large suitcase.

The car then drove off, and Ian walked back to me.

"We're going," he said, opening the door and tossing the suitcase onto the back seat.

He drove us to some place on the outskirts of the city. It was one of those parks for people on holiday; a series of bungalows all centred around a rather characterless courtyard. The carpark was empty – which I guess was the exact reason he had chosen this place. It was out of season. Nobody was there.

He pointed the gun at me and ordered me to get out of the car. I complied. I had no will left to argue anymore.

"Walk," he said, grabbing the suitcase. "It's number seventeen."

I led the way and he followed, the suitcase in one hand, the gun in the other. He didn't have the barrel pointed to my head – he already knew I wasn't too bothered about being given a quick and painless end – but at my back.

When I reached the right door, I stepped aside and there was a brief moment of awkwardness when he hesitated over how to proceed – and it became obvious that he wasn't used to this sort of thing. He was improvising. Possibly out of his depth. I felt a bit of strength in that.

He eventually, after some consideration, dropped the suitcase and, while keeping the gun pointed at me, reached into his pocket for a set of keys (were his hands really shaking, or was that just my imagination?). He then fumbled with the lock for a while – it seemed to be a little tricky – and then, during a moment of rage, he swore and dropped the keyset.

"You do it!" he then growled, taking a step back.

I bent down, picked up the key, and inserted it into the lock. It was, admittedly, a little rusted and fiddly, but I eventually managed to open it.

He then ordered me to step inside.

As soon as we had both cleared the threshold, he slammed the door shut and locked it again.

"Sit," he said, indicating the sofa in the middle of the room.

I did so and placed my hands on my lap. It was during that moment I became aware of just how quiet it was in this place. Gone was the drone of traffic and all that other urban clamour you never quite hear, but always notice when it is missing. We were quite far away from the centre of the city now.

Screaming was not likely to get me out of this situation.

Ian then began to take a look around, checking all the doors and windows. "That's handy," he said out loud, making it clear I was meant to hear him. "The windows all have locks…" he narrated, as he removed all the keys and put them in his pocket. He then went to the kitchen and began checking the drawers. One of the knives was a little sharp for his liking, so he removed it.

He then went to examine the bedroom and bathroom. He kept the doors open as he did so though, and never tore his eyes away from me for more than a few seconds.

Eventually he returned to the living room and sat himself down on the other chair. There was a long silence.

"There is an aqueduct on the outskirts of the city…" I said.

He frowned at me.

"It's on the other side," I carried on, softly. "It's called Tinkinstone. It was part of the canal system which linked the city to the–"

"What the fuck are you on about?" he asked, irritably.

I looked at him. "It was where I was going to walk to today… after the protest."

He turned away – breaking eye contact – and shifted uncomfortably.

"You could drive me there, if you want to," I said. "Just drop me off, and I will do it. You can even watch if you like. Just to make sure I go through with it. You can then drive away and pretend you never even knew me. Problem solved. For both of us."

"How do I know you never told anyone about me?" he asked, after a few moments of silence. I could tell he was considering it though. "You might have told one of your friends where you met me, or given them my phone number. If you die there will be an investigation."

"I didn't," I said. "Honestly."

He stared at me for a long time. "I'm not sure I can take that chance," he eventually said.

"So what *are* you going to do with me?" I challenged. "Keep me here for the rest of my life? Someone will find us eventually. And anyway, if I *did* give your details to someone – which I haven't – there will be an investigation when it's noticed I am missing anyway."

It took him a while to respond. It was clear that, until this moment, he had been acting on impulse alone. He had not thought this through. He didn't have a plan.

"My friend is looking into it. He will handle it all and decide what to do."

"Oh, you mean *Mike*," I said.

He gasped. "How did you?"

"You said his name when you rang him earlier," I said flatly. I then found myself chuckling at his reaction – where did *that* unexpected boldness come from? "Don't worry, there isn't much I could do with just that. There are plenty of 'Mikes' in the world."

"You're too clever for your own good," he muttered. He then reached for the remote. "That is why I can't trust that you never told anyone about me."

He switched the TV on.

It was that moment I saw Jack's face on the screen.

And I was so shocked by it I wasn't able to control my reaction. I gasped openly.

"You know him?" Ian asked, as the newsreader delivered the story.

"New evidence has linked a young man to the bombing,"

she said. “Police are looking for this suspect. If seen, please call this number…”

Ian didn’t like that I had a connection to Jack at all. I played it down, but I don’t think it made much difference. He knew now that I was connected to a key figure in Taxus Baccata. One who was considered dangerous.

The headlines which followed were all about the protest. It seemed that ours was not the only city where the demonstration against the National Conciliation Act had escalated to riots and looting. It made me wonder if Ian was not the only one who had been sent by some shady organisation to stir trouble. I knew better than to ask him.

And then, later that evening, a new headline was announced.

“In an unexpected turn, The National Conciliation Act has been passed by Westminster…”

For the rest of that night most of the national news reporters were fixated upon the passing of the National Conciliation Act. Dozens of people were interviewed, and the fact that the final vote came very close to a tie was mentioned over and over again. Many of the commentators speculated that some MPs were swayed at the last minute in light of the riots which occurred that day. The newly discovered evidence linking Taxus Baccata to the bombing which killed the two farm workers was thought to have played a part too.

And, as I watched it all unfold, it only reinforced my conviction that it was a good thing I was probably not going to be alive much longer.

This world had become that little bit more depressing. A little less full of hope. The future was bleak.

I didn’t believe for a moment that Jack had anything to do with that bombing. True, it was a battery farm, and he, like myself, held some very firm views when it came to animal cruelty, but I could never imagine he would do something as extreme as that.

I was a little more jaded about the world now. I now knew that people like Ian and the men who pulled their strings existed. It didn’t seem that farfetched to me to imagine that evidence could somehow be falsified to suit political motivations too.

I dozed off eventually. I only realised I had fallen asleep when I woke up in the middle of the night to Ian tying a rope around my wrists and binding them together behind my back. He wanted to go to sleep too, I guess, so he was simply making sure I would not cause any trouble during the night.

Not that I would have anyway. I possessed neither the will nor compulsion. I didn't even make any objections as he bound me. I just lay there, still and corpselike.

In many ways, I was already dead.

When I woke the next morning, still lying on the couch, I heard Ian's voice from the bedroom. He was on the phone again, arguing with Mike.

"She says she wants to die anyway..." he said. "So how about you... No... No! *You* do it! You're the one in charge. It's *your* mess. *You* sort it out..." there was a long pause then. "No, it's not my fault. You're the one who...."

I understood then. Ian *wanted* me to die – it would be much easier for him if I simply disappeared – but he didn't have the stomach to do it himself, and he didn't want to clear up either, so he was enlisting his superior. Passing the buck.

It also made me realise how hopelessly out of his depth he was. I felt a little empowered by that.

But my apathy was stronger. I just wanted it all to end.

Eventually he finished on the phone. There didn't seem to be any conclusion reached by the end of their exchange.

Just before Ian returned to the living room again, I closed my eyes and pretended to be asleep so that he didn't know I had heard him.

I experienced something very strange the second day.

Ian popped out for a while – leaving me tied up on the couch – and he returned a while later with food. Neither knowing, nor particularly caring I was vegetarian, he handed me a sandwich which was filled with ham. I couldn't bring myself to eat it, but I did gobble down the bag full of greasy chips he bought me.

Afterwards, he lit up a cigarette, and then, a few moments

later, as he breathed out a cloud of smoke, he looked at me from the corner of his eye.

He then picked up the packet again, flipped it open, and offered me one.

And, to my utter dismay, I found myself feeling something for him I never expected.

Gratitude.

It was just a twinge. It certainly had no bearing upon the anger, hatred, and all of those other emotions I felt for him.

And I knew enough rudimentary psychology to be aware that I was just experiencing my first act of positive reinforcement, and merely mistaking lack of abuse for kindness.

He didn't *have* to offer me a cigarette. He was *choosing* to.

I realised that, in time, I could even start to experience symptoms indicative of Stockholm Syndrome.

I was briefly tempted to turn it down when that thought came to me.

Fuck it, I eventually decided, as I took one and lit up.

It was later that afternoon that everything changed.

We were watching the news – that was what we usually did between Ian pacing up and down the room and making phone calls to Mike – and they had just switched to regional headlines when my face came up on the screen.

"Police are searching for a young girl..."

It wasn't until that moment that the gravity of the situation truly struck me and I began to experience feelings of guilt.

I thought about my grandmother. And my friends. All of them were probably out of their minds worrying about me.

I mean, I know it was hardly my fault I had been kidnapped… but still, if I wasn't here with Ian right now I would probably be dead. That was even worse. If there was a such a thing as parallel universes there was probably one where that very moment my grandmother was being driven to a morgue to identify my body. Or Faye had just received a phone call and been told I had taken my own life. That Jack was… well, I didn't have a clue where Jack was. In this universe, or any other.

It was that moment I began to feel some responsibility to

those around me.

I realised that, by ending my life, I wouldn't truly be ending the pain, just transferring it to them.

It was that moment I began to have second thoughts…

But that moment of revelation was thrown by what came up on the screen next.

Ian's face.

"Tilly was last seen being taken away by this man, who we have yet to identify. He has been described as–"

It wasn't a very clear picture – it had obviously been captured from a street camera. *I* recognised him, but that was only because I already knew it was him. If I had not known I probably wouldn't have been able to identify him from it.

But it still freaked him out. He got up and kicked the table. Began to scream and shout, red-faced. For a moment, I thought he was going to hit me.

Ian spent much more time in the bedroom after that. He kept phoning Mike, and the topic of their conversations shifted from what to do with *me*, to what to do about himself. He begged Mike to find a way to get him out of the country, provide him with a new identity, or even just a better place for us to lay low for a while until it had blown over.

He was irritable the rest of the time. Every time we watched the news he paced up and down the room nervously. He forgot to feed me a few times, but I was too proud to bring it up. Over the course of just a couple of days we had slipped into a routine, but some of our habitual customs began to slip. He always remembered to tie me up before he left the apartment or went to sleep though. I always slept on the couch, and he slept on the bed.

There was one evening however when, shortly after retiring to his room, he opened the door and suggested I could join him in his bed if I wanted to.

Like it was some kind of casual afterthought.

I pretended to not hear him.

The idea that he thought I would even consider such a thing – after everything which had happened since that time we met up in the hotel – turned my stomach.

I didn't sleep well that night. From the moment he had

brought me here, there had always been the fear that he would rape me – and let's face it, if he wanted to it wouldn't have been difficult for him.

Luckily that was a line he never crossed.

He did always insist upon supervising my visits to the bathroom though. I hated those moments.

The television was always on, and I drifted in and out of consciousness to headlines. My dreams were erratic and disturbing. They mostly consisted of disjointed scenes from world events, intermingled with flashes of my friends, my grandmother, Ian, and some of the kids from my old school who made my childhood a living hell. My mother. One night, I kept hearing Faye calling my name. I never actually saw her face though. It felt like she was trying to reach out to me, but I was too far away. There was something very vivid about it.

On the fourth morning everything drew to a head. I woke up to him sitting on the other chair smoking a cigarette.

I knew something was up straight away because he had this strange look in his eyes.

He didn't say anything to me at first. He just stared at the TV.

"We're leaving today," he then said.

"Where?" I asked. I knew it was unlikely he would let me go.

"Mike has found a way to get me out of the country," he said.

Ian had long given up on referring to Mike as his 'friend' by now. He was well aware that I knew his name.

"And what about me?" I asked.

He lit up another cigarette.

"Mike said he will deal with you," he then replied.

Neither of us spoke after that. He couldn't even bring himself to look at me. It was like I was a ghost.

And I knew why.

Ian had probably not even asked Mike what he was going to do with me, but it was obvious he was going to dispose of me. I was too much of a risk to them. I knew too much.

Ian didn't want the responsibility. Letting Mike say he would 'deal with me', and not asking any questions was the easiest way for him to walk away from this without feeling too much guilt.

As far as he was concerned I was suicidal anyway. I had not told him about my change of heart. That I had begun to have second thoughts.

It was tragically ironic. When he first brought me here, I begged him to let me take my own life. Now the tables had turned. I wasn't sure I wanted to die anymore, but it seemed the choice had been taken away from me.

Ian left the apartment shortly after that. He said he needed more cigarettes, but I suspect he was just finding it difficult to be around me. He tied me up before he left though.

It was only after he had shut the door and locked it behind himself that I let myself cry.

I lay there for what felt like hours. I eventually stopped crying. The voices coming from the television were giving me a headache so I wriggled over to the other side of the couch where the remote was and turned it off.

I stared at the ceiling for a while, and then closed my eyes. It was the first time in quite a while that I had heard complete silence. I wasn't sure I liked it, it made my thoughts wander.

I thought about my friends. My grandmother. What Mike was going to do to me when he came. I think I must have drifted off for a while because at one point I opened my eyes and the light in the room had changed. It had become brighter.

And then the strangest thing happened to me. I heard a voice in my head.

Hold on, Tilly. Hold on... Just a bit longer...

I was startled. Just what was that?

We all sometimes have thoughts in our heads which express themselves as inner dialogues, but what I experienced at that moment was nothing like that. It was distinct. It had a persona. It was feminine, but forceful.

It almost reminded me of Ellen when she used to sing back in the days of Sunset Haze. It echoed around my consciousness and sent a shockwave through my body, imbuing me with a fresh burst of energy.

I sat up and began to wonder what exactly it was that I was

doing. Just lying there, waiting to die…

There must *something* I could do to try to get away.

I struggled against the binds but it was useless. In films when people do that they eventually create enough slack to free themselves, but either that just didn't work in real life or I wasn't so lucky. Ian had been thorough and done them up very tight.

I looked across the room to see if there were any sharp edges anywhere – something I could crawl over to and grind the ropes against to wear them away a little – but I couldn't see any.

I was just pondering other actions I could take when I heard a noise and turned my eyes to the window.

It was a squirrel. I almost jumped at the first sight of it. It hopped on the window pane and placed its paws upon the glass. Its little eyes looking right at me.

I realised then that it wasn't just any squirrel.

"Nuttles?" I said. It came out as a croak because my mouth was so dry. I hadn't spoken a single word for hours. "Is that–"

And then another face appeared. I gasped.

"*Jack!*" I yelled.

"Tilly?" he exclaimed, his voice came out all muffled because of the barrier between us.

I twisted around on the couch in an attempt to get closer to them, but I ended up falling to the floor with a graceless thud.

"Get back!" I heard him yell. "I'm going to break it!"

I wormed away from the window and then, a few moments later, I heard a loud crack followed by the sound of dozens of shards of glass shattering across the floor. Jack then hit the frame a few more times to clear the excess glass from the corners.

He then dropped the stick he had used and climbed into the room.

"Tilly!" he exclaimed, looking me up and down. "What the hell is going on? How did you get here?"

"How did you find me?" I asked.

"You go first," he said.

"Okay," I mumbled. "Just… get me out of these binds please."

He shuffled around me and I sat myself upright so he had

better access to the ropes around my wrists. "There's this man," I began to explain. "His name is Ian."

"Is he the one who took you during the protest?" Jack asked as he began untying the knots.

"How do you know about that?"

"I saw it," he said. "We tried to stop him but we couldn't get to you in time. Sorry…"

"It's okay," I said. "How did you find me anyway?"

"It was Naomi," he said. "She just came to my house – I didn't think anyone even knew where I live now, but somehow she found me! She told me to head in this direction and to take my 'nose' with me… which I guessed meant Nuttles. He's the one who found you really… he picked up your scent. Did you tell Naomi about Nuttles?"

I shook my head. "No, I didn't."

"Weird…" he muttered. "Anyway, that's not the only strange thing that's happened. Everyone's gone crazy. On my way here there were all these people running out of their houses and heading towards the centre of the city."

"Why?" I asked.

"I don't know," he said, I then felt the binds around my wrists loosen and he unravelled them. "I didn't have time to check. I came straight here."

"Thanks, Jack," I said as I stretched my arms out. He began to work on freeing my ankles.

"Where is he, anyway?" Jack asked, casting his eyes across the apartment.

"He went out. He said he needed cigarettes but he's been gone for a while."

"He didn't…" Jack then hesitated. He seemed a little embarrassed about the question he was about to ask. "Touch you… or anything. Did he?"

I shook my head.

Technically it wasn't a lie. Since the kidnapping Ian hadn't laid a finger upon me in… well, not in *that* way. All of that stuff happened before.

"So why did he take you?" Jack asked.

"He was sent to the protest by someone," I said. "I don't know who, but someone paid him to cause trouble. *He's* the one who caused the riot. And I knew him, so he–"

It was that moment we both heard the drone of a car engine and we both went silent.

"Shit," I whispered. My heart rate escalated and my entire body froze. "It's him! He's coming back! We've got to–"

"Don't worry," Jack said. "I'll sort this out."

He went over to the broken window and began to climb through it.

"Jack!" I exclaimed. "Don't! He's dangerous!"

He ignored me and leapt from the pane, landing on the grass outside.

I ran to catch him up, pulling myself up from the windowsill, carefully minding out for the remaining shards of glass around the edges as I crawled through. I then dropped, landing clumsily on the gravel – not on the grass like Jack did – and grazed my knees, but I ignored the pain and pulled myself to my feet. The car had just pulled into the driveway and Jack was striding towards it.

Jack was the sort of person who usually walked with a lazy slouch, but during that moment his every stride was channelled with purpose and his hands were balled up into fists, like every muscle in his body was tensed and ready for confrontation.

The car pulled to an abrupt halt and the door opened. Jack carried on marching.

"Jack!" I screamed, as I ran to catch up with him. "He's got a–"

I was too late. I knew from the moment the door opened that there was nothing I could do to stop what was about to happen.

Ian stepped out of the car with the gun in his hand and he pointed the barrel at Jack. He closed one of his eyes as he prepared to aim.

But then something truly unexpected happened.

A pair of birds appeared. They seemed to come from nowhere, but I guess they must have swooped down from the sky. I had been so fixated upon the scene playing out before me I had not seen them coming.

They darted in front of Ian's face in a flutter of black and white. He yelled out and thrashed the air around him blindly, but they dodged out of the reach of his swinging arms and came swooping back in. One of them raked its claws across his scalp and he screamed, falling, planting his face to the ground. He dropped the gun and used both arms to cover the back of his head.

Jack carried on calmly striding towards him and the birds took off, abandoning Ian and flapping away to land upon Jack's shoulders. Two magpies.

Ian finally dared to look up. He was bleeding from several scratches on his scalp but none of them appeared to be serious.

"*How*?!" he screamed. "*How* did you get them to do that?!"

Just then I heard a rustling behind me and turned around to witness three foxes leaping over the fence and sprinting towards us. They ran straight past me and gathered around Jack's feet.

"Don't worry, Tilly," Jack said. "They won't hurt you."

Jack then turned his focus back to Ian and narrowed his eyes.

"I specifically told them to avoid pecking you in the eyes, you know," Jack said, turning to one of the magpies on his shoulder and stroking the back of its head. It chirped. "I could be less kind if you force me to do so again."

"What the fuck are you?" Ian yelled.

"That is none of your concern," Jack said, coolly. "Now. This is what's going to happen. You're going to stay *there*. Do you hear me? Do *not* try to run away, or my three little friends here will have you."

Jack patted one of the foxes on the head and it bared its teeth, making a low growl.

"Now come, Tilly," Jack said, turning away from Ian and walking towards me. "We need to talk."

He placed his hand lightly on my shoulder and led me away. Meanwhile, the three foxes all slowly crept up towards Ian and made a little triangle around him. The birds took off and flew to one of the trees nearby.

"What should we do?" Jack said, keeping his voice low so that Ian couldn't hear us. "We should call the police really, but I'm a wanted man."

"I know," I said. "I saw it on the news… you didn't really have anything to do with the bombing, did you?"

Jack shook his head, but there was a peculiar expression on his face. It wasn't one which made he think he was lying exactly, but it made me almost certain that he knew *something* he wasn't telling me.

Phone Tristan.

I heard those words echo through my mind. It was that voice again. The one which called out to me earlier and gave me the strength to carry on.

He will know what to do.

"What's wrong?" Jack asked. He seemed to notice some kind of reaction in me.

"Nothing," I said, shaking my head "It's just–"

Time is running short! the voice screamed through my consciousness, more forcibly this time. *Do it!*

"Okay, this is going to sound crazy," I said. "But there's a voice in my head and it sounds a bit like Ellen. It's telling me we should ring Tristan."

Jack's eyes widened a little when I mentioned Ellen. That detail seemed to be enough to convince him.

"Where's your phone?" he asked.

"Ian smashed it up days ago," I said. "*He's* got one though."

"Oi!" Jack yelled, turning to Ian. "Give me your phone."

Ian opened his mouth to make an objection.

"*Now!*" Jack yelled. He then narrowed his eyes and the three foxes all stirred back into motion, their bodies' stiffening – as if they were preparing to pounce – and baring their teeth.

Ian complied, carefully reaching into the pocket in his jacket while keeping a wary eye on the fox in front of him. He then tossed the phone at Jack. He threw it so hard I suspect he was hoping it would land on the ground and break, but Jack caught it.

Jack then opened the phone and looked at me.

"Do you have Tristan's number?" he then asked.

"No…" I said. "Do you?"

"I have never even *owned* a phone!" he reminded me. "How would I–"

I then heard that voice again.

Tristan's number is; zero. Seven. Eight–

"Wait, Jack! Quick. She's telling me!" I exclaimed. "Give me the phone!"

He passed it over and I began to type the numbers into the touchscreen. I then pressed the 'call' icon and handed the phone back to Jack.

I guess we were about to find out if I was crazy or not.

"*Is* it Tristan?" I asked as Jack placed the phone to his ear.

"It's just ringing…" he said. "Wait a moment… Oh, hi," his voice changed then. "Is this Tristan? Yeah, it's me… Jack…"

It took a while for Jack to provide Tristan with enough details for them to figure out exactly where we were. He then hung up and sat down next to me.

"What happened to you, Tilly?" he eventually asked. "I haven't seen you for ages…"

"I could ask you the same thing," I said. "You're the one who moved house…"

"You could have found me if you tried," Jack said.

"I guess so…" I said. "But you could have found me too."

He ran a hand through his hair and sighed.

"That morning I found you outside Dinnusos…" he said. "I felt like it was all my fault… like it was *me* who did that to you… I guess I just thought I had been a bad influence and it was best you stayed away from me."

I actually laughed then, which was surprising. It wasn't a happy kind of laughter. It was dry. "Why do adults always blame themselves for the crazy shit teenagers get up to? I knew perfectly well what I was doing, Jack… Look… I've been going through some stuff recently and made some really bad choices… it's no one's fault but my own."

"What kind of stuff?" he asked, looking at me.

I looked down at the ground.

"Lots of things."

I wasn't quite ready to tell anyone what I had been planning to do after the protest that day. I was too ashamed.

"I have feelings for you…" I eventually said.

It felt strange saying it out loud. Especially to Jack himself. I guess I had always figured I would tell Faye first.

Jack stared at the ground with a look in his eyes which was hard to read. He was definitely surprised.

"I was finding it really hard to be around you," I said. "I was worried that you knew, or you would find out and–"

"Why would that worry you?" he asked.

I swallowed a lump in my throat. "I was ashamed… I mean, you know about my past, don't you? The way I was born."

"Tilly," he said, shuffling around so that he was facing me. "I care about you more than you will ever know… but…"

He hesitated. There is always a 'but' during a conversation like this, isn't there?

"I don't know…" he eventually carried on. "I guess I have never even *looked* at you in that way… but not for the reason you think… it's not because of… well… you know," there was a moment of awkwardness then and we broke eye contact. "If I *had* those feelings for you, then I don't think that would matter to me, because I'm not like that. Tilly, the reason I've never looked at you that way is because you're too young and, more importantly, I *respect* you. Don't scowl at me… I know you're very mature for your age and you grew up faster than most people, but that doesn't change the fact that you still *look* very young. Your innocence was ripped away because of the things which happened to you when you were a child, but I want you to keep whatever is left of that innocence for as long as you can because, trust me on this, Tilly, young people spend so much time wanting to grow up, but once you're there, you will look back and want to be young again."

I knew that very well. If I could go back, there were a lot of things I would have done different recently.

I was just about to reply when I noticed movement in the corner of my eye and turned to it.

A group of figures had just stepped out from the trees on other side of the green, and they were walking towards us.

"Jack…" I said, pointing.

We both got up to meet them. There were seven, in all. I soon recognised the one in the middle as Jardair, and the other six were the members of his inner circle. The ones who had always been standing around that table with him in Jack's old house, plotting and scheming. They marched towards us. All of them had messy hair and were dressed in clothes which were tattered and shabby, and yet, they all seemed to possess this unearthly grace which elevated them from ordinary people.

Jack narrowed his eyes at his father.

“So now you decide to show up,” Jack said.

“We never actually left,” Jardair said, crossing his arms over his chest and smiling. “We just laid low for a while.”

“That’s convenient,” Jack said.

“We will discuss that later,” Jardair said. “In the meantime, I believe you have friends arriving here soon and I’m not sure I’m comfortable with the idea of them all witnessing this little spectacle...” he gestured to the group of foxes sitting around Ian. “Can you tell your little companions to make themselves scarce, please? I believe there are enough of us here to keep an eye on that man now.”

Jack complied, turning to the foxes and staring at them. Some kind of communication occurred then. Jack didn’t say anything out loud, but I noticed something in his eyes. It was that same look he always had on his face when he communicated with Nuttles.

One of Jardair’s friends picked up the gun from the grass, where Ian had discarded it, and then pointed the barrel at him.

“You’re going to have to set me free! Or I will tell everyone your secret. I swear!” Ian exclaimed, pointing a finger at Jack. “I know he’s a freak!”

“He’s my son,” Jardair said, coolly. He smiled at Ian. “We’re all freaks. And you’re not going to say *anything*, because you know that no one will believe you anyway. As far as we are concerned, nothing unusual happened here today. *I* certainly didn’t see anything, did you?” he asked, turning to his friends beside him. They all smiled shrewdly and shook their heads. “What about you, Tilly?” Jardair then turned to me. “Did you witness anything out of the ordinary?”

I shook my head. “No,” I said. “When Jack came and rescued me, he was really brave. Ian had a gun and he tried to shoot Jack, but he didn’t realise he still had the safety on so nothing happened… he obviously didn’t really know what he was doing. Jack tackled him to the ground.”

Ian scowled at me, but I didn’t care. He didn’t scare me anymore.

"That is a very plausible story," Jardair said, winking at me.

"But how is *my* involvement going to work?" Jack asked. "The police are after me thanks to you."

"You obviously haven't heard the news," Jardair said, turning to his son. "Is there a television in any of these rooms? There is something you two need to see…"

"Yes, there is," I said. "But get Ian to give you his key. I'm not climbing through that bloody window again."

When we turned the television on the first thing we saw was a scene from our town. There was a massive congregation taking place in the streets. There were thousands of them and the mood seemed quite peaceful and calm – nothing like those riots which occurred just under a week ago.

And in the centre of it all, I saw Patrick. He was playing his violin. Ellen was there too. And Faye. They were all smiling.

The news reporter delivered further details as footage of similar scenes in other cities came up on the screen. Apparently ours was not the only city where a mass protest in defiance of The National Conciliation Act had sprung up, but it had been the first and it started a shockwave. Now people were taking to the streets all over the country.

"There have been reports from several police forces that officers are defying orders and refusing to attempt to bring an end to this newly-illegal behaviour," she said.

She then transitioned to a new story. Photos of two men's faces came up on the screen. "In other breaking news, two men, Andrew Jones and David Yew – both of whom were believed to have died in the attack which occurred in Willowbank Farm just over eight weeks ago – have now both been found alive. They were discovered by a reporter from another network who tracked them down at a location where – it is believed – they have been in hiding since the incident happened. Although exactly *why* their deaths were falsely declared remains a mystery, there is wide speculation that–"

I turned to Jack and smiled. "That's great! I *knew* there was something suspicious about that whole thing."

Jack didn't say anything, he just stared at the screen.

"Did you… have anything to do with the bombing?" I

asked, noticing something in his expression.

"No," he shook his head. "*I* didn't. But my father did… he said he made sure that the building was evacuated so no one was killed though. I guess he was telling the truth that time."

I didn't know how to feel about that. I had always liked Jardair, but that revelation made me a little uneasy.

My attention was then drawn to the television again. The reporter had just abruptly moved on to a new announcement. "We have also just received confirmation that a whistle-blower – a member of the forensic team involved in the investigation into the bombing – has now come forward with accusations that members of her team falsified the evidence which linked the attack to Taxus Baccata. We will give further details of this as and when they come through."

"See…" a voice behind us then said.

Jack and I both turned around. It was Jardair in the doorway. He stepped into the room and one of his cadres followed him. Kendra, her name was. She was the one who always had that messy hair with twigs and leaves caught in it. "Everything happened as it was supposed to."

"What do you mean?" Jack asked.

"We knew that this would happen, and that is why we didn't interfere over the last few days," Jardair said. He gestured to the witchy-looking lady beside him. "Kendra foretold it. Soon, the National Conciliation Act will be repealed. People now know that they were manipulated."

"Who was behind it all though?" I asked. "Who was Ian working for? Was it the same people who did all those other things?"

Jardair shrugged. "I suspect they will have covered their tracks well and not even Ian himself will truly know who he's been working for. They'll never quite get to the bottom of it. But the important thing is, Ian *will* be arrested, and he will confess to *his* part of the conspiracy. It will become known as one of the biggest scandals this country has ever known and people will remember. Everyone will become much more sceptical and distrusting of the ruling classes after this, and that is something, I think we can all agree, this country damn well needs."

"So let me get this straight," Jack said, his voice went

dangerously low then. It was almost a growl, and he fixed his father with a steely glare. “You could have saved Tilly at any point over the last few days, but you *left* her here as part of your plan?”

“Kendra knew that no harm would come to her,” Jardair said, gesturing to me. “Look, see! She’s fine!”

“I am not talking about *physical* harm!” Jack exclaimed. “What about what this has done to her *mind*? Have you got any idea what she has been through, while you’ve been hiding out in the woods plotting your little schemes? You *can’t* treat people like that!”

Jack clenched his fists and, for a moment, I thought he was going to hit his father.

I couldn’t let that happen.

“Jack!” I said, stepping between them and putting my hand on his chest. “It’s okay… If what they say is true – if what happened to me means that The National Conciliation Act will be repealed – then I don’t mind. I’m just one person. This is something much bigger than me. Than all of us… Please, Jack. Don’t make any more trouble over this. I just want it all to be over.”

Jack drew a deep breath and then nodded reluctantly. He looked at his father though and, even though his body language was less tense, his eyes were still filled with loathing. “I will never forgive you,” he said. “I want you out of my life. For good this time.”

Jardair chuckled softly. “Oh, we’ll meet again. Trust me.”

A few minutes later a shiny red car pulled up into the driveway and when it stopped, Tristan, Pikel, Kev, and a young woman I had never met before stepped out.

“We got here as soon as we could. Pandora drove us,” Tristan said, gesturing to the woman beside him. She had dark hair and a gentle face. She smiled at me. “Are you okay?” she asked, looking me up and down. I didn’t know her, but the fact that she was already being so kind made me warm to her instantly. She embraced me. It was nice to have another woman around during a moment like this. Even if I didn’t know her.

“So is this the little cunt then?” Pikel said once the

greetings were over. He looked over at Ian who was still sitting on the grass.

Jardair's friend – the one who was in possession of the gun – nodded. He then handed the weapon to Pikel. "Here. You can take charge of this now. Keep an eye on him."

"Why did he take you, Tilly?" Tristan asked me.

I told them the story of how he had been sent to the protest to incite the riot.

"But how was it that you knew him in the first place?" Pandora asked, narrowing her eyes.

I began to explain, but I stammered and heat rose into my cheeks. I turned my eyes to my feet.

That time Jack had carried me Faye's house was about to become the second most shameful moment of my life.

Everyone was staring at me. I couldn't even look at them.

When I eventually summoned enough grit to explain, there was an awful silence.

But it only lasted for a few moments.

"You bastard!" Jack screamed. He charged at Ian with a murderous look in his eyes that I hope I will never see again.

Luckily Jardair managed to step in. It took three of them in all to restrain Jack and calm him down, and I suspect that if they had not Jack would have killed him.

"I think it is time we called the police…" Pandora said in a rather composed manner which asserted some calm control over the situation.

"I'll handle that," Tristan said, reaching into his pocket for his phone. "I know just the right person."

Once the phone call was over Jardair spoke.

"Well, now that the police are on their way I'm afraid that it is only sensible that the seven of us leave," he said.

"Where are you going?" Kev asked.

"Our work in this town is done," Jardair said.

"But what about the movement?" Pikel asked. "What about Taxus Baccata?"

"Oh, it isn't over," Jardair said. "Don't worry. It has barely even begun. We need to plant more seeds. There is plenty of work to be done. We will leave someone in charge. In fact, we have someone in mind for the role and she is here this very moment."

Everyone turned their eyes to Kendra, but she shook her head.

"No," she cackled. "It is not me. *My* place is by Jardair's side," she patted his shoulder. "He would be hopeless without me… No," she said, her emerald eyes went to Pandora. "It is you, young lady."

Pandora's eyes widened as everyone's focus switched from Kendra to her.

At first she just stared at Jardair and Kendra.

"It was foretold," Kendra said. "You *know* it is your calling."

Pandora cleared her throat. "I have some terms," she then said.

"I am willing to negotiate," Jardair smiled.

"I want to run it under a different name," Pandora said. "No offence, but Taxus Baccata has acquired a somewhat muddied reputation recently."

"Done," Jardair said. "Kendra already predicted that you would go for a more ancillary approach, but I still want you to cooperate with the movement and welcome all of its current members."

Pandora nodded. "There will always be links, but I think it is time for fresh methods. I will work hard for you, but I need to support myself. I want a salary."

"I suspect I won't be able to pay you quite as much as your former job did…" Jardair warned.

"I know," Pandora nodded. "That's fine. I simply want my mortgage paid and enough money to feed and clothe myself. Oh, and a holiday once a year. For two weeks. Somewhere nice."

"Agreed."

"I also want a new headquarters," Pandora said. "A nice place, not one of those decrepit Yesterville dumps. It's time the movement acquired some respectability… I want enough space in it so that I can help the needy too – I have always wanted to run some kind of refuge – I think bringing about change is more than just rebellion, it is about helping the community."

"A little bit flowery, but okay. Done!" Jardair said. "I have resources, but they are *not* unlimited. I will be in contact with you soon."

"I'll give you my phone number," Pandora said, reaching into her handbag and retrieving a card from her wallet. "I–"

"Don't worry about that," Jardair said, waving his hand dismissively. "I will find you… Look, sorry, but I think it is best we skedaddle before the sirens come. Goodbye."

He waved at us and began to walk away. His six friends followed, with impish expressions on their faces as they waved goodbye. They gracefully walked towards the edge of the forest on the other side of the field and then they passed through, into the trees.

I won't go into too much detail about what happened after the cops came. Suffice to say, I spent a lot of time over the days which followed going back and forth to the station to give statements and answer questions. I was physically examined too and, once they discovered I had been self-harming, I confessed to having suicidal thoughts. I was referred to weekly visits to a psychiatrist. That was probably a good thing. I needed it.

I thought my grandmother would give me hell when she found out about it all – especially Ian – but she was surprisingly supportive. She just seemed happy to see me alive. When we were first reunited she had tears in her eyes and she wouldn't let go of me.

I was grounded though. For a very long time.

But it wasn't too bad. It was coming up to my exams anyway and I had a lot of catching up to do. I focussed upon finishing school.

Friends were allowed to come visit me. Faye came several times a week. When she wasn't busy with band practice. I thought she would hate me after the way I had treated her over the last few months but the moment we saw each other, we embraced, and all was forgiven. Steve came to visit a few times too. And Jack, but he only came once because my grandmother didn't particularly like the look of him.

One afternoon Naomi came to see me.

"Hi Tilly," she said, when I answered the door.

I was surprised to see her. The two of us had never spent any time alone before. Whenever we had seen each other in the past it has always been in the presence of Faye.

It wasn't that we hated each other or anything. I didn't really *know* her.

I guess it was my fault we had never bonded. I had always resented her a little since she came into Faye's life because I didn't get to see as much of my closest friend anymore.

I knew now that it wasn't Naomi's fault. Or even Faye's. It was just life. It was part of getting older.

"Hello Naomi," I said. "Would you like to come in?"

"Yes, please," she said, stepping inside.

When I took her up to my bedroom she cast her eyes around the place and then decided to pull the chair away from my desk and sit herself down.

"There's something I would like to do for you," she said.

"What is it?" I replied, seating myself on the end of my bed so that we were face to face.

"It is something you might find a little… sensitive…" she said. "But Faye told me about your–"

"Yes," I said flatly. "I was born a boy…"

"No," Naomi shook her head. "It's not about that. It's…"

She placed her hand upon my arm. "Your scars," she then said, looking up at my face again. "Can I see them?"

I cringed. I was wearing long sleeves, as was usual these days. I wasn't harming anymore but I was beginning to regret the state that phase had left my arm in.

"I think I might be able to get rid of them…" she said. "I would like to try something."

"Really?" I whispered. It sounded too good to be true. "How?"

She raised an eyebrow. "You know I'm a witch, right?"

"Oh…" I said. "Of course…"

I was expecting some elaborate ritual, but it was surprisingly quick. She brought out a phial of oil which smelt very musky and massaged it all over my arm. It was a little painful – some of them were still healing – but I winced and bit back the pain.

Naomi then closed her eyes, and the most peculiar thing happened. Maybe it was just psychosomatic, but I felt a tingling sensation emanating from her fingers. She muttered to herself – not loud enough for me to hear any of the words – but I *did* feel something during that moment. It was in the air around us, like a change in the wind.

She traced her finger across my wrist, stirring an array of even more peculiar sensations. I could feel this energy coursing through my entire arm. I closed my eyes.

"It's done," she then said.

I opened my eyes again and looked at my wrist. The scars were still there.

"Give it a week or so," she said. "It won't be instant, but I think they will heal."

"Okay…" I said. I was a bit sceptical, but I had witnessed all manner of the bizarre recently and would keep an open mind.

"That spell will only work once," she then said, looking me in the eyes.

"Why?" I asked.

She shrugged. "I don't know… maybe it is just the universe's way of saying 'don't take the piss'."

She then drew back her own sleeve and pointed at three little white lines on her forearm. "Trust me…" she said. "I know it won't work a second time…"

That surprised me. Naomi always seemed so composed and confident. I couldn't imagine her doing anything like that.

"I wasn't always as stable as I am now," she said, almost as if she had read my mind. Or maybe it was just my expression.

"I need to go," Naomi then said, getting up. "Faye and the band are having a couple of drinks after practice and I said I would join them."

"I thought you and Ellen didn't get on?" I asked as she made her way out of the room. Faye had never quite told me exactly why the band went into hiatus for a while, but I knew it had something to do with Naomi.

"It wasn't really Ellen I had a problem with," she said, turning around as she opened the door. "It was something else… but it is fine now. We have reached an understanding."

Despite my scepticism, within a week all of my scars had faded away. Which was nice, it was summer and I was happy to be able to wear short-sleeves again without feeling self-conscious. The next time Naomi came to visit me I thanked her and she gave me a hug.

I had gained a new friend.

A couple of weeks later, I came home to find an envelope on my desk. It had no postmark, nor address. It simply had 'Tilly' written in big letters across the front.

My grandmother had not mentioned that anyone had come by to see me…

I opened it. There were lots of papers inside. The first one was a letter, and it was from Jardair.

> *Tilly,*
>
> *I am truly sorry you got caught up in all of this. It is my one regret. You are like a daughter to me…*
>
> *I hope that one day you and Jack both forgive me.*
>
> *Jardair*
>
> *PS. Jack never told me about your problem, but I knew about it. There is a gift for you inside this envelope. I hope it can go some way to making amends.*

I then examined all the other sheets of paper and gasped.

The first thing I found was a prescription. It was for hormones. Conventional ones. God knows how Jardair managed to forge it for me, but it seemed it would provide me with more than enough to see me past my sixteenth birthday when I'll finally be able to get it from my doctor legitimately anyway.

There was more.

Another letter. This one was from a specialist clinic in Thailand, informing me that a donor had paid for my gender reassignment surgery and they were looking forward to seeing me in two years' time.

A plane ticket to Bangkok. It was an open return, but the outward journey was dated for the day after my eighteenth birthday.

There was also twenty-five thousand Thai baht. I was not familiar with that currency, but I guessed it would be more than enough to keep me fed and sheltered between the two stages of my surgery.

I spread it all out across my bed. No matter how many times I examined it all, it was still *real.* Tears leaked from my eyes. I smiled and, for the first time in months, experienced a moment of pure elation.

I still had to wait another two years, but I didn't have to worry about it anymore. I didn't have to worry about anything.

I went over to my bedside table, where the framed picture of my mother was, and picked it up. I looked at her for a while and then held it to my chest.

"I think I'm going to be okay, Mummy," I whispered, as I lay down and rested my head on my pillow. "I think am going to be just fine."

Acknowledgements

Roy Gilham. Who, as always, was the first person I sent each chapter to once I completed the second draft.

Simon Lewis (better known as musician Corporate Christ) for your feedback, company, and all the cups of tea.

Simon Hopkins, who advised on matters of police procedure whilst I was writing 'The Picture Changes'.

Danie Ware and Martin Owton, both of whom gave me constructive criticism and advice during an attempt I made to turn 'A Distant Melody' into a self-contained short story. They gave me recommendations which were so useful, many of them were siphoned into the original version.

The team at Elsewhen Press – Peter, Alison and Sofia – for all their hard work in refining this book and turning it into something that I and many others can hold in our hands.

About the author

Tej has spent much of his life on the move and he does not have any particular place he calls ‘home’. For a large period of his childhood he dwelt within the Westcountry of England, and he then moved to rural Wales to study Creative Writing and Film at Trinity College in Carmarthen, followed by a master’s degree at The University of Wales Lampeter.

After completing his studies he spent a couple of years travelling around Asia, where he took a particular interest in jungles, temples, and mountains. He returned to the UK in 2015 for the release of his debut novel *The Janus Cycle*, published by Elsewhen Press. Since then he has been living in Cardiff, where he works as a chef by day, writes by moonlight, and squeezes in the occasional trip to explore historic sites and the British countryside.

Dinnusos Rises is his second novel and he plans on spending the next few years writing more. He will probably get itchy feet again, and when that happens he has his sights set upon South America.

He keeps a travelblog on his website, where he also posts author-related news:

http://tejturner.wordpress.com